JAIN ZAR
THE STORM OF SILENCE

More tales of the Aeldari from Black Library

• THE PHOENIX LORDS •

JAIN ZAR: THE STORM OF SILENCE
by Gav Thorpe

ASURMEN: HAND OF ASURYAN
by Gav Thorpe

• PATH OF THE ELDAR •
By Gav Thorpe

BOOK 1: PATH OF THE WARRIOR
BOOK 2: PATH OF THE SEER
BOOK 3: PATH OF THE OUTCAST

• PATH OF THE DARK ELDAR •
By Andy Chambers

BOOK 1: PATH OF THE RENEGADE
BOOK 2: PATH OF THE INCUBUS
BOOK 3: PATH OF THE ARCHON

RISE OF THE YNNARI: GHOST WARRIOR
By Gav Thorpe

THE MASQUE OF VYLE
A novella by Andy Chambers

VALEDOR
A novel by Guy Haley

ASURMEN: THE DARKER ROAD
By Gav Thorpe

HAND OF DARKNESS
By Gav Thorpe

HOWL OF THE BANSHEE
An audio drama by Gav Thorpe

THE PATH FORSAKEN
An audio drama by Rob Sanders

Visit blacklibrary.com *for the full range of Aeldari novels,
novellas, audio dramas and short stories, plus many more Black
Library exclusive products.*

JAIN ZAR
THE STORM OF SILENCE

GAV THORPE

BLACK LIBRARY

To Jes, Andy and Rick, for WD127.

A BLACK LIBRARY PUBLICATION

First published in 2017.
This edition published in Great Britain in 2017 by
Black Library,
Games Workshop Ltd.,
Willow Road,
Nottingham, NG7 2WS, UK.

10 9 8 7 6 5 4 3 2 1

Produced by Games Workshop in Nottingham.
Cover illustration by Mike 'Daarken' Lim.

See Black Library on the internet at

blacklibrary.com

Find out more about Games Workshop
and the world of Warhammer 40,000 at

games-workshop.com

Printed and bound by CPI Group (UK) Ltd, Croydon, CR0 4YY

It is the 41st millennium. For more than a hundred centuries the Emperor has sat immobile on the Golden Throne of Earth. He is the Master of Mankind by the will of the gods, and master of a million worlds by the might of his inexhaustible armies. He is a rotting carcass writhing invisibly with power from the Dark Age of Technology. He is the Carrion Lord of the Imperium for whom a thousand souls are sacrificed every day, so that he may never truly die.

Yet even in his deathless state, the Emperor continues his eternal vigilance. Mighty battlefleets cross the daemon-infested miasma of the warp, the only route between distant stars, their way lit by the Astronomican, the psychic manifestation of the Emperor's will. Vast armies give battle in His name on uncounted worlds. Greatest amongst his soldiers are the Adeptus Astartes, the Space Marines, bioengineered super-warriors. Their comrades in arms are legion: the Astra Militarum and countless planetary defence forces, the ever-vigilant Inquisition and the tech-priests of the Adeptus Mechanicus to name only a few. But for all their multitudes, they are barely enough to hold off the ever-present threat from aliens, heretics, mutants — and worse.

To be a man in such times is to be one amongst untold billions. It is to live in the cruellest and most bloody regime imaginable. These are the tales of those times. Forget the power of technology and science, for so much has been forgotten, never to be re-learned. Forget the promise of progress and understanding, for in the grim dark future there is only war. There is no peace amongst the stars, only an eternity of carnage and slaughter, and the laughter of thirsting gods.

I

The silence choked her. It crowded down from near-empty benches that had once held thousands baying for blood. It washed over white sands stained red. From the open roof of the arena silence poured down from a sky the colour of an old bruise.

Hot and stifling, her lion mask was tight against her face. The smell of fresh blood in her nostrils.

Faraethil turned her head left and right as she stepped out into the flickering light. Her shadow danced crazily as the floodlights fell dim and surged back into brightness with sputters and sparks.

Liallath was dead on the sands. Her body was entwined with that of the beast she had faced, spear through its chest, her back and neck a ragged mess of skin flaps and torn flesh. Faraethil's gaze moved past and up to the stands.

There were two dozen figures beyond the wall of the large killing ground, dwarfed by the amphitheatre of death that rose up around them. Half were guards, crackling black staves in their hands. The rest were leering cronies of the arena's sole surviving owner, the Master of the Blood-dance.

Her eye turned to the shadow-shrouded throne that overlooked the arena. Two robe-swathed attendants held ornately laced parasol-fans over their patron, though the sun had not burned for nearly a year since the terrifying apocalypse that had slain so many of their fellow eldar. Beneath this feathery cover a lone figure sat, pale fingers gripping the arms of a chair carved from the bones of fallen gladiatrices. Their skulls formed a stool for feet booted in supple black hide. Of the Master of the Blood-dance's face nothing could be seen except the diamond glimmer of artificial eyes. Eyes that missed nothing.

Faraethil raised her weapons in salute to the Master. In her right hand a three-bladed throwing triskele, in her left a long-bladed polearm. She was naked but for a slatted kilt, the sheath of plated armour down her left arm and a helm through the top of which flowed her mane of white and black like a crest. Her pale flesh was marked with scars, slender lines of darker pink. Before the cataclysm it would have been easy to have such marks removed, but she had refused. The blemishes were her keepsake, each stroke a reminder of an attack she had failed to stop, a mistake made, a brush with death.

She received no acknowledgement from the Master – not since the cataclysm – and instead she turned her attention to the gate at the opposite end of the gore-stained sands. What threat was concealed in the darkness? What foe, what creature had the Master of the Blood-dance chosen for her this time?

A quintet of shambolic figures stumbled into the

fractured light, blinking and crying, prodded on by the staves of their two escorts. Their cuirasses and vambraces fitted poorly, jag-bladed spears and serrated swords held slackly in bruised hands. Fearful eyes roamed the arena before fixing on Faraethil.

Dregs from the remains of the city. Not warriors, not even blood cultists or the body-shaped. Sad, desperate survivors half dead from malnourishment. No challenge at all.

She looked again at the Master, her scowl hidden behind her mask but her aggravation obvious all the same. There was no response from her lord.

Realisation trickled into her thoughts. He was no longer interested in the fight, only the kill. The attention was all on her. Executioner, not combatant. She had become a display piece, a plaything that the Master would turn on and watch and then put away again when he was bored.

It sickened Faraethil.

Swallowing her disgust, she looked at the unfortunates that had been herded in for the Master's pleasure. Moving meat, nothing more. Like bait dangled into a pool so that one could watch a wolfshark's attack.

She was a captive, an animal in a cage, performing tricks for her owner.

Anger exploded through her body. In a moment she sped across the sands, bare feet leaving only the slightest trail. Her hands moved and the triskele flew, slashing the throats of the closest two foes before spinning back to her grip. Even as their bodies toppled Faraethil was amongst the others.

They clumsily swung their swords and thrust their spears. Jagged weapons parted empty air. Her blade wove in three wide loops, near-simultaneously decapitating and slicing the legs from two of her enemies. Leaping through the spray of blood, heart hammering, rage burning, she fell upon the last piece of meat. She discarded her weapons to the freshly soaked sands and used her bare hands, splitting, breaking, turning a living being into a broken carcass, grunting and howling as she did so.

Spattered head to foot, rivulets of blood streaming across her skin, she stepped back, panting, limbs trembling. Everything was white-hot and bright for a few moments.

When clarity returned, the guards had already started to drag away the pieces of her enemies.

She looked at the splay of limbs and organs on the ground, and where she might have seen beauty in the random arrangement, today she saw only a bloody mess. The rage was still there, unsatisfied by the slaughter, swimming in her gut and burning in her chest. Her head spun, her lungs tight, unable to take a deep breath inside her cloying mask.

What was different?

Not enemies. Victims.

This was not combat, it was murder. She ripped off the helm and tossed it away. Its gilded leonine face stared accusingly at her from the reddened sand.

There was movement in the shadow of the throne. One of the Master's attendants called out to Faraethil.

'Put on your mask, bloody one.'

She ignored the command. Bloodstained fingers worked the clasps of her armour. She shrugged and let the segmented plates fall away from her arm.

'The dancer does not disarm in the arena.' The admonition was delivered with testy impatience rather than anger. 'The dancer has not been dismissed.'

Faraethil shook out her hair, and more scarlet droplets fell to the sand around her.

She saw the shadow of the closest guard approaching and heard the crackle of his staff activated.

Faraethil turned, slowly, hands held away from her body as though surrendering. The guard relaxed, lowering his staff a fraction. The gladiatrix took a step and kicked. The heel of her foot connected with the other's chin, snapping back his head with a loud crack of breaking bones.

She ran as shouts of anger echoed around the near-empty arena. The first guard had been taken by surprise but she could not overpower them all, even had she kept her armour and weapons. Speed was her ally, not strength.

Faraethil vaulted effortlessly to the top of the encircling wall. A guard leapt down the steps towards her. She ducked the tip of his staff and dived past, to roll to her feet behind him. She fought the urge to strike. Any delay could be fatal.

Even as he turned she was already sprinting up the steep incline towards the arch of ochre daylight at the summit of the steps.

A hot breeze touched her skin as she sped out into the concourse surrounding the amphitheatre.

Though she had no idea where she was going – had known nothing outside of the arena since the cataclysm – a single thought propelled her on. It mattered not where she was headed. What was important was that she left this place. Even if the outside harboured an uncertain future, the only certainty of the arena was misery and death if she remained.

She did not look back.

* * *

11

The first three days were the hardest – near-endless days in which the darkness of night was barely more than a brief period of dimness, as though a cloud obscured the wound in the sky.

Faraethil put as much distance as she could between herself and the arena on the first day. There was no sign of pursuit. A few scavenging degenerates attacked her, half-physical things tainted by the influx of corrupting power. Her anger had slain them in moments, taking control as it did on the blood-sands.

On the second day she realised she was lost. Even before the cataclysm she had never crossed the skybridges to the other side of the river. The emptiness terrified her. If the silence of the arena, once so bustling with activity, had been unsettling, then to see the whole city empty, every street and building deserted, was a stark assertion that everything had been lost. Everything. There was not a word to describe the disaster that had befallen the eldar people. She knew in her spirit, in her heart, that this was not a localised calamity. It went far beyond the city, beyond even their world, out to the furthest reaches of their far colonies.

Her people were dead, or soon would be.

She cried, sobbing in a garden in the shadow of a phoenix-shaped topiary growing back to its wild, unkempt nature. The slight cooling she took to be evening prompted her to seek out food but she found nothing in the empty house to which the garden belonged, or in the neigh-bourhood. Every dwelling and communal building had already been emptied.

During her search the trickle of water drew her to a complex of white stone cloisters and pearlescent towers.

In one of the courtyards she found a fountain and pool. The ground around it was littered with gnawed bones and droppings. As she approached, a movement in the shadows attracted her attention.

A lyrecat padded out into the light, its shoulder as high as her hip, baring fangs as long as knives, white-and-grey pelt matted with blood. It had probably been someone's pet before the calamity, now returning to its feral state. It circled warily and she noticed brand marks on the skin beneath the fur. Its owner had not been kind.

Its growl was low and quiet; amber eyes did not leave her as she moved towards the water.

Leaves had fallen into the water and started to rot, and there was a slight covering of foam at the edges. It did not matter. Like the lyrecat, she was focused on survival, nothing else. She needed to drink.

Faraethil's eyes darted around the cloister, measuring the distance to the enclosing roof, the windows and arches. Two strides and a jump would take her to a balcony just to her right on the first floor. From there she could quickly scale to the roof if needed.

She met the beast's gaze and slowly crouched, dipping a hand into the water. Its growl intensified but the lyrecat kept its distance. Supping from her palm, Faraethil let the cold liquid spill across her chin and chest. She wiped at the blood from the fight.

The lyrecat's nostrils flared at the scent and its demeanour changed. Ears pricked, tail lashing, it shifted its bulk, preparing to spring into action.

Faraethil cupped both hands into the water and drank as much as she could.

A flick of whiskers, a twitch of tail warned her in the

heartbeat before the lyrecat bunched its muscles. The gladiatrix was already up and running when its snarl resounded around the cloister.

Faraethil leapt, fingers finding purchase on the bottom of the balcony. A swing and a pull brought her up to the slender rail. The lyrecat reared up, swiped claws and gnashed its teeth, frustrated by the escape of its prey.

She knew how it felt.

On the third day she found herself heading back towards the arena. The market squares and souk had filled the approaches in the time before the calamity and she sought the familiarity of the narrow, winding passages and streets.

She found none.

In her flight she had not paid much attention but her cautious return revealed a landscape far different from the one she had known growing up. The winding lanes and alleys had become a nest of shadows and broken lives. Bodies slumped in doorways and glittering eyes stared at her from high windows. Rustling and whispers followed her progress, not of mortal origin.

Her thoughts prickled with tension. She was being watched. More than watched. Something followed her every move, knew her thoughts, its own monstrous heart beating in time to her quickened pulse.

A laugh in the distance, cackling and insane. A susurrant breath of wind on her neck that caused her to turn sharply, forcing Faraethil to fight the urge to flee again.

She had sought safety here and found no sanctuary. The feeling of being pursued, hunted, continued to rise, making her feel sick with pending disaster.

Her steps faltered, feet scuffing on the ground when

once she had danced lightly across the sands. Her breath was becoming a ragged gasping, tightening her chest, causing spots to dance through her vision.

And all the while the predator circled, waiting, ready to seize its moment.

Faraethil staggered from street to alley to plaza in a daze, finding nothing but the dead and the flicker of the immaterial things that now ruled the city in their place. Coming upon a wider vista she spied bizarre towers and spire-like growths that had erupted from the buildings at the heart of the conurbation. Leathery-winged apparitions circled their summits. Sky palaces continued to drift the upper thermals, as devoid of inhabitants as the rest of the city. The burning ruins of others dotted the outskirts where they had crashed. Monorail carriages dangled like entrails from broken bridges and the cadaver of a great starship lay broken at the space dock like a giant, skeletal, beached whale.

Her aimless journey took her into the temple district. She would not have come here before the cataclysm. The shrines had become places of debauchery and sacrifice, of open war between competing sects and stalking shadows looking for victims to splay upon their altars.

Now the area was deserted, the temple steps bloodstained but empty, their doors broken by rampaging mobs while the corpses of the last cultists rotted upon the stairways, savaged by insubstantial claws and immaterial fangs, their last prayers unanswered by the deities they had sought to appease or laud.

A movement caught her eye. Not the half-seen apparition of the things that now haunted her world but an actual motion, like the lyrecat. She headed towards it, suppressing an urge to call out. The Master of the Blade-dance would doubtless still have minions seeking her. It would be unwise to draw attention to herself.

Coming to the corner of a broad boulevard, she found the other eldar standing in the middle of the road. She could not see his face as he stood for some time in contemplation of one of the oldest and grandest temple buildings. Unlike the others it was untouched, still pristine despite the slow decline of the city for generations and the sudden catastrophe that had befallen the eldar civilisation.

Clad in rags, he held a sack over one sagging shoulder, his entire demeanour that of defeat and dejection.

Faraethil started towards him, wary of frightening the other survivor. He ascended the steps with a weary tread before she had taken two paces, and disappeared behind one of the columns.

Following, Faraethil came to the top of the steps and found the great doors were barred. No matter how hard she pushed or teased the locks the massive portal stayed shut.

But the other eldar had made his way in somehow. She retraced his steps and examined the pillar behind which he had passed. Sure enough there was a tiny switch that opened a hidden door to the interior.

She slipped within, feeling the cool and dark like a welcome sheet across her body. She enjoyed the absence of heat and light for several moments, until she heard talking. Moving carefully, she passed into a wider space, dominated by a pool, above which stretched a semi-circular balcony. The light here was ambient, originating from no visible source. Shafts of red light illuminated the upper reaches of the temple from windowed domes above.

She crept closer, ears picking out the whisper from the darker depths of the temple.

'…found more bodies by the orchard alongside Raven's Plaza. The remnants of the gangs are fighting over what's left. I can't go out anymore, it's too dangerous. I found a passageway beneath the second crypt that leads to the Gardens of Isha on the neighbouring square. There appears to be no taint there, perhaps I will be able to nurture fresh food.'

She had no idea to whom the stranger was talking but there was no reply and she spied no sign of any other inhabitant.

'What's the point?' he cried out. His voice echoed back from the vaulted ceiling of the main shrine, diminishing with each return.

She saw him again, as he strode to the mezzanine at one side of the chamber, overlooking the temple floor a distance below. To his left was a tall carving of a wise-looking figure in red and grey stone, on one knee, with a hand outstretched towards the balcony. Water trickled from his hand into the pool, symbolic of… something. Faraethil did not know who the deity was.

The stranger had a dead look in his eye as he ascended, seeing nothing of his surroundings, perhaps confronting a vision from the catastrophe. Faraethil knew the feeling; many nights she had spent staring at the ceiling, reliving the moment when a crowd twenty thousand strong had died in terror and agony as she had carved apart another gladiatrix for their amusement.

The stranger climbed onto the stone balustrade, steadying himself with a hand on the wall. He looked at the stern but caring face of the statue, tears glimmering like blood drops in the ruddy light.

17

Faraethil knew what was going to happen; an instinct, or something stronger. A connection, the delicate mental touch of one eldar and another, a sharing of common consciousness that had been repressed for so long for fear of being vulnerable, of an inner truth being discovered.

'Why? Why carry on?' the other whispered. He glared at the statue. 'Show me you still care.'

Faraethil was running before she had even decided to intervene, though whether to save the stranger for his sake or simply to keep a connection to another eldar she did not know.

He stepped off the rail.

She grabbed the back of his ragged robe just in time, but his momentum swung him in Faraethil's iron grip, causing him to slam heavily into the wall beneath the stone rail. She looked down into a face aged by more than the simple turning of the world, though he was at least twice her age even without the care-lines and haunted gaze. His limbs trembled with fatigue, there was dirt and blood smeared across his face and arms, and broken fingernails scrabbled ineffectually at the stone for a few heartbeats.

She took hold of him with her other hand and hauled. Lifted up, he grabbed the rail and helped, pulling himself back to the mezzanine where he slumped to the floor, eyes vacant.

'What's your name?' she asked. It seemed an odd question but Faraethil didn't know what else to say.

'It doesn't matter,' he replied, shaking his head.

'I followed you in, thought it looked safe. You looked safe. That was a very stupid thing to do.'

'Was it?' He sat up, pushing her aside. 'And who are you to judge?'

'I'm Faraethil. And you're welcome.'

'You're not,' he growled back, standing up. 'This is my home, I didn't invite you.'

It took every effort not to let the rejection become anger. Fighting the urge to lash out, Faraethil turned and ran, heading back to the open air, the shrine suddenly bitterly chill and claustrophobic and dark and full of pain.

She stumbled into the street and gulped down hot air. There was no salvation here.

Faraethil survived. Barely.

Life became a continuous nightmare of flight and paranoia, listening to the screams of the dying and the victorious howls, the chill cries of the daemonic things that had seized their world. An interminable time of scavenging and skulking in shadows to eke out an existence barely worth calling a life.

But eke it she did.

The civilisation of the eldar had prided itself on its lack of personal labour. Intricate machines and carefully devised irrigation, seeding and harvesting systems had supplied all of the city's needs for generations. Though much had changed and all was falling to ruin, if one was daring and knew where to look there was clean water and food to be found – snatched from beneath the noses of the gangs that now guarded farms and aquifers as they had once stood sentry at cult fortresses and narcotic dens.

Less than one in a thousand had survived the initial disaster, one in ten thousand even. Spread across the city they had been scarce, but time brought them together, as prey or companions, but Faraethil desired to be neither. She had seen what lay down that route in the blood-dancers – servility and death for the majority, politics and the ever-present threat of rebellion and usurpation for those whose viciousness took them briefly to the summit of the misery.

And then even the cults disappeared, moving to the webway between dimensions to avoid the increasing encroachment of immaterial fiends that desired dominion over the mortal realm. With each day the world of Eidafaeron slipped further and further into the warp, bringing ever closer the edge of madness that would consume her forever.

It was desperation – a need to hunt and roam on familiar ground – that eventually forced her back towards the racing tracks and arenas of the Kurnussei. She even dared the armoury to retrieve a weapon. A mistake. She was unsuccessful, and worse, roused the hornets' nest against her. Now a very different kind of desperation forced Faraethil to run for her life, the blood-dancers of the Master just behind like hounds on a scent.

She turned left and right without purpose at first, hoping raw speed and guile could outpace them. Yet there was something different, something enhanced about these pursuers. The way they had come upon her so quickly, the means by which they trailed her through the winding alleys, bounding over walls, leaping through windows and across rooftops.

Without conscious decision her route took her back towards the shrines. If she could put just enough distance between her and the blood-dancers she might slip into the great temple where the stranger lived. It was her only salvation for the moment, and she cared nothing for the consequences of leading her pursuers to the stranger's home. Given his mood when she had left, it was unlikely the suicidal eldar even lived there, though the thought of finding his corpse, someone dead by their own hand, gave her a momentary pause despite the hundreds that had died by hers in the past.

She came to the column where the lock was hidden and the side door opened with a click that resounded back from the great space of the temple.

The sound of feet on the steps behind warned that she had not been swift enough. She let the door close behind her, hoping they would not find the catch.

She felt a surge of anger before she saw the stranger sweeping down the stairs towards her. He looked different. Bigger, healthier. His hands formed fists as he ran down the stairs. He slowed and stopped, rage dissipating when he reached the entrance hall and looked upon her. Pity. She saw pity in his eyes.

The others came in cautiously, wary of the rarefied air of the temple. The tranquillity confounded them and they approached slowly, sniffing the air like dogs. Clad in scraps of armour and clothing, long blades in their hands, hooks and barbs passed through skin and flesh as ornamentation.

One of them, a female with red-dyed hair slicked up in spines, snarled then, eyes wild with madness and hunger.

'Who are you?' she demanded, pointing her curved dagger at the stranger.

The stranger looked at Faraethil and then back at the witch-leader.

'Asurmen.'

1

A faint scream lingered in the air, source unknown, echoing far longer from the narrow corridor than was explained by physical sound. Jain Zar felt the ebb of the shrine's power the closer she came to it, while memories flocked around her trying to draw her attention. She paid them no heed, focused entirely on the call that had brought her here.

It was the first time she had returned, but everything was as they had left it. Large, plain, interlocking rectangular stone slabs covered the floor of the shrine chamber. The faded, chipped paint of a mural decorated the walls. What had once been depicted could no longer be discerned, though Jain Zar remembered well the colourful frescos and friezes of scenes from the oldest eldar myths, scenes from the gods' War in Heaven.

The ceiling was covered in a thin coating of iron artfully decorated with threads and beads of bronze. Depending upon where one stood, one saw a different face looking down, each of the six primary Aspects of Khaine, the Bloody-Handed god.

A broad pedestal dominated the centre of the room, its top at waist height inset with an intricate pattern of runes ornamented with bright crystals. The runes and gems had their own glow, six patches of blue, green, red, black, grey and white. Upon the middle of the pedestal was set a single globe, roughly the size of two fists together, swirling with white fog.

Her eye was immediately drawn to Asurmen, who stood at the sky-blue rune of the Dire Avenger, clad in azure and white plate. His longsword hung at his hip, the spirit stone in its pommel dimmed for the moment. Vambraces containing shuriken catapults sheathed his forearms, his head concealed within a high-crested helm with an angular, fierce mask.

Beside the rubies embedded in the sanctum table waited another, his armour the hues of shifting flame. Across his chest he held a weapon with a long barrel of gleaming silvery-gold, matching the detailing on his wargear – a firepike that could penetrate the thickest armour and vaporise bone and flesh in an instant. A triangular-bladed axe, the air around its head distorted by the shimmer of heat, was in his other hand. Overlapping dragonscales hung as a heavy loincloth, matched to other scaled armour in his warsuit. The Phoenix Lord's helm was flanked with broad projecting crests, their shadow long and dark. The air around the figure was distorted by haze, waves of anger emanating like physical heat. This was Fuegan, the Burning Lance, the rune of the Fire Dragon a scarlet gleam upon the pedestal before him.

Opposite waited Maugan Ra, black-clad, his battlegear set with the likeness of bones and skulls. The Harvester of Souls was armed with the Maugetar, a shuriken cannon fitted with a scythe-like blade. The crystal before him burned with black flame.

Karandras was clad in green armour, one hand engulfed by a gem-studded claw like that of a scorpion, a long tooth-edged chainblade in the other. The jade glow of his rune dappled the ceiling.

Their voices were so familiar, as if they had parted only moments before, yet all of them had changed so much since that terrible day. Jain Zar paused a moment longer in the shadows to listen.

'We do not speak of our outer lives in this place,' Asurmen said sharply. Karandras withdrew at the rebuke, his rune faded into dullness to plunge the Shadow Hunter into darkness.

'Apologies, shrine-father, I meant no discord.' His voice was a whisper in the gloom. 'I will speak no more of the outer world and the time beyond.'

Asurmen accepted the apology with a nod and beckoned Karandras to take his place properly.

Jain Zar made her presence known.

'Your tempered manner has always been an inspiration, Hand of Asuryan.' Her armour was the colour of black and bone. She carried a long glaive with a silver head and a bladed triskele hung at her hip. Three quick strides brought her fully into the chamber. 'May it guide us well on this momentous occasion.'

Jain Zar stood to Asurmen's right, within arm's reach of the dais. The runes of her aspect glowed with a clear white. Above her the face of Khaine took on the aspect of the banshee, the horrific face of the Bloody-Handed One screaming its rage amid a curl of writhing vipers for hair.

They waited in silence for some time. Jain Zar, and the others, knew that one more was still to arrive.

With the glittering metal feathers of his winged flight pack furled cloak-like around him, Baharroth, Cry of the Wind, appeared from the corridor. Over his shoulder was slung the tri-barrelled lasblaster he had chosen as his primary weapon, a curved blade sheathed on his belt. Between Jain Zar and Maugan Ra, the rune of the Swooping Hawk broke into a prismatic gleam of every colour and none. Baharroth moved between his companions with only the rustle from his feather-crested helm to disturb the still.

'I feel the call,' Asurmen intoned, 'and I answer it. I come here, to the First Shrine, outside of space, beyond time. I seek guidance.'

He paused and looked at the others. Jain Zar returned his gaze.

'It is rare that all are called together,' the Hand of Asuryan continued.

'Truly rare,' said Baharroth, his voice like the sigh of a breeze. 'My shrine-kin, take a moment to mark the occasion. Be of no doubt that we are each to return to the mortal world with sacred duties.'

'Do you question our dedication, Cry of the Wind?' snapped Fuegan, looking at his shrine-brother. 'Always you speak as the messenger, the doom-bearer, the wings upon which change is borne. What sky-whispers have you heard, tempest tamer, that we should know?'

'No more than you know already, wielder of the pure flame. The storm unleashed follows you like a curse, and it will do so until the Rhana Dandra. You cannot outrun it.'

'Why would I even try?' Fuegan laughed, but there was little humour in him.

'If it is not the End of All that brings us here, why did you summon us, Fuegan?' demanded Maugan Ra, his voice deep, the words rolling around the chamber.

'The fire of war burns bright, searing my thread upon the skein.' Fuegan's attention moved to Asurmen. 'I followed. I do not lead.'

'I followed also,' said Jain Zar. 'Loud was the cry across time and space that brought me here, issued from the lips of the banshee herself. A wail that doubtless brings death to many when I return.'

'It is the will of Asuryan,' said Karandras. The scorpion lord was disconcerting to look upon, never seeming to move, simply assuming one stance instantly after another without intervening movement. 'The heavenly dream falls upon us once more.'

'Just so, shrine-son,' said Asurmen. 'Beneath ten thousand suns have we walked and fought. Timeless and endless is our quest, to bring peace to our people. No more are we living warriors, we have become ideas, memories of glories past and mistakes not to be repeated. We are the teacher and the lesson. Though we share this place now, we are but fantasy and myth, imagined in this place by the dream-wishes of a dead god, our spirits drawn from the realm of fact and reality. Scattered again we shall be when we leave, to such times we left behind when we answered the call. We will each see what we see and act as we will act, as we have done since the sundering of the Asurya.'

They all nodded their acquiescence and turned their eyes upon the great crystal at the centre of the shrine.

'Let us seek the vision of Asuryan,' commanded Asurmen. Each Phoenix Lord placed a hand on their name-rune and the central sphere rose from its resting place and started to revolve slowly. As it turned it formed a kaleidoscope, shedding multicoloured light onto the shrine's occupants.

The light pulsed gently and the walls of the shrine melted away. The six Phoenix Lords stood beneath a storm-wracked sky, red lightning lancing across purple thunderheads above. The rage of thwarted gods made the ground crack and the sky burn. All about the shrine was devastated, a blasted wilderness thronged with daemons from great lords to mindless beasts, held at bay by the rage of Khaine and the blessing of Asuryan.

But nothing outside the wall of power moved, not as seen from within the stasis. The legions of daemons were a frozen tableau, the blazing storm nothing more than a bright pattern across the heavens.

A moment from the distant past, locked away for all eternity by the power of Asuryan's Heart, the Asurentesh that lifted higher and higher from the altar-pedestal, streaming rainbow light down upon the shrine-family.

Jain Zar knew the sensation well, the memory of its first call stark in her thoughts. The experience had not been pleasant, but she allowed her thoughts to be drawn into the Asurentesh despite misgivings. In the Heart of Asuryan she saw a countless number of threads stretching into the distance – the so-called skein, as the farseers named it. Unfolding futures, fates long laid down by the gods and the universe, disappearing into the great unknown of distance. She rode her thread of white fire, and saw others disappearing into the labyrinth, glimmers of gold that soon faded, to be replaced by thunderous noise and a barrage of images.

All is red, of fire and blood.

Screams tear the air and planets burn.

Two craftworlds, tendrils of darkness linking them together, dragging each other to destruction.

The sharp laughter of a thirsting god as it sups from the slaughter.

A savage horde belched forth from furnaces and chimneys, choking and slaying.

A green-clawed fist breaking a crystal eye, blinding it to the peril to come.

Deposited back into the shrine by the Asurentesh, Jain Zar held back a gasp of shock. She looked around and saw that her shrine-kin still remained, their runes diminished, now lit only by the ambience of the shrine itself.

The globe had lowered to its seat, dull white again.

Following Asurmen's lead, Jain Zar took her hand from the rune-table and felt a moment of fracturing, of solitary coldness replacing the warmth of companionship.

'We have seen what must be done, each to their own destiny,' Asurmen intoned sombrely, once more looking at each of his pupils in turn. 'We speak not of what the visions show us, for it is unwise to cross the threads of fate. Our spirits depart, to return to the world of mortals, at such times and in such places as we left, and in the mortal sphere our lives will meet again. Khaine is sundered anew.'

Whispers, lewd and vicious, sounded from the corridors, while baying and howls echoed from further afield.

'Our daemonic besiegers draw fresh strength and so we must leave before they grow bold enough to dare our wrath.'

Jain Zar was not sure of the means by which she had been

brought, nor where she would find herself upon leaving, but it was obvious that the stasis that protected the First Shrine would not last forever. In the world-between-worlds they were all vulnerable to everdeath.

She gave Maugan Ra a nod and turned back to the corridor, leaving with swift steps, the images of the vision burned into her thoughts. The howl of the banshee would sound again, bringing doom for some, salvation for others.

2

It started as a static that ran through Jain Zar. A prickle on skin that had long been discarded by immortality. The soul-shiver was a warning signal from her ship – she did not understand the affectation of naming things that were, at best, semi-sentient. Spirit-bonded, the craft was an extension of her own presence, a larger shell about the armour that contained her essence.

Something else was moving through the webway with her, gliding through the fabric of the walls. Not another ship. The revulsion that accompanied the pulse of feeling betrayed exactly the nature of the presence that coalesced around her: daemons.

Their presence was nebulous at first, undirected, nothing more than a taint on the skeinweave that held the webway suspended between the physical universe and the warp. Yet moments after she first detected the corruption it found her too. The shudder of warning from her ship became a wave of repugnance as malign intelligences focused their thoughts upon her.

There had to be a breach close at hand. The webway had been created to keep their kind at bay, the runic bindings of its semi-corporeal structure aligned in such a way as to provide sanctuary from predatory attention.

She urged the ship to draw more power from the skein-weave, feeding on a burst of psychic energy that threw the ship forward at greater speed. Simultaneously Jain Zar hardened her thoughts, directing part of the energy output into a barrier to ward off the first tendrils of daemonic intrusion.

Their touch was like pawing, groping fingers, seeking ingress not through force but insistent and unpleasant persuasion.

The barrier quivered at their assault, withdrawing and then rebounding to thrust away the unwanted insurgent energy. Jain Zar felt other sensations, of gripping and dragging appendages latching on with barbs as they tried to drag back the speeding craft. Web-like strands splayed across the tunnel ahead, each a net trying to slow and snare.

The Phoenix Lord's burning ire seared through these barricades, but the momentum of her ship was slowed, the leaching effect on the skeinweave starving the craft of power.

Jain Zar fought back anxiety and focused her thoughts on her destination – the Gate of the Pillared Caverns. She was almost there, and if she could reach the portal she would be able to break through to the twinned gate at the craftworld of Ulthwé, free of the pursuing daemons.

Their earlier efforts rebuffed, the daemons switched strategy and sought to tear their way into the impudent physical projectile tearing through their unreality.

In alternating lashes of freezing cold and starfire, their anger battered at the psychic shields; each blow tore away strips of energy. Jain Zar fought back the urge to cry out, reminding herself it was no physical pain – neither for her nor the ship.

The webway was a black tempest of lightning and shadows that writhed around the Phoenix Lord. With each flash of lightning and crash of thunder more of the psy-shield broke apart.

Layer by layer the psy-shield fell into tattered rags while burrowing, questing claws and fangs prised open the defences of Jain Zar's mind. Fragments of soulshield drifted like golden glitter in the wake of her ship, becoming one with the skeinweave again.

The daemons were at the craft itself, scratching and gnawing at the hull. Despite an age of immortal existence Jain Zar felt a moment of despair. This was how she could die. In fact, if the legend of the Rhana Dandra was to be believed, this is how she *would* die, locked in battle with daemons of the Great Enemy.

She trusted to the truth of Fuegan's ancient prophecy, that her time had not yet come. The Howling Banshee snatched the last shreds of power from the psy-shield. She rammed it into the skeinweave itself, detonating the power like a missile. Silver flared, hurling back the covetous Chaos presence, rippling outwards with rings of white fire that bled away the storm cloud.

Exploding from the grip of the daemons, Jain Zar's ship spat from the tunnel into the Pillared Caverns.

She had passed through the crystalline sub-realm several times before, but this time the Pillared Caverns were unrecognisable. Gone was the multitude of ruby, emerald, sapphire and diamond halls. The grand stairs and winding tunnels of faceted beauty had become a whirling storm of multicoloured shards. Swarms of dark wasps issued forth from rents in the skeinweave while purple fire crawled across the crystal walls and ceiling, leaving falling droplets of blackened filth in its wake.

The Pillared Caverns were not empty. Daemons of all kinds materialised out of the raw warpstuff pouring through wounds in the psychic barriers. Cavorting horrors in myriad colours conjured by the Changer of Ways gambolled, cackled and threw fiery blasts as they advanced alongside claw-handed daemonettes – foot soldiers of She Who Thirsts. More of the Great Enemy's warriors rode upon the backs of sinuous, lash-tongued beasts while screaming skysharks and bounding flamers ensorcelled by the power of the Architect of Fate swept through the pocket realm borne aloft by semi-visible waves of magical power.

As Jain Zar's craft punched through the raw daemonic energy crowding into the underspace she arrowed the craft towards the blazing pillar of fire that whirled at the centre of the domain. A thicket of black figures surrounded the webway gate – guardians from Ulthwé alongside striding war walkers and spirit-animated wraithguard. Gliding grav-tanks flew around them, escorted by flights of jet-bikes and, higher still, squadrons of sleek fighter craft. Here and there a splash of colour highlighted the presence of Aspect Warriors; green of Striking Scorpions, blue of Dire Avengers, orange of Fire Dragons.

With them towered the immense shape of a Warlock Titan. The slender-limbed war engine spat death from its long weapons, pulses of ravening psychic energy that left after-shrieks across Jain Zar's senses. From this war machine came a throbbing warp beat that kept intact what little remained of the Pillared Caverns, holding back the encroaching Chaos that fed the daemons their sustaining power.

There were others that had mustered to the defence of the gate. As she wrenched her ship into a braking turn Jain Zar saw several pale-clad eldar amongst the black – White Seers that commanded archaic engines dedicated to the destruction of She Who Thirsts. Their arcane machines looked more like abstract works of art than weapons but they sent out beams of coruscating power that disintegrated the daemons with a touch and scoured forth pulses of cleansing fire.

And lastly the vibrant, multicoloured flare of Harlequins, several dozen of them, though their holosuits and rapid acrobatics made a sure count impossible. The followers of the Laughing God struck deep into the daemonic host, cutting down everything they could reach. When a Harlequin settled for a moment its outline coalesced from a splinter of rainbow hues – figures clad in skin-tight outfits decorated in every imaginable pattern, a dazzling full-spectrum display of jags and diamonds, lozenges, spots and stripes.

The fighting took place not over a single plane but across all the remaining surfaces of the Pillared Caverns. Here the physical properties of the material universe were unnecessary. Squads and floating weapons platforms moved across walls and ceilings as easily as floors, while daemons pushed into the realm's heart along spiralling corridors and through vertiginous tunnels.

In those fleeting moments Jain Zar saw something else.

With the exception of the Harlequins, the eldar were falling back.

The warriors of Ulthwé fought a retreat, giving ground to the daemons in measured withdrawals while the followers of the Laughing God counter-attacked to disrupt the Chaos assault.

Through the systems of her ship Jain Zar felt the energy of the gate waning. As her vessel had experienced in the encounter with the daemons, the Gate of the Pillared Caverns was losing energy. Corrupting influence was creeping into the nexus of the portal, seeping into the whirling white flames from the broken structure of the skeinweave.

Seers from Ulthwé encircled the base of the fiery column, their runes orbiting them like glowing planetary systems. Psychic energy pulsed between them and the gate, fighting back the invading Chaos force while the guardians and Aspect Warriors fought back the semi-corporeal incarnations of daemonic power.

The Chaos insurgency was doing more than shutting down the portal, it was turning its power against the eldar of Ulthwé.

In another moment Jain Zar had discerned the purpose of the battle and the intent of the eldar. The daemons sought ingress to the craftworld through the corrupted gate and the Ulthwé forces had issued forth to hold the breach just long enough for their seers to close the access. The gate could not be saved and if it was lost to the daemons the craftworld would suffer immensely.

As more and more black-clad figures disappeared into the maelstrom of portal fire Jain Zar urged her ship on, faster and faster.

Something monstrous appeared out of the firmament

of breaking crystal and seized hold of the craft in two mighty claws. Jain Zar felt the piercing talons like daggers in mortal flesh. The apparition beat pinions of shadow as it wrenched the craft off-course, its closeness further disrupting the flow of power from the fractured skeinweave.

Jain Zar leapt out of the piloting cradle and seized her weapons. Bounding up steps to the highest level of the ship, she thought to open an access hatch, of a mind to attack the interloper. Yet the moment she sped out onto the roof of the craft she knew it was folly. With powerful beats of its insubstantial wings, the daemon-vulture lifted her further and further from her goal.

Jain Zar turned and with half a dozen long strides leapt from the ship.

She fell towards the gate, mane fluttering around her. Twisting, she turned her descent into a dive. Ahead, the fire column was almost spent, flickers of red and black crackling up and down its length. The last of the Black Guardians had disappeared, leaving only the giant form of the Warlock Titan.

The war engine pulsed a final beat of psychic power that threw back the leading wave of daemons, and then stepped back. Flaming tendrils enveloped its huge frame and within a moment it was gone.

White fire flared and rebounded from the breaking crystal shards of the Pillared Caverns, reflecting and refracting and splitting with prismatic power. The rainbow beams sliced apart Lords of Change and Keepers of Secrets, turned daemonettes and flamers to white ash, horrors and fiends into scattering clouds of aether dust.

The last vengeance of Ulthwé, the power of the gate spent in a final defiance of Chaos.

With the demise of the gate all remaining semblance of order disappeared. The remaining pillars and walls of diamond cracked and fragmented, showering stalactites down around Jain Zar as she continued to glide towards the space where the gate had been.

She landed softly. Crackles of white lightning leapt up to meet her from the rune-wards of the gates' dais. Shrouded with coursing power, she turned.

The daemon army came on, undeterred by the writhing serpents of energy that continued to crawl across what remained of the collapsing subsphere. Creatures that would drive lesser minds insane converged on the Phoenix Lord with baying laughs and hideous roars.

The air shimmered above the host, dancing with myriad colours like the spray of a waterfall. Red and green beams lashed down from the apparition, cutting furrows in the mass of daemonic servants even as a brightly coloured ship with golden sails appeared out of the multi-hued mirage.

The Harlequins' vessel turned tightly, cannons flaring with another volley as it touched down, obscuring Jain Zar's view of the daemonic host. A shadow dappled on its surface and became a doorway from which extruded a slender boarding ramp.

Jain Zar broke into a run before the ramp was fully extended. She sped up to the starship, fixed on the figure in the doorway. The Phoenix Lord was greeted by a mask sculpted into a broad grin, red with elaborate orange swirls on the forehead and down the cheeks, green eyes behind the clear lenses beneath an emerald-studded brow.

'Many thanks, child of Cegorach,' said Jain Zar as she jumped into the lifting ship. The ramp disappeared behind her and the door closed an instant later, sealing her inside.

'When younger I was told by my mother,' replied the Harlequin with humorous lilt, 'that it would be considered highly rude to let daemons feast on a true legend. Welcome to the *Stardance*, Storm of Silence.'

II

Faraethil had lived in the Kurnussei since she had been left there by her parents as an infant. She had seen fighters of all styles and skills and learnt to emulate or defeat most of them. The stranger… was like none of them. He had been a tired, worn creature without hope or will when she had last seen him. Now he moved with purpose, faster and with more focus than anybody – or any *thing* – she had witnessed during the blood-dances.

His face was a mask of serenity. Peace radiated from him even as he bounded forwards and lashed a hand into the throat of the blood-maiden closest to Faraethil. Windpipe crushed, the cultist spun to the floor, choking. He caught the knife that fell from her dead fingers. Faraethil snatched at the tossed stiletto on instinct as the stranger moved to the next foe, kicking his legs from under him, snatching the sabre from his grasp in one movement.

She knew the blood-dancers – not individually but their type. Young and brave but inexperienced. Gawky and slow compared to the efficiency of movement that took the stranger from one enemy to the next and the next in the space of two heartbeats. He drove the sword into the chest of the eldar he had taken it from and ducked beneath a wildly swinging axe. Pulling the blade free, he turned, lifting the sword in time to block the next blow.

As though released from a cage her anger boiled forth, given vent after so much fear and running and hopelessness. Faraethil hurled herself at the blood-drinkers with a feral screech, using her momentum to slam into the closest, stabbing again and again into the blood-dancer's chest.

She did not see what else happened, caught up in the red whirlwind of her own death-dealing. She could feel the presence of Asurmen like a cold light on her back, but she was an inferno of ire, burning so bright and hot, fast and all-devouring.

Faraethil sawed her short blade across the throat of another enemy. Her fear propelled her, turning her into a wild creature of desperate violence, full of passion and fierce need. She leapt from the corpse, blood-soaked and dripping, tumbling to the floor with another enemy, biting and screaming while she plunged the knife down.

Crouching, snarling like a hound, Faraethil bared her teeth. One cultist remained. He scrabbled backwards through the blood of his dead companions. Clarity returned when Asurmen stepped in front of her, blocking her view. His shadow washed over her like a cleansing stream, and she heard the pouring of water from the great statue in the shrine chamber. He turned on the blood-dancer.

'What are you?' the blood-dancer cultist demanded, the dagger in his hand shaking as he lifted it.

'I am your evils returned to you,' said Asurmen. 'I am the justice your victims cry out for. The protector of the weak. The light in the darkness. The Hand of Asuryan.'

The sword sang as it cut the air.

'I am the avenger.'

Faraethil turned her gaze upon Asurmen, trying to hold back the rage that dripped into her thoughts as crimson dripped from the blood-drenched knife in her hands. The edges of her vision were a haze. She forced herself to focus on the other eldar.

Asurmen slowly crouched and laid his sword on the floor. He stood again with equally deliberate motion, his eyes locked to Faraethil's. Hands spread wide, Asurmen spoke softly.

'They are dead. We have slain them. The danger has passed.'

She quickly looked at the corpses. Seeing their still forms settled her for a moment, though her anger had not vanished, fed by an unease she could not identify.

'You remember, yes? You saved me. And now I have saved you. Why did you come back to me?'

Limbs weak and quivering from exertion and thirst and exhaustion, Faraethil straightened. She sucked in a deep breath. She wanted to believe he was an ally, could feel the peace that emanated from him, but his transformation raised deep suspicions. How could he be so deadly?

'You called yourself the avenger, the Hand of Asuryan.' She realised it was not his given name and that was encouraging. 'For me. You took the name for me?'

'Your inspiration. You were the instrument of Asurmen's intervention, now I have become the instrument.'

'You know that the gods are dead, right?' Hunger gnawed

43

at her gut and she felt ill. She looked at the blood on her body and spattered on the floor. For the first time she saw no beauty there, no pattern, no poetry. Just blood, the life of others splashed across the tiles. Her gut revolted and she lurched to the wall to empty it, though there was nothing but bile to bring up.

Asurmen moved closer, but not within striking distance. The knife in her hand wavered, weakly fending him off as she looked back, past him to the bodies.

'Did we do that? Did I do that?' She saw not only the remains scattered on the floor of this serene temple but the countless corpses she had left on the arena floor. What madness had gripped her? How long had she allowed her rage to rule her body? 'How? How could we?'

'It is in all of us, that violence, waiting to be unleashed. Just as the yearning for delight, for adulation, for satisfaction is in all of our hearts. We must resist its lure, be strong against its temptations.'

'Have you done this before? The killing?'

Asurmen shook his head.

'I was a vessel, nothing more. The violence is in me, but I am a being of serenity now.'

'Really?' Faraethil laughed at the irony of his statement. The bloodied carcasses of the cultists did not seem at all peaceful to her. 'Serene is not the word that springs to mind.'

'Violence is an intent, not an act,' said Asurmen. 'I have thought long about this, since the Fall.'

'The Fall? What is that?'

Asurmen waved a hand towards the doors and to the vaulted ceiling of the entrance hall.

'Everything that happened. The loss of innocence. The damning of our people. The doom that came.'

Faraethil eyed him warily. 'You remember the time before?'

'How can you not?'

She did not yet trust him, to share the bloody path she had trodden. Instead, she lied.

'I was a child, I don't remember anything except the death and screaming. My brother survived for a while, looked after me long enough for me to learn how to look after myself, avoid the cults and the daemons. It has been some time, several years of the old reckoning, since I was last here. Have you been alone all that time?'

'For far longer than I had realised,' said Asurmen. He gestured to the blade in Faraethil's hand. 'Let me take that.'

She gave it to him, hesitant, and he threw it away, the metal clattering across stone tiles.

'How am I supposed to protect myself?' she cried, taking a step after the discarded blade. Asurmen held out a hand to stop her.

'It is not safe for you to carry a weapon yet. Your rage will get you killed. It blinds you to danger, fuelled by your fear.'

'So you are not afraid? Really?'

'I have seen the world consumed by a thirsting god, Faraethil. There is nothing left to scare me. I have spent enough time alone. Let me teach you what I have learnt, of the world beyond the cults and streets. Let me help you control the fear and anger, to bring calm to the turmoil in your heart.'

'I will have to fight. Nobody survives without fighting.'

'I did not say you will not fight. I will teach you to fight without the desire for it overwhelming you. Our people have been laid low by our emotions, our desires and fears have consumed us. Those of us that can must learn

45

control. We must walk a careful path between indulgence and denial. We must not pander to our darker passions, but we cannot deny that they exist. Both must be tempered by discipline and purpose. Only then can we be free of the burden of ourselves.'

She looked at him, wondering if he told the truth, or was simply mad from isolation. There was something about his demeanour, the look in his eye and the way he held himself that resonated with her spirit. A manner that was strong, eternal. It reminded her of the statue.

'Is that true? Can we really escape this nightmare?'

'Would you like to try, Faraethil?'

'I need another name. You were not Asurmen when we first met. If I am to be reborn, like you, I need a new name.'

Asurmen thought for a while and then a smile turned his lips, the expression slight and awkward from long disuse.

'I will teach you to channel your rage into a tempest of blows that none can withstand, and your scream shall leave the quiet of death in your wake. You will be Jain Zar.'

The Storm of Silence.

3

Jain Zar's host was called Naemonesh, Great Harlequin of the troupe that travelled aboard the *Stardance*. When the ship had powered clear of the daemon infestation around the Pillared Caverns, the Great Harlequin met with the Phoenix Lord. They convened in a round chamber in the centre of the ship; benches and chairs of many shapes and designs – and species of maker – were arranged in rings around the small hall. Crude ork stools and fentarian pillow pillars sat alongside extravagant craftworld-grown chaises longues and gilded human thrones.

When Jain Zar entered, Naemonesh had already arrived, along with a handful of other Harlequins. The troupe leader sat a few rows back on a plain plinth of black stone, her companions scattered about the hall. Jain Zar sat down on a padded chair with a high back next to Naemonesh. The Great Harlequin shook her head, stood and moved to a bucket-shaped seat opposite.

Other troupe members came and sat down, seemingly without any order or purpose, some in groups, some alone. Holosuits deactivated, their motley was bold and colourful, a clashing storm of colours and patterns. Some bowed in greeting to the Phoenix Lord, others nodded, several ignored her altogether.

Jain Zar detected an otherness about the followers of the Laughing God. She knew a little about their sect – more than many – but the strange rituals that they claimed protected them from She Who Thirsts were as hidden as any of their secrets. Even so, it was common knowledge that they did not wear spirit stones, claiming that they needed no 'soul prisons' to save them from the hunger of the Great Enemy.

It left them blank to her thoughts. Not absent, for they were eldar and still possessed of the mild psychic talent of all their people, an empathic link to others of their kind. But without their waystones their essential thoughts and emotions were hidden, clouded and fractured just as their holosuits split their visual image when they moved.

The ship was the same, its infinity circuit dormant for the most part, running from the power of the skeinweave but little else. There was no flow of spirits through its systems, no ebb of psychic energy in its hull. For a kindred that purported to value life and laughter so much, their vessel was a numb, deadened place to the Phoenix Lord.

A Death Jester arrived, clad in black but for the skeleton design and exaggerated skull mask. With forced slowness the Death Jester approached, stepping carefully between the haphazardly arranged chairs until he stood directly in front of Jain Zar. He bowed, grinning death's head level with her face, and remained there, staring directly at her, obscuring her view of Naemonesh.

'I have faced death more times than all in this room

combined,' Jain Zar said, undaunted by the morbid performer's presence.

'It is too easy to think oneself safe,' crowed the Death Jester, 'when one has already become a wraith. What does proud Jain Zar care for death and pain, with nothing to lose, and nothing to gain?'

'Do not think that Cegorach will save you from my blade.'

The Death Jester remained where he was, defiant and taunting. A flick of the wrist, a simple swipe of the Zhai Morenn – the Blade of Destruction – and his head would be separated from his shoulders. Jain Zar put aside the fancy, knowing that she was being tested, not by the Death Jester but by Naemonesh.

Slowly, Jain Zar stood up, stepped past the Death Jester and sat down upon a fresh seat – an ornately carved block of red stone fashioned with interlocking geometric shapes. Naemonesh nodded her approval, half hidden behind the elaborate green crest of the Harlequin seated in front.

'I am too long in this world for riddles and games, even from the followers of the Laughing God. If we cannot speak plainly then set me down at your leisure. I am not at liberty to spare my time on frivolities – a grave peril must be averted.'

'I saw the light of Asuryan on you, when you came into the Pillared Caverns. A quest, I thought, sent by the Lord of Lords. A Phoenix Lord cuts the web of fate here, let us not worry about the tatters, nor impede the desires of Asuryan. Tell me, Storm of Silence, what of Ulthwé?'

'Fire and broken fates. War with another craftworld that shall see both annihilated and any dream of the Rhana Dandra extinguished.'

49

'Why should Cegorach care for your battle? Mortals and daemons, fragments of dead gods? Nothing will free your kind from She Who Thirsts.'

'My kind is our kind, no matter what you think has passed between you and Cegorach. And more importantly, we both fight the Great Enemy. Or do you teach the lessons of your masques only for others to heed?'

Naemonesh stood up and started to pace through the chairs, passing in front of and behind her fellow Harlequins. She did not take her gaze from Jain Zar.

'We fight the great war against She Who Thirsts. As we have since the Laughing God slipped free on the first eve of our people's destruction. The Rhana Dandra will not save our race, there is no sanctuary even in death.'

'You have nothing to lose, Great Harlequin, by setting me on my way. Passage to Ulthwé is all I require.'

'A pity that is, for Ulthwé hides now, with the Gate of the Pillared Caverns closed, skulking in the Heart of the Last Abyss. Why should she cower there? I do not know. But we are not travelling that way soon.'

'Ulthwé draws close to the Eye of Terror?'

'Into the outer fronds of its embrace. No journey for the faint of heart to take.'

'I know of one that will carry me into those depths. If you are of a mind to aid me, set course for the Winter Tower.'

'The benighted outpost of Commorragh? You still strike business with the dark kin?'

'As you say, I am a legend and that carries respect, even in the Dark City. I have a past with the mistress of the Winter Tower. She will see me to Ulthwé to repay a debt.'

'Very well, it will be just as you ask. The *Stardance* makes for the Winter Tower. After that, your Path takes you where it leads.'

Jain Zar nodded her thanks and stood. Naemonesh turned away and left without a further word. The Death Jester, who had remained bowed for the duration of the exchange, straightened, tipped an impish nod of the head and followed after his leader in a series of skipping jumps and flamboyant turns. One by one the other Harlequins departed, some with sombre step, others with light laughter, cartwheels and pirouettes.

The Phoenix Lord headed to her quarters, seeking isolation from the strange disciples of the Laughing God. Of all the denizens of the galaxy and webway she had encountered, the capricious and carefree Harlequins – Dancers on the Edge of Doom – disturbed her the most.

At the request of Naemonesh, Jain Zar met the Great Harlequin in a viewing blister that bubbled from the side of the *Stardance*. The troupe leader said nothing but simply pointed to the scene beyond the curved transparency.

The ground was white with snow, as the Phoenix Lord remembered from her last visit, but of the verdant purple-and-blue trees that had surrounded the Winter Tower nothing remained. Blackened forest stretched as far as Jain Zar could see, to the shimmering borders of the sub-realm bounded by a mauve twilight sky.

In the distance she saw the fortress itself, a triumvirate of pinnacles that stretched up high above the desolate woodlands. All three were broken, jagged like snapped fangs. A pall of what seemed to be smoke hung over the ruins.

'Our bargain remains unchanged, Phoenix Lord. At the Winter Tower we have arrived.'

Jain Zar eyed the devastation, noting the patches of blackness that marred the purple skies in places, like bruises on reality. Nothing moved below in the woods, not bird or beast or eldar.

'Set me down and be on your way,' said Jain Zar, her foreboding turning to irritation at her host's lack of concern. 'I would not delay your passage any further.'

Naemonesh stepped back and waved for Jain Zar to leave as the viewing port darkened to a milky white. The Great Harlequin escorted her to the main doors, where they had first met.

'The Powers of the Timeless Age care not, either for victory or for mortals. Only the turmoil and conflict feeds them. The game rules are rigged against you, Jain Zar, the only release is never to play. Follow your Path, but do not seek its end.'

Jain Zar said nothing to this unasked-for advice, she simply stepped down the ramp onto the charred earth that had once been verdant forest. With a sigh the *Stardance* closed behind her and lifted away.

The Phoenix Lord stood for some time surveying the devastation. She remembered the woods in full blossom, red and black petals falling like beautiful polychromatic snow while the trees had sung to each other with lilting whistles and hooting, haunting calls.

The songtrees had been burned and slashed down, the ground scattered with black shards that she could feel leaching the last ebbs of life from the artificial soil. The wind carried whispers of lament, from the shades of dead songtrees trapped within shattered, ash-caked stumps. Their voices were a harsh dirge now, cursing all that stepped forth between their broken trunks.

Jain Zar set out, heading directly for the Winter Tower. The ground was soot and dry dust underfoot, all moisture and vitality drained by the black rocks that dotted the ruins. What she had taken for snow were the remnants of leaves and flowers and bark. Ashen flakes fell from the trees at the breeze of her passing, leaving a wake of grey motes.

As she neared the tower she detected a faint keening, at first like a bird of prey, but as the distance shortened she picked out several distinct notes, like a flock of birds in chorus. Jain Zar stopped as she came into view of the tower, the red-stoned base of the three spires. The shadow of the pinnacles left swathes of frost in the darkness and the memory of mortal chill seeped into her as she stepped out of the purple twilight.

The foundations of the citadel were only one storey high, solid but for a narrow gateway – the black metal gate itself lay in glistening droplets of slag at the threshold. There was only darkness within. Of the sky-towers above, the walls were pierced by a multitude of windows and broken in as many places. Pieces of stone littered the ground beneath, cracked and shattered by devastating blows from within the citadel.

Her boots rang from the hard floor as she entered. No more did tapestries and paintings looted from worlds of the old eldar empire adorn the walls – only bare blocks gave cold welcome. The carpets had been taken and the crystal chandeliers, so that the only light came from the gateway and the dim haze that leaked down from the towers through a mist of particles.

The grav-tubes were broken open, their transparent domes left in glinting shards within the three alcoves. Jain Zar could detect nothing of the power that had once lifted her to the heights in moments. The citadel was dead, divorced from the sustaining forces of the realm around it.

She found a narrow winding stair, more an affectation than a sensible mode of ascent given the soaring nature of the tower's structure. Even so, Jain Zar set a booted foot on the steps and started to climb.

The screeching and whistles she had heard earlier echoed down the stairwell from above. She carried the Blade of Destruction pointed before her, ready to strike, though in the close confines of the stair it would be of little use.

It took some time to reach the first chamber. Jain Zar eased through the curtained doorway, suddenly aware of an increase in the disturbing noises.

Their source was immediately revealed. The hall was ringed with skeletons, more than two dozen eldar stripped to the bone and sinew on barbed hooks that had been pounded into the wall stones. Flesh and skin had been left on their faces, captured in the last rictus of terror and agony.

Each was set before a gap in the blocks, so that the wind from outside passed across their bones. Ribs and femurs, vertebrae and clavicles had been cunningly drilled, hollowed and shaped like flutes, so that each breath of a breeze set forth a delightful harmony of sound.

Inspecting the closest, Jain Zar looked for signs of wounds, but found nothing broken or punctured save by the cruel artifice of the bone-music's composer.

The eyes in the fleshy face snapped open and a croak issued from the ragged chords left in the throat.

By some arcane means, their skeletons exposed to the elements, the carcasses decorating the Winter Tower were still alive.

* * *

Jain Zar retreated with swift steps. She turned left and right as the other half-corpses awakened with rattles and moans around her.

'Help us,' pleaded a voice behind her. Jain Zar spun on the spot to find a face with sagging skin, his curls of black hair still falling about the flesh-stripped shoulders.

With horror she recognised the ravaged features of the eldar from the ill-fated expedition when she had first crossed fates with Lady Maensith.

'Mai Dorain?'

'It is. I do not know by what chance of fate or boon you come today, but deliver us from this torment.'

'The Lady Maensith, what of her?' Jain Zar stepped closer to hear the whisper of the citadel's chancellor.

'Taken.'

'She is alive?'

'Some escaped, she did not. Whether she lives I cannot say.' Mai Dorain let out a groan, eyes rolling up. 'End my torment, please.'

'What did this? Daemons?'

Mai Dorain managed to shake his head with a creak of exposed ligaments. His lips drew back in pain.

'Worse.' He took a shuddering breath and fixed a half-dead gaze on the Phoenix Lord. 'Asdrubael Vect.'

There was nothing to be done to ease Lady Alkhask's retainer or the other survivors from the Kabal of the Crimson Talon. Whatever hex had been laid upon them was beyond Jain Zar's knowledge to lift. Instead, she questioned the kin of the Dark City; their desire for a swift end made the kabalites eager to tell her what had happened. She conducted her investigation against a backdrop of haunting corpse-melody, intermittent groans and hissed curses.

'She fell out of favour,' a blond-haired cadaver explained. 'A dispute with Khiadysis Hierarch of the Ascendant Spear, who accused her of stealing his beloved keth-hound.'

'Among other transgressions,' added another underling. 'She stole the heart of his lover also.'

'Maensith did not strike me as the romantic type,' said Jain Zar.

'No, she literally stole his heart,' the Commorraghan replied.

'I see. But what has that to do with Asdrubael Vect? The Lord of the Dark City does not concern himself with the affairs of other kabals.'

'We cannot say,' said Mai Dorain. 'It stopped a bargain being struck between the Ascendant Spear and Crimson Talon, which has displeased our archon. Vect has some favour owed or gained from the hierarch, or perhaps the archon himself. We did not ask questions when he sent Daethrak Demarr to fetch Maensith Dracon to his court.'

'The lady ordered us not to fight,' added another flesh-less kabalite. 'Said that we could not match the power of the Kabal of the Black Heart.'

'She was right, though little good it did us to not resist.' Mai Dorain grimaced with pain. 'I feel the ache in every bone yet cannot move anything but my face. It is more a torment than the burning of the skin I no longer possess!'

'Did Daethrak make any other threats? What did they intend for Maensith?'

'That she would be delivered to Vect unharmed,' said Mai Dorain. 'She argued and struggled, to gain time for others to leave by the slipways with ships and weapons, but some of us remained to cover their withdrawal.'

'So some of her army remains? Her fleet?'

'I do not think they will repay her loyalty.' Mai Dorain laughed harshly. 'Twenty cycles have passed since she was taken, and they have not returned.'

'They have sided with the hierarch or returned to the Archon, I wager,' another said before being racked with dry coughs.

'Why did they raze the groves?' Jain Zar gestured to the wasteland beyond the windows.

'Why not?' said a kabalite to the left, skin loose over the sharp bones of her face. 'Without a dracon to rule it, the Winter Tower is forfeit.'

'Maensith was forced to watch it happen,' explained Mai Dorain. 'And our… internment. She knows that there is nothing here to which she can return. The elimination of all hope of escape or reprieve. I think Vect will have his fun and when he is done he shall discard the lady to the attentions of Khiadysis Hierarch.'

'Was there nothing left by the raiders?'

'What do you intend, Storm of Silence?'

'To go to Commorragh.'

'There are craft, hidden in caverns beneath the dead forest. I think they remain there still.' Mai Dorain slowly shook his head. 'But it is useless. Vect has taken his prize and none can reclaim it from his grip. You cannot go to the Dark City and return. Nobody does.'

'I am a Phoenix Lord, I pass wherever my Path takes me.'

'What of us?' Mai Dorain cried out as Jain Zar headed back towards the steps. 'What of this torment?'

'You are all slavers, murderers of kin, pirates and

torturers. Suffer as you made others suffer. If Vect desires this to be your fate, I will not anger him by changing it. This is where your deeds have brought you.'

Their chorus of pleading, swearing and shrieks followed her down the steps and drifted out through the broken tower even as she made her way back into the wasteland in search of the hidden ships. The wind carried the last syllables of their curses as Jain Zar strode deeper into the dead forest.

Following the advice of the not-dead chancellor, Jain Zar searched for chambers beneath the forest and found a simple raiding cutter close to the ruins. It was a matter of moments to enforce her will on the primitive spirit the kabalites had instilled into its circuitry. Like an experienced stable hand breaking a horse she quickly bent the recalcitrant craft to her will and the blasted remains of the Winter Tower soon gave way to the winding corridors of the webway, leaving behind the echoes of its doomed inhabitants' soul-cries.

The ship she had taken already knew a route to the Dark City so she was content to allow it to steer its own course through the increasingly complex maze of webway gates and tunnels around Commorragh. They flitted across vast domes whose walls still raged with the fires of ancient battles and sped past pocket realms bordered with guard towers like rows of fangs.

Other ships passed in both directions, some alone, others in small flotillas returning from raids, the fabric of the webway shuddering to the psychic misery of the captives crammed into their holds, quivering with the triumphant excitement of their crews.

Her passage attracted occasional attention. A patrol skiff or war-barge would approach, hailing the ship and demanding she stop. Jain Zar knew better than to comply with such demands, that their threats of opening fire were empty this close to Commorragh – Vect discouraged open warfare within the boundaries of his domain, at least without his prior appraisal and approval.

It was a different matter when the ship from the Winter Tower took her into the Cascading Storm. The portal spread across several webway ducts, barring all passage, appearing like a rainbow curtain across the route. Black towers and spire-clad defence posts clustered in a ring, their targeting beams sending a flare of agitation through the systems of Jain Zar's commandeered vessel.

Even here there was no central authority – save the looming shadow of Vect's dominance – as guard boats and war galleys issued forth towards all who approached, vying with each other to waylay and extract tribute from the ships trying to enter the Dark City, exchanging warning bursts of fire when a rival came too close to a chosen target.

Jain Zar found herself under the scrutiny of a large battleship, fully a hundred times as large as her own ship, just one of its energy cannons capable of splitting the vessel from prow to stern with a single hit. With a harsh blare, the approaching battleship hammered its communication signal into the ship systems, forcing its transmission into the relays with brute force, a demonstration of strength and power before even a word had been uttered.

There was no holographic link, only a crystal screen set into the main console above the navigation controls. The slate turned white and then filled with a ruddy glow as the image from the approaching ship filled the screen: a silhouetted head, face hidden within a helm flanked by sharp bladed crests.

'Power down and await the inspection of the Majestic Dominance of Naidazaar Archon!' the shadowy figure demanded. 'By the will of the Kabal of the Barbed Eye you will submit to our boarding party.'

Jain Zar touched a hand to the controls beside the screen, activating her end of the link. The figure on the slate jerked in surprise as her face appeared upon his display – a face modelled from the ancient temples of the eldar people, etched upon a hundred aspect shrines of the craftworlds and known throughout the splintered kindreds.

'I answer to no mortal demand, wretch of Commorragh!' Jain Zar knew that only greater aggression would quell the instincts of the battleship's commander. She was a prize unlike any other, and her status as a Phoenix Lord offered her only temporary protection. 'I am the Storm of Silence, Asurya, daughter of the Bloody-Handed One. If Naidazaar Archon thinks to command me, he is free to come to this ship and tell me himself. If not, I demand you escort me to my meeting with Asdrubael Vect.'

This last was probably the most convincing statement, though nothing had been arranged with the Lord of Commorragh. Even if her own authority did not grant her safe passage, the allusion that she visited at the behest of Asdrubael Vect would gain her some leverage. At the least the archon might think it wise to deliver her to the ruler of the Dark City in exchange for a reward of some kind. At best, Naidazaar might be cowed into simply delivering her to Vect without delay.

The slate turned grey as the archon's herald cut the link

in order to convene with his master. Jain Zar continued to approach the shimmering veil of energy that marked the threshold of the Cascading Storm. The battleship accelerated, the throb of its engines permeating the skeinweave surrounding the portal, leaving a backwash of faint terror and agony coursing through the sensors of Jain Zar's ship.

The communication slate remained blank.

Her vessel's unease turned to a paralysing inner wail as battery after battery of the warship's weapons locked onto their position. Jain Zar fought against the ship's urge to flick on its shadowfield and flee, and held her nerve enough to continue to approach the portal at a sedate but steady pace.

She dared the archon to open fire.

The link screen buzzed back into life to reveal the kabalite from the Barbed Eye, an indistinct figure past his shoulder.

'Naidazaar Archon extends his bountiful greeting to the Storm of Silence and offers invitation to join him on the *Daggerwraith* for your journey to the palace of our great lord.' The herald glanced back for a moment. 'In fact, he is most insistent that his hospitality is not rebuffed.'

The squeal of the ship's sensors quietened and became a groan of apprehension as the battleship's guns powered down, to be replaced by a locking beam. Doors in the belly of the gigantic ship slid back to reveal a red-lit docking bay.

Jain Zar quickly weighed up her options. Whatever the intent of the archon, she believed her survival was better served in person than in a ship that could be destroyed in moments. Even if Naidazaar intended to hold her captive, as a hostage for Vect perhaps, he would convey her to the heart of the Dark City – a journey that was not without perils if she was somehow to elude the warship and proceed on her own.

'I welcome the archon's flattering offer of escort and look forward to thanking him in person.'

The vague figure behind the herald gave a nod of approval and then the screen darkened. Jain Zar slowed her ship and allowed the locking beam to envelop the craft, its coils slipping around like a constricting serpent.

With a crackle of energy, the beam drew Jain Zar into the shadow of the *Daggerwraith*'s bay. The doors closed and all became darkness.

4

Contrary to the many-shadowed depths of Commorragh, the warship of Naidazaar was bathed in light. Escorted through the high corridors by a guard of twenty kabalites, Jain Zar had reason to wish that the decorations of the archon were not so well lit.

Every wall was covered with flayed skin. The high craft of the haemonculi had perfectly preserved every hair, pimple, scar and pore. Stitched together with hair-thin silver wire, the skins came from many different races, creating a changing plateau of dark and pale browns, shades of orkoid greens, purples and even the pure white of albinos. Some were missing limbs. Many had wounds from blade and splinter rifle, welts of burning plasma and marks of electrolashes.

The vaulted ceiling was made of bones, most likely taken from the same victims judging by the myriad lengths and thicknesses representing different species, including strangely shaped skeletons from corpses Jain Zar did not recognise.

The skulls were missing; they had been saved to pave the floors of the vessel. They were lacquered and polished in all colours, the path laid out in vibrant hues and many different precious metals. The Phoenix Lord and her escort moved easily, their natural nimbleness compensating for the uneven footing.

Great chandeliers held the gleaming crystals that lit the scene – immense constructions made of talons and teeth. Garlands of preserved viscera looped from the walls like obscene bunting, their fluids still glistening within the stasis-embalming.

The doors to Naidazaar's inner quarters were built from gigantic bones three times Jain Zar's height – the creatures they had been taken from would have towered more than four times that again in life.

The Phoenix Lord stopped a little way from the closed doors, earning a scowl from the leader of the guards.

'How do you start?' Jain Zar asked the sybarite.

'I don't understand,' he replied. 'Start what?'

Jain Zar waved at the macabre ornamentation.

'This. When you began, you couldn't have possessed enough bones for the whole ship. It would look stupid with a few dozen skeletons nailed to the walls. So, how do you start? Do you save up enough bodies for a corridor at a time, or put them away until you have enough to decorate the entire vessel?'

The sybarite snarled, hand straying to the agoniser lash that hung on his belt. Jain Zar moved her fingers to the triskele at her waist and tilted her head towards him. A moment later the kabalite raised his hand away from his weapon.

'We shall see what humours you when Naidazaar Archon is done.'

Jain Zar set off again, impervious to the kabalite's threats. Far worse adversaries than Naidazaar Archon had tried to end her existence, yet here she still was. Continuing, even if not quite living and breathing as once she had.

The grand doors opened at their approach, unleashing a peal of triumphant music from within the hall beyond. Clarions signalled a salute while harps added a melancholic harmony and some other strings touched rawer notes that undercut the score with a harsh edge. It was quite perfectly orchestrated, as far as Jain Zar knew such things.

The hall itself was surprisingly plain; near-white walls with railed galleries beneath a domed ceiling, on which the archon's favoured followers sat on marble benches viewing proceedings. Usually kabal leaders elevated themselves above their minions with stages and daises, but the hall of Naidazaar stepped down through five levels, forming an amphitheatre at the centre of which sat the lord.

Jain Zar had seen many kin of Commorragh but she was quite unprepared for the apparition that waited for her in the centre of the hall.

Four identical figures sat on white thrones, facing the cardinal points of the chamber. They were naked but for jewelled necklaces, torcs, vambraces and greaves, and short kilts of scarlet scales. Each had skin of black flecked with gold, their bodies emaciated to the point of cadaverousness.

Their faces were indistinct. Eyeless, noseless and lipless like abstract sculptures, only the jutting of their cheeks gave them any defined shape at all. Bald-headed, their skulls were elongated into curving spirals from which slender silver wires linked them to each other.

The hands that lay on the arms of the thrones had fingers that turned into pulsing tubes, looped up to hooks in the ceiling to hang like creepers until they converged into a throbbing brain-like mass overhead.

Open gutters ran down the levels of the hall, one to each of the seated figures. Down each gutter trickled a different fluid – one obviously slick with red blood, the others a thin yellow, vibrant orange and sluggish grey. Tendril-toes hung into the pools of fluid beneath each throne from which tiny tongues lapped at the seeping liquids.

Save for a single winding route down to the thrones, the steps of the auditorium were filled with the plunder of innumerable raids. There seemed to be no pattern to the display. Pieces of jagged alien technology sat alongside trophies made of stuffed rodents. Ingots of precious metals piled unceremoniously next to furs and outlandishly patterned textiles. Broken pieces of pottery painted with alien marks were heaped on mouldering furniture. Ork-dung totems were used to hold up fine tapestries looted from some unfortunate craftworld. Step after step, the pillaged detritus continued, stolen from a thousand worlds and a hundred different races and civilisations.

The display was not intended to impress, Jain Zar realised. These trophies were not laid out as an exhibition to others, but for the pleasure of the one who had hoarded them.

The quiet was unsettling. Not a sound came from the viewers up on the balconies, not even a flutter of cloth or whispered remark. Jain Zar looked more closely and saw that the kabalites positioned on the benches were immobile, their faces locked in expressions of surprise and delight, hands raised in flamboyant gestures, part of the display along with the vanquished foes in the passage-ways outside.

The doors closed silently behind her, leaving her trapped in the still hall.

Jain Zar regretted her earlier confidence. A hoarder like Naidazaar would be overjoyed to acquire the armour of a Phoenix Lord, and certainly if anyone possessed the means to separate Jain Zar's essence from her suit it was the Commorraghans. Perhaps they might even extract her spirit intact for their collection.

She stood looking at the four figures seated below. The skin of the one closest to her peeled apart at the eyes, revealing red gems within the sockets. They sparkled with an inner light that also glowed from the mouth when the figure spoke – words that issued in unison from the other figures, each accompanied by its own nimbus of green, yellow and blue. No other movement stirred the seated bodies.

'At first I did not believe the reports of my dracon.' The words were clipped, delivered with precision from some mechanism inside the figures, for the lipless, tongueless mouths could not form the sounds themselves. 'Imagine my delight and shock that I, Naidazaar of the Barbed Eye, should encounter the legendary Jain Zar. My peers shall not believe the tale!'

'Few cross paths with the Asurya without lament,' Jain Zar replied solemnly, starting down the path between the piles of stolen treasures.

'Assure yourself that I wish no harm on you, Storm of Silence. Your invocation of Vect's name was unnecessary, though I have made enquiry and it seems his people are unaware – yet – of your impending arrival. No, I would not damage something so precious.'

The organic fronds from the ceiling quivered and detached from the fingers of the closest figure while tendril-toes shrank into the feet. The silver wire dropped from the back of its bizarre skull and it stood up, mechanical in its stiffness, though Jain Zar could feel the faint ebb of soulstuff in its centre as she drew closer.

'I collect,' Naidazaar said simply, waving a hand at the contents of the room. 'We all do, of course, to show off to each other. But for me, my collection is not about status, it is about knowledge. What can I learn from these things? Of our past, and perhaps our future. You are one of the few beings, along with the majestic Vect himself, who remembers the time before the Fall. I would not damage such an oracle of myth.'

'You are to be disappointed – I will not indulge your curiosity. Those times should be forgotten.'

Naidazaar ascended towards Jain Zar with faltering steps.

'Stay away from me,' said the Phoenix Lord.

The mannequin stopped a short distance away. There was no expression on its face but the sag of shoulders and tilt of the head betrayed sadness.

'These things exist for the memory of their taking,' said the archon. He bent and awkwardly picked up a silver salver decorated with rubies and opal. Running a finger along the stones, he was lost in reverie for a moment. 'A human piece, taken from the castle of a warlord. He was a large male, dark-skinned, bearded, with long curls of raven hair. My warriors trapped him with shardnets and we forced him into one of the chimneys of his great hall and lit the fires underneath.

'He climbed to avoid the flames, but there was another shardnet across the opening. I watched as he pushed himself further and further into the mesh, slicing his own flesh to escape from being burned alive.

'I looked into his eyes as he clawed at the net and his fingers fell away from the strands. I drew out his essence as he fell into the fire, savouring every particle of his terrified soul.'

Naidazaar's animatron bent his mouth in an approximation of a smile.

'Good times.'

'I want nothing to do with you. Take me to Vect and our business is concluded.'

'Business? So this is to be a barter, an exchange of goods or services?' The mannequin held out its hand, as though inviting Jain Zar to dance. Gold dust sparkled on ebon fingers. 'You wish to see Vect. What do you offer for your passage through the Dark City?'

He twitched his hand, renewing the offer. Reluctantly, Jain Zar stepped forward and laid her palm in its grip. The mannequin was icy cold to the touch, an empty shell devoid of any soul-warmth. It shuddered with pleasure and turned, their hands held up as if courting at a ball. Jain Zar easily kept pace with its uncertain stride down through the heaped treasures.

'My company,' Jain Zar said before they reached the centre of the hall. 'If you take me to the palace of Asdrubael Vect I will stay in your company for the duration of the journey.'

Naidazaar stopped and turned, stepping even closer, their chests almost touching. Jain Zar had not realised just how frail and skeletal the mannequin was, but it looked as though she could snap it with a single blow of her empty hand.

'Perhaps you could offer a little... more?' The mannequin's other hand hovered, as though he reached for her cheek but stopped himself.

'You misunderstand the nature of a Phoenix Lord,' said Jain Zar. 'Even if I had the inclination, it cannot be done.'

'Not the crude physical interaction.' Naidazaar seemed genuinely offended by the suggestion. 'I speak of something more spiritual. I have it in my power for us to commune beyond the physical, for our souls to meet in ways you cannot imagine.'

Now he placed his hand on the moulded mask of her helm, sliding fingers across the sharp cheeks, caressing the shrieking grimace of the psychosonic projector.

'Let me taste the essence that lies within this suit. Let me savour an age of bloodletting and history. Let me feel as an immortal feels, see as an immortal sees.'

The thought revolted Jain Zar but she held back her rebuke. It made no sense to alienate Naidazaar and she was in no position to exact any leverage on her 'host'. She stepped away from his hand, still holding the other, and continued down towards the thrones.

'How would it work?'

'One of your spirit stones...' Naidazaar gestured towards the many spirit vaults that dotted her armour – receptacles from those that had passed on to sustain the force that was a Phoenix Lord. 'I need to use it as a conduit. I must admit, I had never considered the possibility that I might use such techniques on one of the Asurya. My experience has been limited to delving the minds of our mortal craftworld kin while extracting their dread for my sustenance and amusement. It is quite exhilarating to experience them simultaneously as the drink and the drinker.'

Again Jain Zar swallowed back her revulsion as she considered the mental intrusion to which the mannequin alluded. If she resisted, would Naidazaar try to make such a connection by more demanding means?

They reached the thrones. The silver wires that hung from the heads of the other mannequins twitched into life, rising at their master's approach. He let go of Jain Zar's hands and took up the strands in his palm, gem eyes turned towards the Phoenix Lord with an enquiring glint.

'Shall we, Storm of Silence?'

Jain Zar nodded and plucked a red spirit stone from her armour and held it out to Naidazaar. The Archon took it with a reverent sigh and clasped it to his emaciated breast for a few moments, eyes fluttering with ecstasy. He then laid the three silver wires onto the oval gem. They probed and slid across the surface like questing digits. Jain Zar gasped as she felt the insidious touch of them inside her thoughts.

She remained calm, trying not to resist the intrusion, knowing that to do so would make the contact worse. She thought to steer the tendrils reaching into her memories, guiding them away from the deepest recesses of recollection. The filaments of silver light creeping through her essence split and split again, seeking out every part of her.

Their presence awakened memories long dormant, flashing images of battle and death through her conscious mind. Jain Zar relived the experience as she slaughtered orks beneath a blood-red pair of moons. She bounded along branches as long as sailing ships in the rainforests of Nammeainmaresh, driving back the kroot mercenaries sent to pillage the Exodite world. Crystal-walled chambers in the broken core of craftworld Nebreith resounded to the roar of flesh hounds and the shriek of banshees. In every vision the Blade of Destruction was a blur of silvered doom, the Silent Death a whirling arc of black flame.

Deeper and harder the filaments delved, seeking out every part of her. The whirl of memories became a blur, each vista of bloodletting segued to the next with increasing rapidity.

She felt the hunger of Naidazaar, devouring every stolen moment, feasting on the carnage and second-hand bloodthirst of Khaine's daughter unleashed.

Even as Jain Zar suffered the intrusion she became aware of the other mannequins standing, moving around the thrones to encircle her, hands outstretched. They meant to take everything, to strip away all that was left of her for themselves. Naidazaar would never be sated until he had gorged himself on every shred of her soul.

He meant to betray her.

She had feared as much but a fleeting contact with the archon's mind broadcast his intent. She saw in the glint of a crystal eye the cannibalistic intensity of the creature she had invited into her thoughts.

A mortal might have panicked, but Jain Zar had been assailed by the psychic and daemonic many times and was not prepared to relinquish herself to this treacherous thief. She did not resist openly, though she knew she could repulse the questing tendrils if she desired. That would lead only to the stalemate that had existed before the connection had begun – a lock between her desire to see Vect and her ability to do so.

Here was opportunity instead. Naidazaar's greed, his

overpowering desire to possess her, left him vulnerable. While she amused him with the most gratuitous scenes of slaying she could recall, Jain Zar followed the tendrils back to their roots, teasing herself along their lines until she met with the thoughts of Naidazaar.

In the instant of contact she was struck by a counter-surge of images from the past of the archon – sickening scenes of defilement, torture and execution. She pushed through waves of stolen torment, devoured terror and grief-thirst and into the older memories of Naidazaar.

She found what she was looking for bound beneath layers of pain and redirected rage.

With a triumphant flash of power, Jain Zar tore open the archon's memory vaults and plunged his consciousness into the worst nightmares of his childhood.

She felt the internal scream building within him as he was forced to confront his own degradation and physical torture at the hands of those that passed him around like a possession. Even he, heir to a grand kabal, born into one of the noblest families of the Dark City, was a plaything for his betters.

His hate boiled, an infant's hurt and rage made manifest over and over, amplified by the ruination he had brought to others in his quest to drench the agony of his own past.

And in the heart of all, the overwhelming truth of the eldar existence – the brooding, watchful, ever-present attention of She Who Thirsts. No matter how many were slaughtered in his name, no matter how much dread and sadness he supped in lieu of the Great Enemy's soul-draining existence, he would never escape the fate sealed for him from birth. Damnation, utter and ethereal, awaited his soul the moment he lapsed, the instant he allowed himself to relent on the path he had set for himself; She Who Thirsts would take her fill and empty his spirit until it was a dried husk. He could hide in as many bodies as he liked, erect as many walls of misery and murder as he could, but still his doom followed only a step behind.

With a wail that filled the hall, Naidazaar ripped himself from the grip of Jain Zar. Howling like demented sunwolves, over and over, all four mannequins enacted his manic flailing.

Jain Zar snatched at the closest animatus and seized it by the throat. It did not breathe as a living creature but the psychic intent from the Phoenix Lord still caused the mannequin to cough and choke. Bony, weak fingers tried ineffectually to prise away her grip.

'You will deliver me speedily and unharmed to the palace of Asdrubael Vect,' Jain Zar told the archon. She tossed the mannequin to the floor, and the others fell in unison around her. Drawing free the Silent Death, black fire licking along its three bladed arms, she gestured towards the writhing fleshy mass in the ceiling above. 'Shall I sever the cord? Shall I pitch you into that black nightmare you have glimpsed? It does not matter what your underlings try to do to me, I will see you into the heart of She Who Thirsts before I fall.'

The archon rolled to his knees, all four incarnations of him, and looked at her with featureless horror. Anger flared in the ruby eyes and then dimmed, cowed as the Daughter of Khaine raised the Silent Death for a throw.

Broken, Naidazaar lowered his gaze and dipped his heads in submission.

III

'Where did you learn to fight like that?' asked Jain Zar. She circled to the left, the duelling baton held easily in her hand. Asurmen said nothing as he matched her, stepping to his right to close the distance. He moved with consummate ease, a continuing motion from one stride to the next without the slightest pause while his weight transitioned across his steps.

Around them the shrine to Khaine the Bloody-Handed had started to take shape. This central dome was a training area and inner sanctum to the god of war and murder from the time of the ancient eldar. Its shape reminded Jain Zar of the blood-dance arena and she knew deep down that it was no coincidence that such a place shared similarity to the architecture of a bloodthirsty deity. The blood-dances had been generations old even when she had begun, and now she was learning that it traced its roots back to a far older and even more sinister ancestry.

'You are rage-filled and reckless, but you are no stranger to a weapon,' the Hand of Asuryan replied, switching his stance to bring up the baton to a guard across his chest. 'Perhaps you should answer the question first?'

Jain Zar swallowed hard. She knew the lie she had told would not stand much scrutiny but she was not yet prepared to bare her guilt to Asurmen.

They continued to measure each other in silence, eyes locked. Starlight filtered through the semi-transparent forcefield around the half-completed dome above, a silver sheen on their skin. Underfoot the bare rock was hard, unforgiving, like the surface of the moon that stretched beyond the basic accommodation blocks they had started to erect.

Jain Zar changed direction, quickly retreating, wary of Asurmen's apparent defensive state. She had seen the speed with which he had attacked the blood-dancers at Asuryan's shrine and knew that the calm surface concealed a whirl of energy waiting to be unleashed.

'Coward.' His one word hung in the air, spoken so softly Jain Zar thought for a moment that she had imagined it.

'What?'

'You are a coward, Jain Zar.' Asurmen straightened and lifted his baton to his shoulder, assuming a defenceless pose.

'Why do you say that?' Her jaw tightened. 'You know nothing of what I have done.'

'You can no more confront yourself than you are willing to confront me,' said the Hand of Asuryan. 'You are a physical and moral coward.'

She thought of the times she had stepped into the arena, blade in hand, to face some scaled beast or trio of armed foes, her heart steady, palms dry. Not once had she taken a step back from danger.

'From one that hid in a shrine while our people destroyed themselves? I did not see you fighting on the streets.'

'Why must everything be a fight?' There was an annoying swagger to his step as he turned towards the arch that led from the inner sanctum. 'Sometimes it is better to walk away.'

'That is the talk of a coward!'

Asurmen stopped, his back to her.

'What happened to your brother?'

She kept her silence, knowing that he already had the answer. He made her wait, neither of them moving or saying anything. Jain Zar stared at his back, her irritation at his smug arrogance turning to something fiercer.

'I lied. So? The past is dead, it means nothing anymore.'

'Your past lives within you.'

'Hypocrite! What right have you to demand to know my past? I saw what you were before – it is not a source of pride for you.'

'And I shed those times, with your help. I am Asurmen, not Illiathin. You are becoming Jain Zar but Faraethil holds you back. It is her anger you must control.'

'My anger has kept me safe, before the Fall, and after.'

'You are a foolish child.'

His dismissal broke the dam that had been holding back her rage. Raw emotion flooded out in a high-pitched scream as she launched herself across the sanctum, baton aimed for the back of Asurmen's head.

The Hand of Asuryan hardly moved. He pivoted on a heel, ducked beneath her wild swing and struck his own weapon against the side of her jaw.

The impact was not heavy, but enough to jar her senses and buckle her legs. She stumbled to the floor, elbow cracking heavily on the rock, air forced from her lungs. Asurmen crouched, hooked his baton around her throat – to provide leverage rather than to choke – and pulled her up. Snarling, she was helpless to resist as he half dragged her from the dome, her feet moving quickly to stop herself from falling as she stumbled after his long strides.

He marched her relentlessly along the plain corridors that surrounded the shrine, face impassive. Jain Zar tried to tear away from his grasp but the baton moved just a little further up her throat, to a point under her jaw that made her legs feel numb.

Their journey ended outside, on the expanse of matt-black refabricated ground that surrounded the growing suite of temple, villas and store rooms being erected by an autonomous construction system they had salvaged. Asurmen let her go, softly lowering her to her knees. In front of her sat the four surface-to-orbit shuttles they had accrued on recent journeys, the beginnings of a fleet Asurmen desired to make much larger. Such was his grand vision, which apparently no longer included Jain Zar.

'Pick one,' he said.

'I don't...'

'You are leaving. If you are not willing to learn, I cannot teach you anything.'

Jain Zar sat with shoulders sagging, her anger swept away by the chill wind that blew around the shrine complex. Her sullen silence was the only answer she could muster.

'You want to stay? Then you must listen.' Asurmen held out a hand and helped Jain Zar to her feet. 'Your anger controls you.'

'My anger has kept me alive.'

'But you know that cannot last.' He looked deep into her eyes, as though seeing the thoughts that had run through her mind at that moment she had chosen to leave the arena. 'Your past and your anger are bound together. We cannot shed them like a skin, but we can hide them beneath a new layer.'

'But the anger will still be there. What if it escapes? What if I hurt myself, or harm you?'

'You will learn to release it. My despair almost ended me, and like your anger it was born out of a deeper fear. Let go of the fear and the rage will be yours to master. Not gone, but subject to your demands. It will become your weapon.'

Jain Zar stepped forward and let the baton fall from her fingers. She threw an arm around Asurmen and buried her face in the soft material of his robe. There were no tears, but as his arm embraced her in return, she could feel the grief breaking through the barrier of the anger, becoming something more real, more accessible.

'Tell me your story,' he said.

'Not yet,' Jain Zar replied, stepping back. She met his gaze with a single assured nod. 'Soon, I hope. But not yet.'

5

The shuttle from the *Daggerwraith* deposited Jain Zar on a high landing balcony of Vect's palatial towers and then lifted away without delay to power back to the warship hovering overhead. Two other vessels, each a match for the battleship, prowled close to ensure that Naidazaar did not have any strange ideas while within weapons range of the palace.

After his encounter with Jain Zar, the Archon of the Barbed Eye had no mind for further danger and his warship had already started to turn away, abandoning the shuttle and crew he had despatched with the Phoenix Lord.

As Jain Zar had expected, a sizeable number of warriors from the Kabal of the Black Heart waited on the broad expanse of the docking balcony, their weapons trained on the Phoenix Lord. Still chastising herself for the unfortunate situation she had placed herself in with Naidazaar, she was in no mood to be threatened again.

As the first kabalite stepped towards her, Jain Zar

snatched free the Zhai Morenn and hurled it. She followed its course, sprinting towards Vect's warriors in the trail of the triskele's ebon fire. The Jainas Mor flashed across the chests of four kabalites, felling them instantly, another two despatched by the Blade of Destruction in the following moments.

It was too late for the kabalites to fire their splinter rifles, shredders and blasters; the press of their own kind shielded Jain Zar from attack. A pair fell, beheaded by the Silent Death returning to her outstretched hand as she ducked beneath the serrated bayonet of another kabalite.

Blades and agonisers drawn, others circled around the Phoenix Lord, nimbly avoiding the flying heads and limbs from their companions as Jain Zar whirled and slashed into their midst. She turned, armour slick with the blood of the dead.

She screamed, releasing her pent-up frustration and the wash of filth and guilt left in her soul by the delving of Naidazaar. The shriek cracked open the armour of a kabalite directly in front of her, blood spraying from the fractured plates and shattering mesh. Behind the warrior, her kabal-kin were flattened by the psychosonic blast, jerking and stumbling as their nervous systems sparked with agony.

Jain Zar fell upon the trembling victims, slicing open armour and bodies with her blades. She rolled and dodged, expecting the others to fall upon her, but they fled, scattering through the dark arches of the palace like insects whose stone had been suddenly upturned.

It became clear that they had been ordered to depart, leaving the dismembered remains of their kabal-kin in rings around Jain Zar.

A solitary figure was left at the largest of the gateways. Dressed in black robes, skin as pale as snow, silver amulets and piercings chiming as she moved, a withered haemonculus advanced, a long staff in one hand, the striking of its point on the stone floor like the crack of splitting rock, sparks of power flickering along its length.

'Enough.' The word was spoken in a hoarse whisper but carried the length of the quay easily. 'This is childish.'

Jain Zar pulled back her arm, the Zhai Morenn flaring with black flame in her grip.

'You are all foolish children to me, haemonculus. Take me to Vect or he will lose many more of his warriors.'

'If the great majestic lord wished your body brought before him, you would not have set foot upon the stones of his palace.' The haemonculus raised her staff and pointed to the warships, and then moved it to gun turrets in the black towers to either side, their cannons directed at the landing dock. 'I am Suivaneth. Follow me. Lord Vect awaits.'

She turned, dismissive of the threat of the Phoenix Lord, and started back towards the gateway.

Jain Zar hesitated. What she contemplated was madness. There was no guarantee that Maensith was still alive, and even if she had not yet been killed or turned over to her enemies, what could Jain Zar offer Vect for her release? The bargain with Naidazaar had been dangerous enough; any deal with Vect would potentially be even more costly.

Yet here she was, her current mission set in motion by the will of Asuryan, and she had to trust that she followed its course. She needed to reach Ulthwé swiftly, and it was likely Maensith remained the surest way to do so – few others would wish to travel with a Phoenix Lord, for the heralds of Asuryan were seen by most as harbingers of war. If Jain Zar freed the fleetmistress she would have no option but to accede to Jain Zar's need.

Flicking blood drops from the Silent Death, Jain Zar followed Suivaneth into the palace of Asdrubael Vect, Supreme Leader of the Black Heart, Lord of the Dark City. The most dangerous individual from across the scattered kindreds.

Keeping pace at the shoulder of the haemonculus, the servant of Vect within striking distance, Jain Zar advanced warily along the corridors and rampways of the palace. The passages were thronged with eldar, most of them armoured warriors openly carrying weapons, bearing the marks of the Kabal of the Black Heart. Others from lesser kabals moved among them, in flowing robes and studded gowns of black and blue and purple. They were not permitted armaments but the whim of Vect protected them more surely.

All turned to watch the Phoenix Lord, distracted from their politicking and mutual antagonism by the presence of such a novelty in their realm. Those faces she saw regarded her with a mixture of surprise, delight and hatred. Whispered conversations followed along the vaulted halls, and preceded them down galleries.

By stair and grav-lift Suivaneth took Jain Zar further up the spire of Vect's palace, to an immense plateau that overlooked the Dark City. Overhead was open to the sky and the flaring black suns that bathed Commorragh in eerie twilight – open but for a faint aura of a protective energy dome. The floor was made of translucent red crystal that revealed the sprawling city below, cast as though seen through a bloody lens. Smaller towers that yet housed thousands of eldar dwindled like anthills below, swarms of skyboards and skiffs, shuttles and barges moving between them while bat-winged scourges flocked about the peaks of these lesser pinnacles.

So high was the summit of Vect's fortress that returning star-ships moved beneath the level of the floor, carrying raiding parties seeking the relative sanctuary of their home docks to offload their captured wares and the freshly enslaved. Jetbikes seemed no larger than flies, grav-yachts and pleasure barques like oil-winged beetles sculling across a pool of crimson.

Of the lowest depths nothing could be seen but shadow, but Jain Zar knew well the tales of that abyssal realm, where carnivorous ur-ghuls stalked the unwary and clashes between kabals continued their bloody rivalries beyond the sight – or care – of the city's overlord.

The audience plaza was no less thronged than the rest of the palace; a small army of warriors, attendants and slaves waited on the whim of their all-powerful master. There was subtle hierarchy at work, each cluster of kaba-lites arranged along loyalties and associations so complex that many dark eldar made a lifelong study of the inter-necine struggles and feuding blocs that vied for control and favour in Commorragh.

Some danced in weaving formations, feeding and drink-ing from trays carried by agile serfs who moved effortlessly through the interleaving lines and twirling partnerships. Fighting pits had been erected where the kabalites wagered and shouted, urging on the beasts of their favour whilst gambling away the souls of hundreds of lesser beings. Jain Zar averted her gaze from these, their spectacle paling in comparison to her experiences, yet the lure of that old life ever-present in the back of her thoughts.

Here and there heavily black-plated figures stood watchful and silent, immobile as statues. Incubi, mercenaries ready to strike down any that looked to be moving or plotting against their employer. Contempt welled up in Jain Zar at the sight of the sell-swords – unworthy of the skills that had been passed to them, bastardised descendants of the Asurya. Their path had taken them into darkness, their mastery of Khaine's gift sold to the highest bidder.

The crowds parted at Suivaneth's approach, while more stares of loathing and desire followed Jain Zar. The splitting of the crowds revealed an open path to Vect.

The Lord of the Dark City lounged on a throne of midnight stone, its back spired in the same fashion as the palace itself, six ornate blades rising from the flanks like the horns of a daemon. Vect wore a diaphanous weave of black across his pale flesh, wrapped about torso and waist in loose folds, eschewing armour in his inner sanctum. He bore no weapon here. Upon his head he wore a crown of dark grey metal, studded with black and dark green gems. From its brim hung a veil that concealed his face but for the sneering twist of thin lips.

Though the supreme lord of Commorragh seemed at ease, his dais was filled with armoured figures – a dozen more incubi, their powered halberds throwing a gleaming blue light upon their master. Around them a favoured few were allowed to recline on the steps. They were fed dainty morsels by flitting demisylphs with gossamer wings. Domesticated starfeys filled their goblets from golden ewers, their heads flayed to expose their crystal skulls.

Vect raised a beringed hand and all chatter fell silent, the quiet rippling out from him in a wave. He leaned forward to rest an elbow on the arm of his throne, chin on fist as he watched Jain Zar. With the merest flick of a finger he dismissed Suivaneth, who departed with a deep bow.

'The Storm of Silence comes to the court of Asdrubael Vect.' He spoke with quiet assurance. 'Had I known earlier, I would have prepared a more suitable exhibition to welcome you back to Commorragh. I must admit to a certain pleasure that you have finally deigned to grace my palace with your presence, after shunning my invitations on your previous visits.'

'It is not by choice that I come before you, Vect.'

'Few do. In fact, none of these cretins wish to be here.' He gestured dismissively at the others around him. 'They are bound to me by dread or need. A few by hate, I am sure. Except my incubi, of course. They fight for me simply because I pay them to do so. It is the most efficient and therefore least interesting exchange in this entire place.'

'I...' Jain Zar paused, choosing her words carefully. Vect's veil cast a shadow over his features far darker than the gauzy material warranted. She suspected he viewed her with some augmentation device. 'I ask a boon from the Lord of Commorragh.'

She expected taunting. Triumphant gloating. On the journey from the docking bridge she had steeled her pride against the barbed tongue of Vect.

None came. He peeled away the veil to reveal his hawkish features, dark eyes fixed on Jain Zar. The eldar on the step murmured praises of his handsomeness and declared themselves blessed to have laid their eyes upon his true features. A scowl furrowed the lord's brow as he looked down at the courtiers.

'There is some litter on my step,' he remarked to the incubi. 'Dispose of it.'

Protests and wails were lost in the hiss and crackle of the mercenaries' glaives hewing down the unfortunates. The demisylphs and starfeys scattered into the crowd, their silver chains tinkling and rattling. Slaves with punisher gorgets around their throats stumbled out of the crowd, thrust forward by their slavers. Humans and other eldar, they cast terrified glances at Vect and set to the task of cleaning up the bloody remains that slicked the steps. Under the threat of agoniser lashes they gathered up heads and limbs and licked at the blood and gore to clear the dais.

Vect had not taken his eye from Jain Zar.

'How I despise interruptions.' He smiled, but the expression had all the warmth of a serpent's charm. 'Apologies, I should really hold my temper better when in polite company.'

'You are a devious, murdering, ruthless coward, Vect, and I am not intimidated by these displays.' Jain Zar reversed her grip on the Blade of Destruction and plunged it into the crystal of the floor. She crossed her arms, displaying her disdain for his warriors.

'Not a coward!' Vect snapped. He fluttered a hand as if swatting at a particularly persistent and irritating wasp. 'Those other things, yes. A thousand times, yes. Proud of it. But never a coward. A coward would have bowed to the lash, would have accepted his lot with the lowest dregs. A person of ambition is never a coward, because they risk all to achieve their goals.'

'Then fight me, if you are so brave.'

'Do not be ridiculous, Jain Zar.' He sat back as if physically struck by the notion, his face contorted with a look of horror that turned to one of condescension. 'I did not crush my enemies, lay waste to the houses of the nobles, raze Shaa-dom and rise to be lord of all Commorragh so that I could soil my hands with personal combat.'

Jain Zar knew there was no point in avoiding the inevitable confession of her need. Vect was the most manipulative, callous ruler the eldar had ever spawned, and his mind was able to weave plots more convoluted than any other. And though he possessed an almost over-powering pride, so strong was his arrogance he cared not one bit for the opinions of others. He had to court no favours nor concern himself with the good opinion of others. His word was absolute, his grip on power unshake-able. She would not trick him into a bargain, she could not force his hand with threats. The unpleasantness with Naidazaar had left her deeply uncomfortable with offering anything else, but she had no leverage except her presence.

'I have come for Lady Maensith Drakar Alkhask Dra-con. Is she still alive?'

Vect scratched his temple with a gilded fingernail, brow furrowed. One of his court nervously ascended the steps with much bowing and whispered something to the over-lord. He nodded and the courtier swiftly retreated with a look of relief.

'Maensith Dracon? Why?'

There was no point lying. Jain Zar suspected it mattered nothing to Vect except as an exercise in authority, and to deny her reason would only invite refusal.

'I need to reach Ulthwé, but the craftworld has hidden in the outer reaches of the Eye of Terror. Maensith knows a route I can use and I need her to take me through it.'

'A Phoenix Lord travels to Ulthwé. A curious incident, to be certain. Why should that concern me?'

'I have been despatched on a sacred mission by Asuryan.'

Jain Zar knew Vect cared nothing for the old gods, but if she humoured him there was a chance he would acquiesce. The truth was that she had nothing to lose. He had likely already made up his mind. 'I have seen disaster blaze free from the black flames. Ulthwé will fight a terrible war against another craftworld. Their conflict will break asunder part of the webway and the Great Enemy will pour his power through the breach and doom many more of our people.'

'This incursion, does it threaten Commorragh?'

'The apocalypse that unfolds will be the greatest disaster to our people since the Fall. Divided, we shall be consumed in the fires of war. The Rhana Dandra will not come to pass and we shall all be doomed.'

'So… yes. In the longer term.'

'We all perish, Vect. One day even you shall pass from the mortal plane. The doom that devoured our people… She Who Thirsts will never be sated, no matter how many other souls you feed to her.'

'So I should hide myself away in one of your little magic stones, Jain Zar? I should imprison myself in life and death, be a good slave as Asurmen would teach us?' Vect leaned over and said something to one of his functionaries. The eldar disappeared into the subdued crowd, who listened to their lord's tirade with studied indifference or feigned admiration. 'Is that the grand plan to save our great people? To hide forever? To smother She Who Thirsts with the blanket of our deaths?

'I look upon the doom that we created, every cycle. I feel the gnaw of it, the lure of subservience, the promises of glory. I face it, accept the whole truth of what it is, and I fight. Am I a predator, feeding others to the beast that stalks me? Yes. And a scavenger too, for I will fling whatever morsel I find into that maw to keep it busy for a few more moments. Every heartbeat is precious to me, but do not think I am afraid of death. I have drawn more out of life than any other of our kind.

'And who are you to judge me, Phoenix Lord? Whose spirit did you last drink to resurrect this shell you call a body? From whose ashes did you rise this time? You are nothing, a spectre trapped in a suit. If Asurmen had promised you this, you would not have followed. You would have fled into the webway with the rest of us, to live out whatever life you could prise from the dead grip of the galaxy.'

He became more and more agitated, voice rising in pitch, features contorted with aggression though Jain Zar felt that his rage was born from some other source than her presence.

'You are not immortal! You are dead! You think and move and fight and... There is nothing to you. A puppet of Khaine's memory, strings twitched by the death gasps of Asuryan. I live! I am truly immortal! Let the Prince of Pleasure court me, I do not need his favours. I have a city, a kingdom of countless souls to command. I can extinguish suns and destroy worlds, what do I care for the trinkets of power the Great Enemy dangles in front of me?'

And there was the confession, masked as denial. The whisper they all heard, the constant demands and promises and threats from She Who Thirsts, to serve, to subdue, to submit. Except for the Phoenix Lords – rightly no longer truly alive as the Lord of the Dark City professed – Vect was one of the few hundred living eldar to remember the

Fall. The nobles that had come before had died by his machinations, the craftworlders and Exodites had passed a generation, only the longest-lived were born before the arrival of the Great Enemy, the younger had known nothing but its shadow on their lives.

Vect had endured the teasing and the threats and the knowledge of his certain damnation for all of that time, for a generation living and dying, and clung to his delusions of immortality as one who lies upon a deathbed knowing that there is no cure, but calling for the physician all the same.

She said nothing, there was nothing to say that would assuage his anger or steer his mood. Vect settled into brooding silence, slumped back in his throne, eyes downcast. None of the hundreds in attendance dared utter a word or make a sound for fear of disturbing him and incurring his instant wrath.

It reminded Jain Zar of the frozen retainers Naidazaar had arranged about his throne room. Vect needed no embalming stasis, just total power and the certain knowledge that his favour could elevate a kabal to the heights of dominance but his displeasure would be fatal.

After a period of unsettled quiet during which Vect sulkily stared off into the distance, a disturbance behind Jain Zar drew accusing stares. A troop of kabalites pushed their way through the silent throng. All eyes moved back to Vect, trying to predict his response to this intrusion. Jain Zar saw that the warriors brought with them a slender figure in a long gown of red, with white hair that hung to her broad-belted waist. There were no restraints upon her, but the crackle of agonisers acted as a reminder of the consequences of defiance.

The lady looked up, her hair parting to reveal cruel beauty – a cold indifference as she scanned the onlooking courtiers and petitioners.

Jain Zar barely recognised Maensith Drakar Alkhask – her hair had been black and she had always worn armour aboard ship. Her emerald eyes fell upon Jain Zar and widened in surprise. The group passed the Phoenix Lord and Maensith's attention switched to the ominous figure on the throne, whose fingers fidgeted with the thin gauze of his clothes.

The kabalite in charge of the prisoner escort darted a look at his companions and approached the steps of the throne. The incubi stiffened, ready to act. The kabalite fell to his knees, head bowed.

'Lord Vect, your guest has arrived.'

Lugubriously, Vect roused himself from his sulk and looked at Maensith. Some semblance of animation returned as he laid eyes upon the prisoner and moved his gaze to Jain Zar.

'This? This is what you need from me?' he asked.

'Yes.'

'And you expect me to just let it go, to wander free, an insult to my allies, an encouragement to my enemies?'

'I need her help. Tell me what you want in return.'

Vect flexed his fingers like a merchant readying to haggle for his wares. His gaze moved back and forth several times between Maensith and Jain Zar, a calculating look in his eye.

'It took some effort to acquire Maensith Dracon. While she was wise enough not to fight against my warriors, the expedition wasn't without expense. Daethrak Demarr had to be rewarded for the risk, and his work on the lady's retainers required certain elements that are awkward to acquire. Khiadysis Hierarch would be willing to extend me considerable concessions for her safe conduct to him. The Crimson Talon controls much of the Blizzardway. With the Winter Tower destroyed, they will be forced to relinquish control of their docks in the Spire of Shadowed Stars and the Talon. All of these things please me. Maensith will be part of that price. What can you offer that is of equal interest?'

'I have nothing but what I carry with me. I am a Phoenix Lord, I have no possessions, no territories.'

'You have exactly what I want.' Vect pointed to the Blade of Destruction still pushed into the floor. His slender finger moved to the Silent Death.

'My weapons? I do not think they are as remarkable as you hope, but they are yours. I can fashion more.'

'I don't want them for myself, Jain Zar. I want you to use them. A place where you have some experience, I believe. You will fight in my arena.'

'Don't.' Maensith shook her head, defiant in the presence of Vect, earning herself a scowl from the tyrant of the Dark City. 'You'll die. And I'll still be a prisoner. A waste of your life.'

Jain Zar wondered just how much Commorragh's tyrant knew about her, and her past. If he wanted to destroy Jain Zar he had ample resources to do so. He wanted her alive, for the time being. The spectacle of a Phoenix Lord fighting in a wych stadium would reinforce his reputation as the paramount power in the Dark City. But there had to be more than that to Vect's plan, a goal she could not see. To see her die beneath the blades of his champion? That would be a statement few could dispute.

Or did he think to awaken something in her. Did he know that much of her past? Something to unleash, something he hoped to control, perhaps.

'I accept,' she said to Vect and then looked at Maensith. 'Send your best champion against me. There are worse things than death.'

'Yes, for certain,' said Vect, lips twisted in a sinister smile. '*You* will bear my colours. *You* will be my champion in the arena. I am sure you will not disappoint me, Storm of Silence.'

6

A whole civilisation had died and new societies been born in the age since Jain Zar had last waited in the shadows of a gate looking out into an arena of death. So much had changed, but she could not deny the visceral thrill of the experience. Everything she had learnt – all that she had been taught – had been directed at controlling and channelling the sensation. But she had never relinquished that sense of expectation in the moments before battle.

The arena was so much vaster than anything she had seen before. The dome of Eidafaeron's blood-dancers looked like a provincial slaughterpit in comparison to the bank after bank of stands and terraces that surrounded the fighting ground. The view through the gate revealed only a narrow fraction of the space but still she could see many thousands.

There was an expectant hush. The shuffle of feet could be heard as spectators still made their way to their places, while the shrill cries of vendors split the quiet, offering exotic delicacies, intoxicating vapours and more esoteric services.

GAV THORPE

From behind, in the corridors and chambers below the killing field, the echo of preparations continued. Whetstones gliding, las-torches sparking, the murmur of pre-combat rituals by those about to face each other. It was so familiar she thought she might turn and see Venanesh or Amareith waiting behind her.

And in the reverie was a dark pill to swallow. This had not changed. In all of the time that had passed, this was exactly how it had been at the blood-dances. Every depravity she believed the dark kin were capable of came from the time before the Fall. As much as she despised the wyches of Commorragh, Jain Zar knew that except for a moment of clarity and a chance meeting she would likely be one of them – or more precisely would have been, because it was not an existence that lent itself to longevity.

What would her former self have thought of this moment? Would she have been proud or horrified?

A swell of noise from the gate signified an increase in the intensity of the crowd. Jain Zar knew what that meant before she saw the figures emerging from the other gates out into the white sands.

White sands. White, the colour of death. The perfect canvas to paint with the blood of a foe. Even the smell of it was an invitation to memories she had ignored for longer than the lifetime of a mortal eldar. Its legacy was within her and it was to that place she had to return.

She did not understand how it could be that the dreams of a dead god could turn events of the future, but she had to wonder if Asuryan had known this would come to pass. Or did fate simply give way to circumstance and serendipity, its patterns created by ignorance and hindsight?

Always she had fought for survival, but this time she

entered an arena with something far greater at stake. If she failed here, two craftworlds would die.

'They're waiting for you.' The prompt came from a raven-haired wych standing at the bottom of the ramp behind Jain Zar. The gladiator was clad in scant armour, only the most vital areas protected by plate, leaving him free to move and fight. He nodded past the Phoenix Lord. 'They're getting impatient.'

Jain Zar could hear the murmurs of discontent. They had been promised a spectacle like no other, though Vect had made it clear to all within earshot that if just a hint of his new champion's identity was known in advance everybody privy to that information would suffer.

She knew that her entrance would not disappoint. As much as she desired to end this affair, to be gone with Maensith to fulfil her quest, the part of her that was still a blood-dancer could not resist the opportunity to entertain.

'Let them wait. The more frustrated they get, the greater their delight when their desires are satisfied. If you live past today, perhaps you will remember that.'

The wych sneered and shrugged.

'I am Druath the Serpent, victor of forty contests. My face is known across the city. Three archons vie for my patronage. What do you know of the blood sands, craftworld bitch?'

The Silent Death left her hand in a fluid motion, taking the warrior's head from his neck before spinning back to her. She chastised herself for her petulance even as she hooked the triskele to her belt. The Phoenix Lord marched down the ramp, stooped to lift up the severed head by its topknot and turned back to the sands.

'Let's see how well your face is really known.'

She advanced up the ramp and, just as she was about to step into the light, threw the head arcing into the arena. Shouts of surprise and delight became roars of appreciation – evidently Druath the Serpent had indeed enjoyed some fame. The calls increased in volume, demanding Vect's new champion be revealed.

Jain Zar stepped out from the shadows with swift strides and the arena exploded with noise.

There were seven others waiting, wyches armed with a variety of weapons – splinter pistols, impalers, razorsnares, falchions, shardnets, hydraknives and other wargear. Like everything else, Jain Zar knew them all well from her time in the blood-dances. Little had changed in the style of the combats. The wyches' arrogant smiles fell away as they saw the nature of the combatant Asdrubael Vect had hired them to face.

Where before they had been spread across the sands, wary of approaching each other too closely, by unspoken agreement the wyches drew together, forming tacit alliance against the outsider. They formed small groups, a trio and two pairs of warriors, experienced at teamwork as well as individual combat.

Jain Zar stopped about a quarter of the way to the centre of the arena. The killing area was far larger than anything she had seen before and she assessed her tactics accordingly.

A pair of wyches moved to her left and opened fire with their pistols. Toxin-tipped shards splintered across Jain Zar's armour as she broke into a run, heading for the two other groups; the pistol fire was a lure, of little danger to a fully armoured warrior.

The others split as Jain Zar sprinted towards them,

moving in opposite directions to outflank the Phoenix Lord. She let fly with the Silent Death at the trio directly ahead and instantly changed direction to bear down on the other pair. She knew from the excited gasps of the crowd that at least one of her targets had failed to dodge the curving path of the triskele. She held up her free hand as she ran, snatching the weapon from the air as it spun over her shoulder.

One of the wyches she ran towards had a barb-covered shardnet and long three-tined impaler. The other wielded a heavy blade two-handed. The wych with the net took a step and hurled it at Jain Zar from just a few paces away while the falchion-armed warrior sped past, hoping to land a powerful blow against a freshly entangled target.

The Phoenix Lord lashed the Blade of Destruction through the net, letting the barbs entangle around the haft. She ducked beneath the falling shardnet and released her glaive, diving into a roll that took her under the swing of the wych directly ahead. Coming to her feet in front of the impaler-armed gladiatrix, she thrust hard and the points of her gauntlet-clad fingers punched up through the throat and jaw of her foe.

The appreciative roar of the crowd made the stands shake. Through the tumult she picked out the hiss of a blade through the air. Jain Zar fell and rolled to her right, anticipating the fresh attack from the other wych. The falchion parted several hairs of her elaborate crest as she came to her feet in a spray of sand. She spun and swept out the Silent Death like a three-bladed dagger, opening up her target from groin to chest, parting armour and straps with the blow.

She threw the Jainas Mor at two more wyches running

towards her – the survivors from her first attack. They quickly cartwheeled and somersaulted out of its deadly path, but the delay gave Jain Zar time to recover the Zhai Morenn and face them with both weapons.

More splinters cracked against her armour from the left, but rather than injure her the shots were intended to distract, just as the other pair charged. Jain Zar leapt into their attack, meeting their charge with her own. The Zhai Morenn flicked left then right in her hand, parrying a hydraknife of one foe and slashing open the throat of the other. A turn and a sweep took the legs from the remaining gladiator, spilling a wash of fresh blood across the sand.

Now she was left with the warriors armed with the splinter pistols and punch-daggers. By unspoken agreement her foes fired on the move, one breaking to the right and the other to the left. Jain Zar headed after the one to her left, not directly towards but across his line, cutting the arena in half.

Like a herding beast, she tracked back and forth, darting forward when one or other of her adversaries tried to break past, the threat of the Silent Death forcing them back.

She had them almost caught at one end of the bloodfield. To their credit, they abandoned any pretence with their pistols and stood a little distance apart, each with a cestus at the ready.

The crowd fell deathly silent, intrigued by the subtlety of the contest, watching the game playing out with rapt interest. In the quiet Jain Zar heard the echo of a whine from a gateway behind her, a few moments before the crowd roared in greeting to a newcomer to the fight.

She did not take her eyes off the wyches in front, but listened as a pair of jetbikes shrieked from the entrance, cruising high to make a lap of the arena. Hooted calls and shouts of encouragement followed them around the stadium like a sonic wake as they dipped their machines towards the ground, accelerating behind Jain Zar.

The wyches ahead seized their moment and charged with defiant shouts. Jain Zar let them speed closer, trusting that they had timed their attack well. She could see the eyes of one tracing the approach of the jetbikes and the sound of the engines further betrayed the angle and distance of the attack.

She ducked and turned, holding the Blade of Destruction in both hands. The jetbike screamed overhead, the rider's slashing blow missing its mark while the engine of his mount let out a tortured shriek as it ripped itself apart along the waiting blade of the Zhai Morenn.

Flaming pieces fell around Jain Zar, the rider tumbling into the sand to land heavily a few paces away. The Phoenix Lord was on him without hesitation, splitting his body as she had split his jetbike.

The second rider banked hard and tried to wrestle his machine into a fresh attack run. The two wyches on the ground were almost on Jain Zar, drawing her attention away from the mounted reaver coming from behind again.

An instant before the rider was upon her, Jain Zar leapt acrobatically, bending her body to somersault backwards as she flung out the Silent Death in the same movement. The flaming triskele arced gracefully towards one of the incoming wyches, his eyes widening in horror a heartbeat before it slashed off the top of his head.

The Phoenix Lord's leap took her over the head of the

rider, his lance slashing thin air. She landed behind, driving the Zhai Morenn down through his chest and gut. The jetbike jerked as the dying pilot fell into the controls. Jain Zar rode the dip and jumped again, snatching the returning Silent Death from the air before she landed.

The baying and cheering of the crowd was a tangible thing; the atmosphere writhed with bloodlust that Jain Zar could feel as a pulse in her soul. Their adulation drew the eye of the Great Enemy, even here in the heart of Commorragh behind layers of warding. Perhaps they no longer felt it, but to Jain Zar their savage bloodlust and hunger for the kill were a lure to Chaos she could not ignore.

The surviving wych sagged even as he was forced by momentum to follow through with his attack. His aim was good, his speed incredible, but neither was enough to catch Jain Zar. The glinting edge of the cestus passed a hair's breadth from the side of her mask, at the same moment that the point of the Zhai Morenn entered the wych's heart.

She sidestepped the falling corpse, a fresh arc of arterial blood coating her cuirass like a crimson sash.

Jain Zar turned and found the immense balcony where Asdrubael Vect viewed the proceedings from the shadow of an immense awning. She could see the tyrant standing at the balustrade, gripping the stone, a savage grin on his face – triumphant rather than defeated. Various slaves attended to his guests behind and Maensith stood between two incubi. She had a hand over her mouth, caught between fascination, hope and anxiety.

Setting out across the sand, Jain Zar held aloft the Blade of Destruction, saluting the crowd in response to their deafening roar of approval. She needed them to add weight to her demand. Vect did not need to court the favour of these people, but he gained little by directly denying their desires. Jain Zar would appeal to the mob if need be, to demand that Vect handed over the prize she had rightly won.

The tyrant of Commorragh guessed her intent and straightened, face turning serious. He lifted a finger and wagged it in admonishment, a slight shake of the head. He moved his gaze, from the Phoenix Lord to something behind her.

The crowd's cheers faltered, replaced with shock from some, from others delight that the entertainment was to continue. They pointed and clapped with excitement, exchanging animated chatter even as they continued to gorge on sweetmeats and inhale deep draughts of narcotic smoke.

With a sense of foreboding, Jain Zar turned to see what fresh foe had entered the arena.

Two haemonculi escorted their creation onto the sands amid the hush and a ripple of excited applause. The crowd stared down upon this novelty with appreciative gazes, exchanging querying looks and whispered conversation regarding this intriguing development.

At first Jain Zar thought it silhouetted against some light in the grandstand, but a moment's consideration revealed that it was dark in itself, surrounded by an umbra of power. As it approached with long strides the details became more distinct.

It stood over thrice Jain Zar's height. The monstrosity was fashioned in the likeness of a four-armed giant, its dark flesh bound and reinforced with organopolymer plates and braces, as though the curved armour and ribbing was intended to contain its bulk rather than protect it. It wielded a selection of oversized wych weapons – shard-net and impaler in one pair of clawed hands, whip-like razorsnare and long-bladed falchion in the other.

It had no head as such, simply a multifaceted diamond where neck and head would have been. Witchlights danced within the massive gemstone, coalescing and separating, forming the ghost of a face before splitting into random whorls.

Spirit stones stolen from the craftworlds gleamed on its breastplate and two flared chimney-like appendages towered from its back. Glimmering with the souls captured within, the spirit stones powered the exo-skeleton with psychic energy and left faint ripples of silver and gold dancing across the unnatural flesh of the haemonculis' creation.

Jain Zar could feel the wash of dread that emanated from the stones embedded into the compound creature. Beyond their metaphysical wails she could sense the presence of the monster's spirit – alive in some sense but wholly corrupted.

With shock she recognised the spiritual component of the titanic gladiator. Within the carcass of flesh and artificial systems the haemonculi had bound a daemon. Its core was a corrupted waystone, a miniature gateway into the raw warp to sustain the daemonic presence within.

The gem-lights gathered, becoming piercing points that stared directly at Jain Zar. A wave of pleasure emanated from the flesh-construction. It flexed its arms and purred like a nightmarish cat.

IV

Heat washed through the opening door of the lander but Jain Zar felt a chill run through her body as she saw where Asurmen had taken them. He stepped past and strode out onto the landing pad adjoined to the great dome atop what was unmistakeably the blood-dance arena.

'Why…?' She did not step onto the ramp, one hand tight on the edge of the door lip. 'What are we doing here?'

'Foraging,' said Asurmen. 'We need proper weapons and armour. I believe there is a working armoury system here.'

'It's dangerous. These blood-dancers…' How could she tell him? Was he really blind to the threat? 'What if someone finds us?'

'It is deserted, Jain Zar.' Asurmen turned with a look of confusion. 'It is quite safe.'

She took an uncertain step. Asurmen turned away, at ease it seemed. His confidence was infectious and she moved after him. Even so, she drew the slender sword from her belt, more assured with the monomolecular-edged blade in her hand.

Around them stretched the city, more broken and twisted than when they had last been here. The air seemed to writhe at a distance, giving glimpses of a shattered, star-lit universe as though a reflection seen in a dark, cracked mirror. The presence of leaking daemonic energy was palpable, making Jain Zar's skin itch, leaving a dull throb in the base of her skull.

Asurmen was heading towards a gateway that led into the upper part of the dome above the main entrance. He was going the wrong way, the armoury was in a sub-level close to the rear of the arena, but Jain Zar held her tongue.

'Where did they go?' she asked, feigning vague interest as they moved from the heat into the shade of the great awning that sheltered the upper stands. 'The blood-dancers?'

'Into the web like the others.'

He stopped and Jain Zar stepped beside him, looking down into the oval of pale, bloodied sands. She thought she could see figures fighting – shadows played across the sand, swaying and flickering but unmistakeably those cast by an ongoing blood-dance. She stiffened at the sight.

'Echoes,' Asurmen told her. He laid a reassuring hand on her arm but the touch of his fingers made her flinch. 'Psychic ripples from the cataclysm bouncing back from the stones, from our minds. This world is slipping into the other-realm and as the veil thins more phenomena are emerging.'

Jain Zar only barely heard his words, still enraptured by the shadowplay of a fight progressing on the floor of the arena. Though she could see only the vaguest remains of what transpired, she could follow the cut and thrust – both metaphorical and literal – as the two combatants moved back and forth over the sands. Intrigued, she started to descend the steps for a closer look.

Asurmen grabbed her shoulder to hold her back. She turned sharply, heart pounding, sword raised at the sudden contact. As her eyes met his, so their minds conjoined for an instant also.

In the moments she shared the mind of Asurmen before his mental barriers slammed like a fortress gate she was swept into a fierce recollection. She was in almost exactly the same place, just a few rows forward and to the left, but the blood-dance arena was subtly different. There were no sands, the floor covered with an artificial turf marked with lines and symbols. A variety of hoops and nets jutted from the wall on poles, just out of reach of the swirl of eldar streaming below. She found herself absorbed by the memory from her companion, experiencing it as he had.

The crowd shared a collective wince and gasp as one of the Void Ravens' players folded to the floor, blood spraying from his lacerated gut. Sirens screamed, announcing the opinion of the adjudicators that there had been foul play. The player that had made the offending slash pleaded her innocence with a shout, her begging turning to screamed threats as enforcer automatons entered the court and dragged her away. The visitors, the Sunkillers, jeered and snarled as the Void Ravens' playmaster called for a pause while she reorganised the team on the sideline.

'You know,' Illiathin told his companion, 'I had my doubts about some of these rule changes. When they allowed punching and kicking, it turned the game into a boring brawl in the middle of the court, but the introduction of blades is bordering on an act of genius. That you can only cut the ball carrier has turned this back into a sport of manoeuvre and passing, feint and speed. There's so much more skill again.'

He turned to his friend when there was no reply.

'Myrthuis?'

His companion stared down at the courtside, a look of such intensity on his face that Illiathin wondered what could warrant such scrutiny. He looked and saw that his friend was fixed by the sight of the wounded player. A slick of blood surrounded the wounded Void Raven, patterns made in the red-soaked grass by his flailing arms and grasping fingers.

Illiathin could see there was a strange beauty in the scene below, the slow leaking of vitality from the injured player, the desperate desire to cling to life. The colours were so vivid, bright red against the yellow of the court-side area.

'Is he… Is someone going to help him?' Illiathin asked, dragging his eyes away. He was disturbed by his own fascination, and even more afraid when he saw the glimmer of cruel delight in Myrthuis' eyes.

'No courtside assistance,' his friend murmured, eyes locked on the tableau of death below. 'New ruling yesterday.'

'I need to…' Illiathin realised he did not need any flimsy fabrication to leave; Myrthuis was barely paying him any attention. His friend did not even look around when Illiathin stood up.

Illiathin looked at the rest of the crowd, listened to the chants and songs. The Void Ravens' supporters were calling for vengeance, demanding that their players retaliate. For their part, those in the crowd that held the Sunkillers as their favourites shouted taunts and insults, seeking to stir up the home team supporters even more. There was

already fighting around the fringes of the crowd and Illiathin could sense the growing tension.

Jain Zar staggered back, dizzy for a moment as her own
psyche reasserted itself over the impression made by her
companion's thoughts. Asurmen's stare was glazed for several heartbeats, distracted by the separation.

Clarity returned as he looked at her.

'What was that?' Jain Zar demanded. 'That was not...'

'I had forgotten,' Asurmen whispered. 'Forgotten how
this place had once been. Forgotten how sporting achievement and team pride had been consumed by competition
and tribalism.'

'That was here, before the blood-dances?' Jain Zar had
never considered the possibility that anything but the
blood-sports could have played out in the arena. She
wondered how old Asurmen really was, but a different
question reached her lips. 'What actually happened to us?'

He said nothing at first, shaking his head to dismiss
whatever images continued to linger in his mind. Stepping away from the seats, towards the descender carousel,
his movement drew Jain Zar with him.

'You remember nothing of the time before the Fall?'

'I certainly remember nothing of this place as... a stadium for harmless ball games.'

'Harmless?' Asurmen stopped as a gateway lensed open
in front of him to reveal the spiralling path of the carousel. He stepped on and the moving walkway whispered
into life. Jain Zar walked quickly to follow him, taking
several strides to come alongside him on the descender.
'Even before the players were incited to violence, before
our desire for victory demanded the sacrifice of those that

strove for it, there was little enough that was harmless about this place. My transformation has given me perspective on what occurred in my earliest life, but objectivity is a shadow-goal to chase. Even so, I see that what occurred on the court was simply an extension of the desires of those of us who watched from afar. We identified too strongly with these false notions of teamwork and aspiration, falling upon the hollow achievements of others to hide from the emptiness of our own existence.'

'But…' Jain Zar realised she had not phrased her question properly. 'What was the point of it? The ball, I mean? Why bring a ball to a combat?'

Asurmen turned, a sudden flux of expressions crossing his face – confusion, amusement and then concern.

'It was used to score points, to determine who won the contest. Do you really not know that?'

Jain Zar considered this for a moment.

'Why would you score points? Surely the survivors are the winners?' They were nearing the ground floor and Asurmen made moves to step off the carousel. Jain Zar knew they had to continue down into the subterranean levels and held back, pretending to be distracted by her thoughts. 'That would mean the fighting was, literally, pointless. That is… obscene.'

Realising that she was not going to follow, Asurmen remained on the edge of the descender. He glanced out through the arch to the main thoroughfare that surrounded the arena seating and then back to her.

'That was the point I was attempting to illustrate.' He sighed and pointed to the spiralling carousel. 'We were sucked into a vortex of our own creation, a disaster born of apathy and hedonism. Our desires, our own refined senses and sensibilities were our downfall, craving ever more outrageous stimuli, fuelling our desires so that we were never quite satisfied.'

The descender came to a broad opening at the bottom level and they dismounted before it slid beneath the floor. Asurmen looked around, seeking some sign of where they were, where to go. Jain Zar stepped down the shadowed corridor ahead of him, feigning impatience.

'Let's just try this way – the armoury has to be down here somewhere.'

'What started as a need for more excitement, a desire for more than simple pride at stake, escalated,' Asurmen continued as he walked alongside Jain Zar with swift, long strides. 'The destination, winning, was no longer sufficient. The journey had to be more dramatic, more… visceral.'

Jain Zar led them onwards. She paused at the next turn, gave a shrug of indecision and then turned to Asurmen.

'Any ideas?'

He silently pointed to a plaque on the wall. It was inscribed with a neat schematic depicting the lower level, different areas annotated in a key beside it. The armoury was clearly marked, as Jain Zar knew it would be.

'This way,' she said, after a show of examining the map. She took them along a passageway that cut directly beneath the fighting floor above. Rib-like structures braced the ceiling, to bear the weight of not only the sands but also some of the larger creatures that had occasionally featured in the most extravagant performances and galas.

The armoury was at the far end. She had thought to find it empty, ransacked of all weapons and armour, but the hooks on the walls and mannequins were still laden with all manner of deadly blades, whips, spears, nets, curved plates and scale armour.

'I think the occupants left in a hurry,' said Asurmen in answer to her unspoken question. 'Or whatever took them did not need their weapons...'

Without thought, Jain Zar moved to the trio of dummies that held the enlarged vambraces and chest plates that she had once worn, her eye darting to the triskeles and glaives on the wall behind them. She reached out a hand.

'Leave it,' said Asurmen. He pointed to the alcove at the back of the chamber where the artificer station was kept. 'We need the means to make this wargear, not just the weapons themselves.'

They investigated the multi-limbed device that sat dormant in the alcove. Its various limbs were capable of ejecting, moulding, cutting and beating a variety of complex shapes, a plethora of materials that could be conjured at an atomic level from the microforge inside its main cavity. The pair were able to open the fastenings that held it to the wall, and it drifted out at a touch, carried by a suspensor field. Asurmen gave it a gentle push and it glided easily through the air.

Jain Zar stopped beside the weapon rack on their way out.

'It will take time to manufacture fresh armaments.' She lifted her sword as if in explanation. 'These are crude blades in comparison to what is on display here.'

'I cannot stop you,' said Asurmen, though Jain Zar had hoped for a little more enthusiasm.

She eagerly disrobed and pulled on the arm sheath and cuirass. She cinched the straps tight and unhooked a throwing triskele from the wall. Lastly she took up a duelling glaive, its long, curved blade catching the lights of the armoury on its crystalline edge.

They stepped back out into the corridor and, after consulting another map plaque, sought the nearest carousel to take them back up to the roof. However, they had barely started walking when Asurmen turned sharply in reaction to something Jain Zar did not – or could not – see.

'What was that?' said the Hand of Asuryan.

Jain Zar did not reply. She felt movement around her, like the touch of a breeze on her bare arm and cheeks, half-seen shadows gliding past. She thought she saw figures in armour passing by from the armoury. She and Asurmen continued on but as they passed a side corridor – one that led to the healer's chamber, she knew – she would have sworn she spied two insubstantial figures dragging a third between them, leaving a trail of ghostly blood that disappeared into the floor.

'What do you see?'

Jain Zar realised she had stopped to look. She ignored Asurmen's question, her attention drawn not by a sight but a sound. A roar of the crowd above, distant and muffled but unmistakeable. The thunder of stamping feet. She knew well that reaction to a particularly vicious or elaborate death. Asurmen spoke but she did not hear the words. Her blood was seething through her body, a reaction to the sights and sounds that drifted through her consciousness. The half-imagined tremble of the stands echoed as shivers in her limbs.

She knew it was not real, in a detached, isolated part of her brain. The rest of her body did not want to cooperate. Glaive in her grip she marched along the corridor and up the ramp that led to the sands.

In reality the arena was lit only by the ambient light

that streamed from outside the dome, but in her mind's eye she remembered the glare of lamps highlighting her as she stepped out of the shadowed gate and into the full gaze of the waiting masses. Her breath came easily, the glaive in her hand light. The swish of its keen edge broke the expectant hush she heard in her thoughts.

Jain Zar turned slowly, seeing row after row of cadaverous faces leering down at her from the stands – a crowd of the deceased, some little more than dead skin tight on skeletons, others with split skulls, gashed faces, slit throats, pierced breastbones and savaged ribcages.

Her opponents. Her victims.

All had come to watch her final fight. Their silence was not expectation, it was accusation.

Whirling about, she sought a foe, feet moving effortlessly across the sands as she turned her blade first to one of the entry gates and then back to the one by which she had arrived. She saw a figure there, could barely remember who it was.

'Jain Zar!'

The words meant nothing. A shout that vanished with the draught of air that drifted from the gates.

She took two steps towards the apparition, noting the sword at his waist, the easy way he held himself. Full of latent energy and motion. A threat.

'This isn't you.'

She could smell blood, fresh and pungent and intoxicating. The sand beneath her feet shifted, every grain trembling in anticipation of her next move. The crowd – her crowd – watched expectantly.

'Where are you? Tell me.' The voice was insistent but not aggressive. 'Jain Zar, talk to me.'

The request was an odd one, unexpectedly puncturing the fog that clouded her thoughts. The lights seemed to dim, the blood-scent grew stale. She looked around again, saw decay and ruin, the dilapidated stands and empty seats, the old blood dried into the particles of white sand.

The stamping died away, replaced by the furious pulse of her heart to the same beat. The glare of spotlights became a shaft of ruddy sunlight through a crack in the dome.

'I...' Forcing out the words helped her focus. 'I know this place well.'

The confession brought a little more clarity. She saw Asurmen, recognised his face, felt his gaze on her.

'A trick.' The thought that he had brought her here to force this confession riled her more than the phantasms of the past. Her voice became a shriek. 'You tricked me!'

This place, the feeling that surged through her, flared into fresh life. She was running, glaive at the ready, before she had made a conscious choice. Her hand moved to the triskele at her hip, but before she could pull it free Asurmen reacted. His arm moved in a leisurely arc, its languid pace belying the power and accuracy of the projectile that left his hand.

She did not even see what it was he had thrown before it struck her between the eyes. Stars danced across her vision as she fell, the glaive slashing into the sands with a spray of white and crimson dust.

Shaking her head, Jain Zar felt the shadow of Asurmen move over her. She looked for his eyes, found sanctuary and understanding in them. He pulled the armoury machine behind him, one hand extended to help her to her feet.

'I did not know, I swear,' he told her. 'This place, I mean.

I knew you had to be a gladiatrix, that was obvious, but I thought it was in one of the lesser pits. Not here, not in the grand arena.'

'These echoes... They were inside me, taking me back.'

'I was wrong,' said Asurmen, with a sad shake of the head. He looked at the apparitions that ghosted around them, exchanging silent blows, screaming unheard taunts and uttering death-cries. 'Not echoes... They stayed here, became part of this place, reliving their bloody existence over and over. Trapped.'

Jain Zar shuddered, but her eye was drawn to that place where she knew the Master of the Blood-dance would be. Sure enough, the canopied throne was shrouded in a darkness she could not penetrate, but she spied two silvery glints. She tore her eyes away.

'How many times are you going to pick me up?' Jain Zar asked, grabbing Asurmen's hand to haul herself from the sand.

'However many times I need to.'

Even so, she noted his foot was on the haft of her glaive, pinning it to the floor.

7

All consideration of entertainment vanished the moment Jain Zar heard the otherworldly mewing of the wychbeast. She launched at the creature and unleashed a nerve-shredding scream, letting free the disgust that welled up at the sight and sound of the bastardised monstrosity. The psychosonic attack set sparks flying from the monster's spirit stones and churned ripples across its half-flesh.

The wychbeast fell to one knee, crystal head bowed against the storm of power that erupted across it, the lights within converging into an angry red glare. Jain Zar levelled the Blade of Destruction, aiming at a point between the crystal and shoulder.

She was half a dozen paces away, still accelerating, when the wychbeast answered with its own bawl. A bass thrum pulsed outwards, ripping the air with a wall of shadow, a bow wave of white sand thrown up before it. The storm of particles engulfed Jain Zar for a moment before the roar hit her like a detonating shell and threw her from her feet.

The misery of the wychbeast coursed through her thoughts

and entwined her limbs, crushing organs, smothering all thought. Darkness sucked down at her, blinding, deafening, numbing. A seeming eternity passed during which it occurred to her with slow foreboding that she hadn't yet hit the ground.

The impact jarred all sense and feeling back into her, replacing a void of sensation with crashing pain and searing heat. More sand sprayed, braking her momentum. The stench of burning flesh was everywhere, though she had neither body nor nostrils, a constructed memory inside her consciousness.

She lay helpless, half buried in a white drift, dazed and trembling.

Thirty paces away the wychbeast advanced, whirling the shardnet about its head. The razorsnare, impossibly long, snapped out to lash agony across Jain Zar's chest. The shock of its touch jolted energy through her, powering limbs that had been deadened by the beast-roar.

She rolled sideways, avoiding the next lash. In one fluid motion she flipped one-handed to her feet and threw the Silent Death with the other. Its course flew true, crashing against the crystalline face. But the triskele glanced awkwardly from a vertex, landing in the sand some distance away rather than returning to her outstretched hand. The slightest of scratches marred the crystal face.

It threw the shardnet, the mesh spreading as it whirled, barbs catching Jain Zar's leg as she leapt aside. A score of hooks sank into the armour of her thigh and the rest of the net contracted, digging into the sand like a creature hauling her into its trapdoor lair.

One leg immobile, she only just avoided the razorsnare aimed for her face, ducking beneath the whispering tip as she slashed at the shardnet with the Zhai Morenn. Fibres parted under the blow that left a furrow through the sand beneath, but the net responded by coiling tighter, wrapping itself around her greave and boot.

The wychbeast loomed, coils of blackness undulating along its limbs and body. Its crystal face had taken on a purple and pink hue, emanating amusement.

The crowd screamed their approval, stamping and yelling so hard that the stands shook like thunder. Dodging another flail of the razorsnare, Jain Zar caught a glimpse of Asdrubael Vect on his viewing platform. The tyrant of Commorragh seemed disappointed, perhaps believing the fight would soon be concluded.

His indifference sent a fresh rage boiling through Jain Zar. She saw the falchion blade descending towards her and pivoted, avoiding the strike even as she ripped her entangled leg out of the sand, dragging the shardnet with her. The thorn-mesh slapped into the wychbeast's falling arm and constricted on contact, snaring the limb.

As the wychbeast pulled up its arm in confusion, Jain Zar swung, her leg still bound within the shardnet. She twisted and used the pendulous momentum to fling her free leg around the limb above, and thus anchored swung the Blade of Destruction two-handed at the carapace protecting the monster's chest.

The Zhai Morenn blazed with purple light as it struck, carving open a furrow of twisted psychoplastic, parting the unflesh beneath. Splintered ribs splayed in the wound, springing out to widen the injury.

The crowd whooped their appreciation, their curses turning to shouts of encouragement.

She was too close for the wychbeast to use its weapons,

clinging spiderlike to two of its limbs, blade whirling around to deliver another crippling blow to the exposed torso. Shadows streamed from the lengthening wound, forming a flux of darkness around them like a swarm that hissed and crackled.

The wychbeast dropped its impaler and seized hold of her free leg. The arm crushed her against its body, stifling all movement, pinning the Zhai Morenn between Jain Zar and the gaping wound. Claws sank into the armour of the Phoenix Lord's leg as it prised her away from its upper arm, parting the cords of the shardnet as it did so.

Pressed up against its protoflesh, Jain Zar could feel the beating of several hearts inside the chest cavity, but more overwhelming was the sense of lust and hunger that swelled from the wychbeast's spirit. It wanted not just to destroy her, but to possess her, to enslave every part of her body and soul.

A fresh dread sent icy shivers through the Phoenix Lord as she realised the nature of the daemon trapped within the artificially grown shell: an emissary of the Great Enemy. Had this been Vect's aim? Not just to break her mortal form, but to see her immortal essence consumed?

As always her fear became ire, channelled from terror into soul-searing rage. She screamed, just an arm's length from the wychbeast's crystalline head.

The shockwave hit the creature like a las-beam and sent stress fractures webbing across the surface of the crystal. This close, Jain Zar was caught up in the backwash of her own fury, launched as though hurled by a blastwave.

She twisted from the wychbeast's grip, arcing her back to turn her fall into a somersault. The Phoenix Lord landed on her feet, somewhat unsteadily, the Zhai Morenn ready to deflect an incoming attack.

The parry was not needed. The monstrous gladiator staggered back, empty hand raised to its cracked crystal face, rivulets of thin oil streaming through its fingers and streaking over the open wound in its chest.

Jain Zar flung out a hand, willing the Silent Death back to her grip. The triskele tugged free of the sands and flew to her waiting fingers.

The wychbeast heaved, emitting an odd moan. It pulled at the crystal mask, glass-like shards falling away from its body. Straightening to its full height, it tore free the final pieces of the crystal, chunks of breastplate falling with it, sloughing away broken bones and torn flesh to reveal the cavity within.

Jain Zar's gaze was dragged into a bottomless void of shadow. It seemed as though the innards of the wychbeast descended into an unending abyss, deeper and deeper, darker and darker, until nothing was left but the Phoenix Lord and the lightless hole.

She was not alone. She felt hot breath on her neck, the pawing of clammy fingers on flesh long since lost.

Two diamond bright points regarded her from the darkness, ever-watchful, assessing and calculating, weighing up her worth, nothing more than a commodity to be exploited.

Memories fought each other in their desire to be seen. Terrible recollections of slavery and debasement beneath the blood-dance arena.

And being watched. Always those diamond eyes regarding everything with cold clarity.

The Master of the Blood-dance.

The thought made everything spin. Was it really him, trapped within this mortal-daemon frame? Or a conjuration of the wychbeast, her worst nightmare dragged free from the depths to which she had consigned it?

Reality returned, and with it the absence of sound. The crowd waited in abject silence, the air thick with tension as the two fighters stood opposite each other. Jain Zar could see Vect again, more animated at the rail as he stared down in triumph.

Yet not for her death. His eyes were not on her, but on the wychbeast.

The rage this time was unlike anything she had felt before, not even in the depths of its grip in the arena or when she had harnessed its power under the guidance of Asurmen. Feral, self-destructive, untrammelled anger consumed every part of her. It wanted control. It wanted her to let it free, to give it her body so that it might rip asunder this affront to all that she was, to avenge wrongs that had festered in the darkness.

Revenge, hot and bloody, would be exacted upon the source of all her fears.

She was a leaf caught in the thermals above a furnace, about to drop into the flames and be consumed. In that moment, as she was held aloft in the white hot draught, she understood what Vect had intended all along.

This was what he wanted to see. This was what he wanted to unleash. The Howling Banshee free of all restraint, giving in to the basic rage at the core of her being. To become the thing she had left behind – the thing he and all the kin of Commorragh represented. Indulgence, excess, gratification.

If she let the flames take her, there would be no return. She would be trapped inside the rage for eternity.

Vect wanted Jain Zar to fall.

V

The smell of freshly drying lamination masked the slightly older scent of newly composited weavewall, and stronger but more distant was the perfume of blossoms and the earthiness of freshly tilled soil. Eyes closed, Jain Zar allowed the sensation to trigger an image, picturing the tower that now rose up above the shrine room, the dormitories spreading out into burgeoning gardens.

'Hone the thought.' Asurmen spoke softly but insistently. 'A single image, a single moment, a single thought.'

She focused, narrowing down the inputs. She tried to shut out the touch of cool air on her ankles, the faint but unmistakeable buzz of the hydroponics. It was hard. Life in the arena – and its ever-present companion, bloody death – had taught her to open up to every sense, to be ready to react without thought to the slightest change or warning. What Asurmen asked seemed physically impossible. She could no more shut away these things than stop her blood flowing and her heart beating.

'Our openness destroyed us,' said Asurmen, repeating the

lesson he had begun on their return from the blood-dance stadium three dozen cycles earlier. 'Our lack of control robbed us of choice, of knowing ourselves. To regain our freedom from these impulses we must learn to isolate them and tackle them one at a time. We are each one against many, so we must choose a foe and best it before moving on to the next. Your anger comes from fear, your fear from lack of control. If you cannot concentrate your thoughts and emotions in a single aspect of yourself you will be overwhelmed by the sum of your experience. We must learn to act, not react.'

A thought.

One singular consideration, the essence of an idea.

Growth.

Everything else seemed to drop away from Jain Zar as she spiralled towards this instant, possessed by the fundamental notion of growth.

The moment she achieved clarity was the same moment she lost it. Her thoughts expanded again into success, pride, achievement, and the singular place of balance evaporated in a wash of her returning senses.

'Hone. You are not honing!' Asurmen betrayed no impatience, just positive assertion. 'Do not seek to plunge into the pool, but to sink slowly into the depths.'

Jain Zar opened her eyes, the dim light of the shrine to Asuryan bright as they adjusted. Blinking, she turned around and faced her teacher.

'What if I cannot do it?' she asked. 'What if you are unique in this ability to portion your mind into manageable compartments?'

'I do not think I am,' said Asurmen, ignoring the first question. 'I was nothing special. Less than special, I was arrogant, egotistical and easily distracted.'

'But how did you learn? There was nobody there to teach you.'

Asurmen smiled and glanced away, eyes moving to the half-formed shape of Asuryan that was being grown by a matter incubator to one side of the new shrine room.

'Perhaps I had a guide.' He waved for her to follow and started towards the arch that led from the sanctuary space. Jain Zar caught up with him and stepped out into the corridor at his side. 'When you saved me, in the space between my last heartbeat and my next, I had a moment. An awareness devoid of all ornamentation and past. I knew who I was, and I was nothing. And that was good.'

He led her to the other sanctum, the shrine to Khaine with its iron weapon racks and blood-hued floor. Immediately her tranquillity disappeared, replaced by a darker instinct. Asurmen picked up a training baton from a table and threw it to her before taking another for himself.

'Life,' Asurmen continued. He moved out into the duelling space that now adjoined the shrine and Jain Zar followed. 'I realised I was alive. When all else had fallen, when our entire people, our whole civilisation had been struck down by terror and death, I remain. That was my singular thought, the centre to which I continually return. That thought gives me strength and purpose. To make a meaning out of the meaningless.'

They stood opposite each other and raised batons in preparation to fight. The Hand of Asuryan looked sharply at Jain Zar, his expression intense for several heartbeats.

'I have made an error,' Asurmen said, turning his wrist so that the tip of his baton made slow circles. He smiled. 'Truly failure teaches us more than success!'

'An error? Failure?' Jain Zar swallowed hard, fearing he

spoke of her recruitment, of some deficiency in her person that could not be overcome. She could not stop the venom in her heart reaching her words. 'Maybe I erred, in thinking you could be of any use to me.'

'My journey is not your journey,' Asurmen said, paying no heed to her barbed accusation. 'We each begin from a different place and though our paths cross they will also take us to separate destinations.'

'I do not understand. You told me that we need to strive to control ourselves, that our goal is the same.'

Asurmen nodded.

'The goal is the journey.' He stepped back and lowered his baton. 'This is not a change-of-state that can be achieved and then forgotten. Our development must be continuous, an ever-present awareness of ourselves.'

He became quite animated, talking as much to himself as he was to Jain Zar.

'We each tread our path... There is no destination, simply one step after another, which we each take on our own but guided and assisted by those who have taken that step before.'

'You are making even less sense than I have come to expect, Asurmen.'

He looked at her, reminded that he was not alone. Eyes narrowed, he stalked closer, his stare boring into Jain Zar.

'My fear was of loss, as is yours, but you manifest that dread as anger. Let us forget other moments, and focus on the rage that fuels you. Become mistress of that rage and you will eliminate the fear. You cannot suppress it, you must harness it. I called you Jain Zar, the Storm of Silence. That is what you must become, not what you are.'

'Is there a point to this?'

'Scream.'

'What?'

'When your anger breaks free you scream. You have done it several times now. The scream is your fear being released.'

'How is this going to–'

'Scream!'

He slapped her hard. The sting burned through her, indignation and shame forcing its way into her gut and then exploding outwards in a wave of irrepressible ire.

Her arm shot out even as the shriek left her mouth. The tip of the baton barely touched Asurmen's chest but a heartbeat later he was lying on his back several paces away.

Even more surprising was the calm, cool tide that welled up in the wake of her outburst. Previously she would have set upon her discommoded enemy, consumed by the need to strike and slay out of survival instinct, an uncontrollable outpouring of bloodthirst. Now she watched dispassionately as Asurmen struggled to one knee, nursing his chest with a hand.

The ire was still there, an inferno-fist in her chest.

Jain Zar took a breath and allowed the anger to ebb away, satiated by release, not bloodletting.

She dared not move, her hand still extended with the baton, as Asurmen tentatively regained his feet and approached.

'How do you feel?' he asked.

Jain Zar was unsure of the answer – the conflict of emotions bottled up inside made her legs weak and set the shrine slowly spinning. And yet she could recall the singular moment Asurmen had talked about. Not for her life – she had been a servant of death too long. Something else had focused her being into one encapsulated idea.

When she replied, a tear rolled down her cheek at the recollection of that perfect moment.

'Free.'

8

The wychbeast peeled away its outer form as though shucking off a discarded robe. Armour and altered flesh fell to the sands, leaving a thing of shadow in its place; an absence rather than a presence. The darkness that had consumed Jain Zar regarded her with the icy glint of star-eyes.

The scream still threatened to burst free, taking with it the last vestiges of Jain Zar's control. Like a hound straining at its leash to hunt, the last gift of Khaine snarled and spat in her breast.

But to let it go would be surrender. It would be to accept its dominion over her, and never again would it be chained. If not, the wychbeast would slay her, break open the ward that bound her spirit to this plane, and the daemon within would drink deep of her soul.

With a susurrant cry, the wychbeast attacked, forming hard blades and spears from its shadow-limbs.

An impossible choice.

Death and damnation, or life enslaved to her basest emotion.

Jain Zar chose another way.

She closed mental fists around the shriek, turning the wail into a pulse of energy that filled her body and flowed along her limbs. Ignoring the lure of its wrath she remembered the cooling, calming words of Asurmen. She looked upon the wychbeast and through it, seeing the shadow monster behind, the Master of the blade-dance that had been so cruel and possessive.

The Silent Death left her hand as a star of black flame. She followed a moment behind, the Blade of Destruction held two-handed above her head.

Where the triskele struck, flame and shadow combusted into a burst of white that turned darkness into falling pale dust. Silent, powered by the internal scream, Jain Zar swept the Zhai Morenn towards the point of impact, channelling Khaine's gift not in hot anger but cold vengeance. In a blizzard of swirling white flakes she struck.

The fire became ice that crackled across the wychbeast's immaterial form. The impact of the Zhai Morenn turned the freezing apparition into a splinter of needle-like shards that showered outwards even as the momentum of the two combatants took them past each other, so that Jain Zar emerged from a shattering cloud of black fire and white fragments.

The Silent Death curved in a broad arc and then came back to her hand. She caught it and turned in one motion, thrusting out the Blade of Destruction towards Vect's balcony. The master of the Dark City looked down with a mixture of astonishment and barely controlled indignation.

The cheers started to her left, quickly taken up by more and more voices, spreading around the arena until hundreds of thousands bayed and chanted and shrieked with delight. She took no pleasure from it, the wave of naked lust and adulation too close to the hunger of Khaine's gift for her to enjoy.

With visible effort, Vect started to clap, jaw twitching. Around him his sycophants and retainers added their measured applause, casting glances at the tyrant, trying to gauge their reactions appropriately.

'Lady Maensith, free passage and a ship,' Jain Zar called out. 'My prize, as you promised.'

Asdrubael Vect mastered himself, his glare turning to a smile. He cast his eye around the stadium, calculating the best way to profit from the reaction of the crowd. He gave a single nod and turned away, disappearing into the shadow of the awning.

Escorted by a squad of incubi whose presence set her soul on edge, Jain Zar met Maensith on a boarding gantry in the mid-levels of the palace. The former dracon was as she remembered now, in that she was clad in dark blue plate and mesh armour, a splinter pistol and long blade at her hips. Her hair was still pure white, tied back with a black band, her expression haunted.

'This could just be a cruel taunt,' Jain Zar said, eyeing their guards. 'It would be typical of Vect to snatch away hope when it would cause the most despair. Be ready.'

'I do not think that is his plan,' said Maensith. 'While he has never cared for his word as his bond, to appear magnanimous and lordly gives him renewed influence over the masses. For the price of a prisoner and a ship, and the promise of good faith in the future, he can recruit thousands more defectors to the Kabal of the Black Heart.'

'Even though he lost?'

'You do not understand Asdrubael Vect,' said Maensith, turning towards the waiting ship. 'He never loses, he just changes the definition of victory.'

Absorbing this nugget of wisdom, Jain Zar followed her up the ramp. Whatever Maensith's assertions, it would be better to be far away from the Dark City as swiftly as possible.

And all things considered about their destination, she concluded that this unplanned excursion to Commorragh was not even the most dangerous part of the journey to Ulthwé.

'Vect certainly didn't do us any favours with this ship,' Maensith told her companion. The pilot's hands constantly moved from one control to another, setting the trim through the keel-field, filtering the fluctuations that stuttered through the energy nucleus. It felt as though the ship were fighting her every moment, possessed of the same contrary spirit as the tyrant of Commorragh. It slipped along the webway more like a dart rattling down a chute than a ship riding a wave. 'I wouldn't be surprised if he didn't have the personality core spiked just to spite us.'

'There's fresh blood in one of the compartments,' Jain Zar replied. She stood at the door to the tiny piloting suite, her armour too bulky for one of the small ship's flying cradles. 'I think the previous owners were reluctant to let it go.'

Maensith shook her head, partly in surprise but mostly in appreciation.

'Vect! He loses a wager on the wych games and orders his warriors to steal a ship to pay part of his bet...' She shuddered at the recollection of being his 'guest'. It was best not to dwell on what had happened, to focus on the positives – being the fact that she was no longer within the tyrant's clutches.

'Four cycles out from Commorragh, we lost the last of Vect's shadows in the Serpentine Coils, just open webway and a ship. There are worse fates.'

'There are,' said Jain Zar. 'And we have one. You know my intent. We must reach Ulthwé as soon as possible. More delays will be catastrophic.'

Reluctantly, Maensith set the scow's crude mind to take over the controls. She spun the piloting web to face the Phoenix Lord. The gleam from the control gems dappled the black of Jain Zar's armour with greens and blues.

'Not in this ship. I wouldn't make a run between the Blind Peaks and the Winter Tower in this half-wreck.'

'The Winter Tower is no more. Vect's people destroyed it.'

'I know, thank you for the reminder.'

'I mean to say, where else will we get a ship capable of running the webway into the Eye of Terror?'

'We'll need more than one ship, if Ulthwé is hiding where I think it is. The Gulf of the Hydra. We'll need at least three vessels to open the gate, and another to watch our backs while we do it.'

'And you have a suggestion where we might find such a fleet? I have nothing to offer for payment, and your list of allies has been shortened of late.'

'I know exactly where to find the sort of fleet we'll need for this, but I can't offer guarantees.'

'Nothing in life is certain,' said the Phoenix Lord.

'Except death,' Maensith completed the adage.

Jain Zar tilted her head, amused.

'Not even that, Lady Maensith. Not even death.'

It took another two cycles to navigate the webway conduits around the outlying realms of the kabalites, slipping through unused tunnels and half-hidden kinks, skulking from one gate to the next to avoid detection. Maensith was well versed in such manoeuvres as a captain of a ship but it had been a considerable time since she had experienced the thrill of it at the piloting controls.

The ship's reluctance to obey her wishes added to the drama, as though it were trying everything in its meagre power to betray their presence or delay them. Two cycles of constant course management and wrestling with the scow's fractious personality left Maensith with a short temper, to the point that she dismissed Jain Zar to the control suite to avoid further distractions.

Alone in darkness but for the dull glow of activation runes and control crystals, she drifted between conscious and semi-conscious states, feeling her way through the webway as much as navigating by chart and position.

This was how she had started life, in the lowliest service to the kabal, smuggling cargoes of slaves, souls and physical treasures, hidden from the sharp eyes of Asdrubael Vect's 'tribute' collectors. And secretly taking a cut each time, of course, to the point where she was able to pay an assassin to kill Neaderith Dracon and take command herself.

Miserable days, even then, beholden to the whims of the hierarchs and archons, surviving through a combination of luck, wits and an interminably complex web of favours and loyalties within the kabal.

It had helped that she was true-born, which conferred a degree of status beyond her lowly employment. Though most of the old nobility had been wiped out by Vect's coup and purges before her birth, a few of the ancient lines remained and she had been, in theory at least, heiress to sizeable assets including the Winter Tower.

All that was gone now. Proof that complacency was always rewarded with treachery.

Which brought with it another line of thought, bobbing through the surf of her half-dreaming mind. What did she owe Jain Zar? Nothing. The Phoenix Lord had freed her from Vect's clutches, but only for her own ends. Theirs was a bargain of mutual benefit, and as far as Maensith could figure it, the Phoenix Lord had already fulfilled her side of the bargain without exacting any promise in return.

Maensith now held the surfeit, not the deficit, in the equation of power – Jain Zar needed her service and knowledge yet offered nothing but hazard and potential death in return. Though the Phoenix Lord had been correct in her assessment that Maensith had lost all leverage within Commorragh, there were others that might be allies – the very same ones that she would need to recruit to help Jain Zar. Why should she not remove the Storm of Silence from the picture and employ them for herself, rather than act as third party?

Lost in this chain of reasoning, Maensith only vaguely registered the whisper of the door opening. She roused herself from her weary somnolence to find Jain Zar standing at the threshold. She held the Silent Death, its black flames licking around her raised fist, and the Blade of Destruction.

'What...?' Maensith blinked against the light that crept in from the corridor.

'Your thoughts leak,' said the Phoenix Lord. She ducked into the small cabin. The Blade of Destruction passed a hair's breadth from Maensith's throat. She felt the crackle of its power on her skin, her hair trembling from static discharge.

'I do not understand.'

'The dark kin have allowed their psychic potential to stunt, leaving it to wilt and wither rather than risk attracting the gaze of the Great Enemy. But it is still there. I am a Phoenix Lord – the souls of those close at hand are laid open to me. And the ship is an amplifier, resonating with your desires.'

Maensith swallowed and dragged her gaze away from the gleam of the Zhai Morenn. She looked directly at the Phoenix Lord and knew that denial was not an option.

'I cannot help but be what I am. You know my nature, yet you chose my company.'

'I will offer you reward enough for your assistance. And any others that we need so that we can reach Ulthwé. I may not have physical means, but I have seen many things and walked many dark roads. That will be your payment. Troves and vaults hidden from the knowledge of your people for generations. Enchantments and opening words, ward-sigils and pathways.'

'Tell me more.'

The Phoenix Lord shook her head, drawing back the Blade of Destruction. It seemed as though the flare of the Silent Death crawled across her whole body, filling the chamber with unlight, leaving only two ruby eyes piercing the gloom.

'Remember this: you cannot destroy me. Vect thought he had found a way to possess me or end my existence, but he failed. Whatever power you think you have, it cannot defeat the gift of Khaine and the will of Asuryan. I am the banshee, the doom yet to come. Turn on me and your life is forfeit. No matter how far you flee, how well you hide, you will not escape my wrath.'

Maensith shrank back in the cradle, her skin crawling with dread. She thought she could smell charnel smoke, the metallic hint of freshly spilled blood – scents with which she was intimately familiar that now made her want to retch. Since her earliest memory she had been aware of the all-consuming power that lusted after her soul, had spent her whole life like her kin avoiding that fate by feeding on the spirit of others, by extracting exqui-site terror and agony from her victims as a submission in place of her own essence.

Now she looked into the eyes of something even older still than She Who Thirsts, a bloody-handed death-dealer that would usher Maensith into the Great Enemy's damn-ing embrace without hesitation.

The flames guttered, leaving Jain Zar standing in the doorway, an elaborately armoured warrior silhouetted against the glow, but nothing more.

'Are we of accord?'

Maensith nodded, mouth too dry from fear to speak. Jain Zar regarded her for a heartbeat more and then with-drew. It was as though fresh air flowed into the room. Maensith took a deep draught and licked her lips. Hands trembling, she turned back to the controls.

9

This was the part Maensith hated.

The ship was trying hard not to approach the gate, feeding on Maensith's own reluctance. The transition point looked like a black obelisk hanging in the centre of the vast golden sphere that encompassed the ship. White lightning crawled across its surface, occasionally throwing out fronds of power to the distant walls.

It looked broken, but Maensith knew appearances could be deceptive, altered even. Fighting back her apprehension, she eased the ship closer to the portal needle, as though edging with tiny steps towards a precipice. At their approach the sparking intensified, reacting to their presence.

Maensith stopped their forward momentum, holding back just out of translation range. She knew she had to cross. The former dracon had examined her other options and all of them were even riskier than the course she had chosen. Logic was certainly in favour of entering the portal, but personal preference was a hard mistress to betray.

With almost physical revulsion, Maensith forced her fingers back to the controls. She took three long breaths, eyes closed, feeling the wash of power flickering through the ship as the portal energy tried to find purchase in its systems.

She almost reversed course, like a steed shying at a hurdle, but in the same moment of action activated the aether impeller instead, flinging them into the grip of the gate.

White lightning struck the hull and earthed along the navigational systems, searing into her cortex. The sensation of opening was not unpleasant, a release of potential energy that made her heart skip a beat.

And then the reassuring warmth of the webway disappeared and Maensith felt like a babe ripped from the bosom embrace of its mother. Cold, the gnawing, ever-hungry chill of the void, ripped and scratched at her soul.

Yet even this was nothing compared to the aching vastness that threatened to pull her inside out. The thunder of a god's thoughts hammering at her soul, a deity's claws seeking to prise open her mind, to snuff out the pitiful candle-flicker of her life, to suck her spirit from her as a beast devours the marrow from a cracked bone.

The emptiness and the cold became one, a freezing abyss in her chest, paralysing all action and thought.

She Who Thirsts. The Great Enemy. The Doom of the Eldar.

Naked and alone she drifted, cast away from the sanctuary of the webway that had dulled the roar of her race's nemesis, reduced it to a throbbing itch. Beyond the warded bounds of the interstitial system Maensith was set before the gaze of the hungering god.

And it did not end. There was no shelter here, no respite from the gaze of that lustful immortal. Every moment was filled with stark awareness of the doom the eldar had brought about. One heartbeat, then another, and another, all of Maensith's energy focused on just surviving those fleeting moments.

The crushing power did not diminish but her own defences strengthened. With practised care she turned her thoughts away from horrific destiny, using her breath, the tingle on her flesh, the gleam of the controls to anchor herself in the present.

Awareness drew Maensith back into the ship, into the cabin, into the cradle and finally into her own body. She glanced back and saw Jain Zar, who had taken up position in the doorway yet again, despite Maensith's repeated assertions that her presence would be a hindrance rather than assistance.

'We have left the webway.'

'Yes.' Maensith struggled to form the words, to remember physical action. It helped, distracting her from the thunderous pulse that echoed in her soul. Perhaps it was better to have Jain Zar there. There seemed to be an aura of defiance around her, which extended across Maensith, soothing the crackle of dread that still sang along her nerves. 'Yes, we are in real space.'

'Where exactly have you brought us?'

'A place where Vect's hand cannot easily reach. The Balance.'

Maensith waited to see if this name meant anything to the Phoenix Lord. Evidently not, judging by Jain Zar's silence.

'Exactly my point.' Her thoughts gathered speed, returning

to some semblance of normality. Every word, every action was an affirmation that Maensith was still alive, still a physical being. The leaching of She Who Thirsts dragged at her but it was becoming bearable again. 'The Balance lies outside the webway, so most of the crews there are craftworld outcasts, not kabalites. We... We do not like to dwell beyond the webway for too long.'

'And you think you can entice these outcasts into joining our venture?'

'The craftworlders do not like to cross paths with a Phoenix Lord any more than kabalites, but outcasts... They live for adventure. When word spreads that you are leading an expedition to the Gulf of the Hydra the hardest job will be picking which ships are the most trustworthy. Craftworlders value honour, duty, respect. Commorraghans we can trust just so long as we keep it in their interests to work for us. Outcasts are entirely more fickle.'

'I will impress upon them the importance of my quest,' said Jain Zar, 'and the value of my goodwill.'

'And I will labour the point about how dangerous it will be, the slim chances of survival and the variety of perils to overcome. That should bring the right sort of thrill-seekers to the cause.'

'Won't they be the most unreliable?'

'Possibly, but we only need them for a short time, and we should encourage a certain amount of independence.' Maensith smiled and turned back to the controls. 'Nobody likes bait that attracts attention to the hand that placed it.'

Jain Zar watched the former dracon fitting her enviro-mask. Clad head to foot in the insulated, sealed suit Maensith looked like a hybrid of eldar and insect with antennae-like propulser vanes along her spine, coupled with the compound-lensed eyes of the full helm.

'Can you hear me?' Maensith said.

'Yes, quite clearly.'

They moved to the ship's hatch. It hissed open with a breath of wind escaping from the air-locked passage, which tousled the Phoenix Lord's mane-crest and fluttered the red ribbons Maensith had tied around her upper arms and wrists. Apparently they were some kind of signal in the world of the outcasts.

Stepping out of the ship, they left the artificial gravity field and floated into the cavern that formed the dock of the hollowed-out asteroid called the Balance. There were no docking gantries here, no spires and palaces. Tall-sailed and broad-winged ships floated in the vacuum, circling globular cluster-habs suspended in nothingness while the Balance slowly rolled around them. A few of these groupings were linked by sealed walkways, nascent settlements spreading like fungal growths. Three great gashes in the surface opened to the star-filled void through which a handful of ships came and went.

It was almost a small moon in size, drifting in the outer reaches of a nameless system as it followed its leisurely orbit around a dying star. Jain Zar had seen long solar-banners stretching into the aether from the surface, catching scant particles of the solar wind. This meagre harvest was supplemented with a background hum of psychic energy that passed through a rudimentary infinity circuit – craftworld spirit stone technology and Commorraghan engineering combined. It was enough to maintain a thin ward against daemonic incursion. Jain Zar had felt Maensith relax as they passed into its protective embrace, a step removed from the full glare of She Who Thirsts.

The vanes of Maensith's suit vibrated gently as they carried her down towards the closest of the multi-cluster collections. Suspensors built into the fabric of Jain Zar's arcane armour performed the same function, finding traction even in the miniscule gravity of the Balance.

It took some time to fly down to the structures, during which Jain Zar examined her surroundings. A few shuttle craft flitted across the void but mostly the eldar travelled as they did, on solo skimmers or within gravitic suits.

A gathering emerged onto a bridgeway at their approach. They wore all-enclosing suits of void armour, outlandishly decorated with helm crests of bright foil streamers, their armour chased with motifs of jewelled animals, diamond stars, sunbursts of precious metals. They were armed, Jain Zar noted – a mixture of craftworld shuriken catapults, Commorraghan splinter weapons and laspistols – but did not appear belligerent.

With their faces hidden it was impossible to be sure of their mood but Jain Zar felt no hostility, only excitement and curiosity. The outcasts parted to leave a space for the pair to land close to one of the airlock doors. One of them, who wore a sleeveless dark green coat over her white voidsuit, tapped a finger to the bulge on the side of her helm, indicating the internal transmitter. Maensith nodded and Jain Zar mentally commanded her warsuit to seek out the transmission channel.

'...you hear me? My name is Answea Delleaneth Taihou, captain of the *Swiftriver*.'

'I can hear you,' replied Jain Zar. 'I am–'

'You need no introduction, Storm of Silence,' Answea

said with a curt laugh. She turned to the Phoenix Lord's companion and continued in a more subdued tone, 'Do you vouch for your kabalite friend?'

'This is Maensith, my pilot and navigator of the moment,' said Jain Zar. 'We seek ships to accompany us on a vital mission to Ulthwé.'

She was going to furnish more details of her requirements but Maensith stepped forward, insinuating herself into the exchange. She allowed the former dracon to steer the conversation, trusting her to know the best way to proceed.

'Jain Zar needs you to convene a captains' congress,' said Maensith. 'We require several ships for the journey. As soon as possible, time is not an ally.'

'I will send word to the other crews,' Answea said, turning slightly as she holstered her laspistol. Around her the other corsairs relaxed their weapons. The captain indicated the sealed door behind her with a tilt of the head. 'We are quartered here, if you would care to join us.'

Jain Zar looked up at the cruisers, frigate-class escorts and other vessels drifting in the outer reaches of the Balance. The smallest was as big as the cluster-hab.

'There would be more room on your ship,' said the Phoenix Lord. 'Which one is the *Swiftriver*?'

'That one,' Answea told them, pointing to one of the largest vessels, its hull like a huge offspring between a shark and manta, the masts of its vast solar sails flexed back along the spine whilst inside the asteroid dock. The skin of the ship was turquoise rippled with stripes of dark grey, the light from dozens of ports gleaming silver. 'And no, we shall hold the congress here.'

'Neutral ground,' explained Maensith when they started towards the door.

There was not much room inside the interconnected spheres of the cluster, barely enough for the twenty-two rogue captains to fit, and their entourages were required to wait in the adjoining chambers and bridges. The attendants wore a clashing plethora of outlandish costumes, all of them enclosed in exotically decorated voidsuits whose ostentation seemed in direct competition with each other.

Inside the double-layered protection of the domes the corsairs removed their masks, revealing an equally varied array of facial tattoos, paint, piercings and modifications. Jain Zar had spent time with outcasts before, mostly those that chose to become rangers and pathfinders, but the corsairs of the Balance were a tribe unto themselves. They prided themselves on their individuality, eschewing any allegiance to craftworld or kabal.

There had always been some caught between the rigid requirements of the Path and the wanton excess and indulgence of the dark kin – eldar that could not conform but relied upon a waystone to protect their spirit from She Who Thirsts. Most left the craftworlds for a time, exorcising whatever complaints and desires had forced them to seek seclusion, ready to answer the call for aid from the craftworlds of their birth. The corsairs of the Balance did not seem like such a group – their designs, their language, their names had broken all links to the places from which they had come. Jain Zar could tell by their mood and behaviour that each of the captains had been away from the Path for so long it would be very hard for them ever to return to the controlled, sedate lifestyle of the craftworlds.

In the absence of gravity the captains drifted and floated in the spherespace, some of them using tethers to the wall, others cross-legged as though sitting, or reclining in mid-air. Maensith propelled herself to the centre while Jain Zar kept to one side, though all eyes were fixed on the Phoenix Lord.

'The Gulf of the Hydra,' said the former dracon.

The name alone drew their attention, along with a chorus of exclamations and whispers. Two of the captains left without further word, shaking their heads and eyeing the others with patronising glares.

'Cowards,' muttered another, clad in white patterned with mauve and red like the pelt of a hunting cat.

'The Gulf of the Hydra,' Maensith said again. 'A coiling labyrinth of the most dangerous paths of the webway, much of it unwarded, open to intrusion and attack. Three gates that must be opened simultaneously. On the other side, Craftworld Ulthwé, our destination.'

'If the Storm of Silence requires it, the faithful of the *Phoenix Risen* will answer,' said a captain, gently pirouetting inverted above Jain Zar. 'We serve the will of Asuryan also!'

Jain Zar was not sure what to make of this. All manner of strange sects continued to thrive in the craftworlds and beyond, but few actively worshipped the dead gods. Maensith answered before the Phoenix Lord had to respond.

'And you are welcome. It is Andaenysis, is it not?' The captain nodded in response. 'The *Phoenix Risen* will be our flagship.'

This caused a storm of protests to erupt, several captains declaring the *Phoenix Risen* incapable of such a task, unworthy as a flagship of the legendary Jain Zar.

Counter-offers flowed, each accompanied by escalating boasts of speed and prowess.

'The *Swiftriver* will be the flagship,' Answea said suddenly, her voice cutting across the others. 'If the price is right. Don't think to manipulate us into spending our lives in your service for the goodwill of a Phoenix Lord, fugitive of Commorragh.'

She turned away from Maensith and Jain Zar to address the bulk of the corsair commanders.

'I have flown the necks of the Hydra. We all have our reasons why we are here, seeking different rewards, be it exhilaration, purpose, fame or physical luxury, but do not be rash today. Of those that leave with the Phoenix Lord, not all will return. That is a truth we must all face. When I passed the Gulf of the Hydra, we had seven ships enter. Only three escaped, and of those we had lost a third of our crews.'

'What others will you bring?' asked one of the captains. His face was covered in black and red paint, carefully blended to accentuate the contours into a devilish mask. 'Harlequins? White Seers? Kabalites?'

'None, Janneh,' said Maensith. 'We do not have time to recruit for a full expedition. Speed and daring will be the key to passing the Gulf of the Hydra. For those that come, the promise is simple – the favour and wisdom of Jain Zar, Storm of Silence.'

Answea looked doubtful.

'Do not judge the worth of a Phoenix Lord,' declared Andaenysis.

More arguments and enquiries followed, demanding details of what the journey would entail, the scope of the reward being offered. Maensith started to field these questions as best she could. A few more captains left during the exchanges, not enamoured of the offer being presented.

The Commorraghan was handling the situation poorly. Despite her earlier words her bias influenced the way she engaged with the corsairs. She haggled like a stallholder, but what they desired was greater than simple commerce. Jain Zar knew it was not in the detail that the bargain would be struck. Whatever they claimed on the surface regarding treasures and fees, the outcasts had all left the craftworlds for a singular purpose: adventure. However it was defined, they sought novelty, excitement and danger.

'I come before you, the Storm of Silence,' she began, gliding into the centre of the sphere, the Blade of Destruction held out like a banner. The Phoenix Lord's long mane-crest flowed behind her like the tail of a comet, the corsairs parting to let her through as Maensith slipped aside, conceding the metaphorical stage to her employer.

'I have come in need, dire need. If I fail, catastrophe will follow. If I succeed… Those that join the voyage we are about to undertake will be hailed for generations to come. The names of their ships will be written into the legends of the Phoenix Lords, the titles of their captains shining resplendent in the stories of children and adult alike.

'In the same hushed tones that they speak of Eldanesh and Ulthanesh, Diareceth and Khavan Lyanden will they speak of you.' She fished into her memory for the names she had heard when the corsairs had assembled, and pointed to the captains in turn. 'Samanet of the *Lucid Wavewalker*, slayer of the hydra. The holder of secrets, vaultbreaker Kasogareth from the *Insinuous*. Faeodne, the Princess of Gold, they will cry, who sailed at the shoulder of Jain Zar.

'In life or death you will be immortal, your stories woven into the skein of our people like no other. Treasure hunters will whisper your names to bring fortune, warriors will think on your deeds for inspiration. Fate calls!'

She turned and slipped towards the door amidst the renewed clamour of affirmations, leaving Maensith to arrange the details.

VI

They stood at the pinnacle of the main tower and looked down at what they had built. The campus around the buildings extended some distance, a network of fields and organipods to provide food, fed by an underground irrigation system burrowed out by sentient root systems. Harvester-mite nests had been placed at strategic points to ensure the crop would be processed at timely intervals.

The habitation dorms could house two hundred people, spreading in a series of roundels from the parapet-linked hexagonal structures of the two shrines at the heart of the complex. And the tower itself, destined to be a repository for all of the knowledge banks they could find on their excursions. Everything pulsed with nascent energy, drawn from the ground itself.

Jain Zar suspected she should feel pride at the sight, but her overriding feeling was of foreboding.

'It's empty,' she said, not looking at Asurmen.

'We will find others.'

'That is what frightens me.' She stepped back from the

smooth false-stone of the parapet and settled her hand on the broad belt of her robe. Asurmen did not allow her to carry weapons outside of the Khaine sanctum, for which she was both uneasy and grateful. She felt vulnerable in their absence and yet unburdened by their presence. 'We cannot send out a message inviting all to come, there will be terrible groups that would seek to destroy what we are going to build.'

'You are right, we cannot broadcast our presence. We must seek out those that can benefit from walking the Path with us.'

'And then? When we have two hundred kindred spirits?'

'Two hundred more, and then another two hundred.'

'You think to rebuild our entire civilisation from this place?' Jain Zar did not know whether to be amused, inspired or shocked.

'All journeys begin somewhere. Our ancestors were born on a single world, without knowledge of the greater cosmos, and yet we managed to span the stars. Who are we, armed with the mistakes they made, to aim for anything less?'

She did not answer, because she did not want cynicism to rule her thoughts any more than fear or anger. But she could not hope, either. Hope had been lost when her entire race had destroyed itself with its own excesses.

'Let us begin,' announced Asurmen, heading towards the grav-tube that would take them down the tower.

'We arm ourselves first?'

Asurmen nodded. 'I am an idealist, not an idiot.'

The silence no longer perturbed Jain Zar, nor did the empty streets, abandoned homes and desolate landscapes they searched. City after city, world after world, she grew numb to the near annihilation of her people. There was nothing else to feel, so deep was her grief, so utter the dread of what had happened.

Only Asurmen kept her sane, his focus the relentless teaching of the new Path he had discovered, channelling her fear and hate into a near-tangible energy that she could unleash through her fighting.

The disaster continued to unfold with each foray from Asur. Every planet they visited evidenced more and more corruption. All of the ancient core worlds were gone entirely, sucked into an immense unnatural storm that stretched across hundreds of star systems that had once teemed with billions of eldar lives. Now it was a pulsing, semi-material wasteland where daemons made playthings of eldar spirits and ruled from towers built of spite and jealousy.

As on Eidafaeron, each world was littered with inert gems, each dull egg marking the place where an eldar had been devoured by the malevolent being their hedonism had birthed. Jain Zar and Asurmen salvaged as many of these waystones as they could find, under the belief that somehow the spirits they thought trapped within might be freed. The stones certainly seemed to possess strange qualities, for the daemons shunned them, while flickers of energy played on their surfaces at a living touch.

After many fruitless quests it became clear that they would find nobody alive in the purely physical realm – only those that had fled deep into the webway could have survived the constant predation and the influx of warp energy that characterised the heart of the eldar stellar empire.

So it was that they learnt to navigate the semi-material strands that linked together the gateways of the Old Ones upon which the foundations of the eldar empire had been built. Travelling neither in the real universe nor the warp but through an interstitial layer between, Asurmen and Jain Zar moved further and further from their damned worlds in the hope of discovering fledgling settlements and new civilisations.

The daemons that encroached into the space between realms were not the only threat. The majority of survivors from the Fall were former members of the sects and cults that had dominated society in the slow decline to cataclysm. Blood-worshippers, body-changers, warrior creeds and half-corporeal spirit walkers – all manner of deviants and pirates continued to vie with each other, seeking to dominate the webway tunnels and pocket realms as they had the streets of the cities now consumed by a ravening god.

'We cannot be the only sanctuary of sanity,' Asurmen insisted on one of their journeys deep into the labyrinth of the webway. He piloted their small ship, a former pleasure yacht that they had augmented with defensive fields and a few short-ranged weapons. Asurmen had dubbed it *Stormlance*. 'It stands to reason that those seeking to avoid the madness would be the best hidden.'

'But we have found nothing in all of our searching. Not even a hint that anything but selfishness and deprivation are now the law. What if the Fall was a judgement by Asuryan, a punishment for thinking the gods dead? Neither of us is clean of taint. I was a blood-maiden, the murder of countless eldar stains my hands. We are the wicked, left to dwell in our own misery while the righteous have ascended to another plane. The wrath of Khaine has been unleashed at last, unending war to please the Bloody-Handed God.'

Asurmen turned, his piloting cradle swaying with the movement. The gleam of the control gems marking the panel in front of him caught his sharp cheeks and brow, throwing his face into stark shadow, almost skull-like.

'What else would you do?' he asked. 'Return to Asur and contemplate our fate until we are also devoured or wither away? No. We shall not pass idly to our doom. Not only the cults survived. Before the Fall, before the end came, there were some that fled on the craftworlds, and before them the Exodus that took many from the madness that we could not see. I think they survived. There is life out there, Jain Zar, and we must search for it.'

'So where next?'

'The memory banks of the yacht contain the location of an old victualler port – a waystation between worlds where pleasure cruisers could restock on the freshest produce for their passengers. I do not think any supplies will remain, but it is a hub of several webway strands and thus important.'

'It will be a battleground, if it is that useful.'

'Perhaps, but not everyone that fights might have dire intentions. Are we not warriors? Yet we have a higher ideal.'

'I'm not so sure,' said Jain Zar, earning herself an irritated glance from Asurmen. 'We have become followers of Khaine, the foe of our people, the Bloody-Handed slaughterer. I have read as much from the texts we saved. War and death, what else does our future hold? Are we any different?'

'We can be, if we choose as such.' Asurmen laid his hand on hers, his touch unsettling but she forced herself to endure the closeness knowing there was no intent but to comfort. 'I have made the journey, you are on the Path, others can learn the same. I believe this. I believe this with every part of me, in body and spirit. We are saviours, not judges. Asuryan has returned to us in need, not to punish but to guide.'

Faced with such sincerity, knowing how much her own mind and spirit had changed under Asurmen's tutelage, it was impossible for Jain Zar to argue.

They did not speak for some time, each with their own thoughts, until a green alert gem started to shine on the console just by Jain Zar's left hand.

'What is that?' she asked.

Asurmen shook his head. 'Activate it and find out.'

'Really? Just activate a random system? What if it's something dangerous?'

Asurmen pointed to the row of dormant amber gems in front of him. 'Then it would be red, like the other warnings.'

Uncertain, Jain Zar gently touched her fingers to the gem and felt a moment of contact. It was as though part of *Stormlance* passed into her. She felt a crackle of energy inside her eyes, just the faintest trace of connection.

A face appeared in her vision, hovering about an arm's length away. It was a female eldar, older than Jain Zar, her hair tied back in tight braids. An untended scar on her lip made her look as though she were snarling.

Out of reflex, Jain Zar prodded the gem again and the face disappeared. Judging by Asurmen's reaction he had seen the apparition also.

'What was…?' Jain Zar began.

The jewel gleamed into life, this time flashing insistently. Asurmen gave her a reassuring nod.

'I think it is the communicator. Someone is trying to contact us.'

'And you think we should answer? Did you see how she looked? People that keep scars treat them as badges – I should know. Not our kind of person.'

'And her facial appearance is enough information to judge her intent?' Asurmen sighed. 'You have just admitted you have trophy scars, and yet here you are, sitting next to me and very much an ally on my quest. We are here to find people – we cannot shun an opportunity like this.'

Jain Zar shook her head.

'We can't attract attention, though, not like this.'

Asurmen's reply was cut off as two more runes sparkled into life above them, projecting a display onto a glass-like plate at the centre of the console. Jain Zar felt a thrill of urgency pass through her from the ship. A scale representation of the webway conduit glimmered into view, a small rune depicting *Stormlance* at its centre, another blinking point ahead along the undulating webway tunnel.

Asurmen looked surprised. 'So that's the scanners…'

'They're coming closer!' Jain Zar pointed at the display. At her thought, a golden line appeared between the two ships and numerals coalesced in her vision, counting down the distance. It would not be long before the ships met. 'Turn around!'

'Think of it this way,' said Asurmen. 'Everyone we have met so far has tried to attack us on sight. There has to be some credit to the fact that they attempted communication. Answer the message.'

She reluctantly conceded to this logic and moved her hand to the communications gem again. As before, the scarred face appeared directly in her vision, intermingled with the scanning display.

'Hello?'

'Greetings, travellers.' The other eldar smiled, diminishing the intimidating effect of her scar. The voice was quiet and measured. Jain Zar thought she could hear it, like an actual soundwave, but knew it to be projected directly into her mind via the texture of the webway. The effect was slightly distracting and she did not catch the start of what was next said. '… and require that you do not power up any weapon systems. If this is agreeable, we shall guide you to a docking station.'

On the scanner the other ship had slowed and now reversed, keeping position ahead of *Stormlance* at the extent of weapons range.

'We bear no ill intent, Mahagrati,' Asurmen assured the other eldar. 'We are simply seeking contact with others who have survived the cataclysm.'

'Then you are welcome to Nir Erva Vanamin, travellers. Might I know your titles and names that I might convey them to our master, the merciful Davainesh?'

'I am Asurmen, a teacher, and this is my pupil, Jain Zar.'

Mahagrati's eyes widened at their names and then her brow furrowed.

'What manner of travellers are you to bear such titles?'

'Messengers,' said Asurmen. 'Bearers of hope. Your welcome gives us heart that our mission is not without merit.'

'Very well.' Mahagrati was stiff and businesslike compared to her earlier demeanour. 'I can see that you are novices at piloting. With your permission I will send a guidance core to your vessel.'

'That would seem sensible,' said Asurmen. 'What must we do?'

'Simply greet the program when it arrives. Your ship will know what to do.'

Jain Zar wasn't sure what this meant, and was equally unsure that they should allow some strange routine into the system of their ship. The first doubt was answered when she detected a slight pressure in her thoughts, as though someone were gently pushing inside her mind. Before she could voice the second concern Asurmen thought a welcome to the psychic packet and with a whisper through their thoughts it disappeared into *Stormlance*'s core data systems.

'That could have been anything!' snapped Jain Zar. 'A corruption, an attack!'

'If we are to prevail we must learn to trust as well as to fight, Jain Zar.'

'A little suspicion goes a long way. It's kept us alive so far.'

Asurmen swung back in his cradle as a gleam of energy pulsed through the control console. By its own volition *Stormlance* accelerated, following Mahagrati's ship as it turned and powered towards Nir Erva Vanamin.

'We shall soon find out which of us is correct.'

'Just to be sure, we are taking our weapons? If they attempt to disarm us, we leave?'

'Very well, I will give you that guarantee.'

They tagged behind Mahagrati, turning and twisting along the arterial webway route for some time. Eventually the transit realm opened out into a broader space, wide and high enough for several large vessels to berth at the same time. At the heart of the city-sized chamber was a much smaller hub, a tapering structure suspended in the air, no bigger than the Kurnussei district where Jain Zar had been raised. Spired docking bridges arced out in different directions, ten of them, all but two empty.

Several ships no bigger than *Stormlance* circled patrols around the outpost, while at the dock were two grander vessels. One was clearly a stellar liner, deck after deck of baroquely ornamented galleries banked upon each other to form an elegant shark-like hull beneath three massive solar sails. The other was a battleship, prow cannon like the horn of a narwhal, its twin sails more like fins, extended to either side of its sleek hull.

The piloting system guided them in a slow arc around the cruise liner, spiralling twice around the hub, gradually slowing until they reached a spar that jutted almost vertically – as much as terms such as up and down applied to an interdimensional space that existed within its own pocket reality.

Docking calipers embraced *Stormlance* and drew it to the quay, which undulated like a tendril of vegetation in a current, bringing ship and wharf to a seamless connection. What felt like a sigh from *Stormlance* announced their safe arrival.

They unstrapped from the cradles and made their way to their chambers to pick up their weapons. By the time they opened the main portal a small welcoming party was waiting on the docking spar. The ramp of *Stormlance* extended like a tongue to the floor and formed steps for them to descend. Jain Zar felt a breeze on her cheek as she stepped out of the ship, and looked around to find that there was no covering, not even a field to shelter them from the raw elements of the pocket space. In the distance swirled multicoloured darkness, like oil on water, a shifting miasma that enveloped the whole chamber, through which she could dimly see distant stars and nebulae.

She tasted incense on the wind, wafted up from the hub that extended several storeys below them. Feeling Asurmen at her shoulder, she glanced back to see the ship's iris doorway closing behind them. The faintest glimmer of power indicated locking shields engaging. At least Asurmen wasn't going to be that trusting...

She descended, eyes on the eldar that waited at the bottom of the ramp.

There were four of them, unarmed as far as she could see. Mahagrati was not one of them. All four stood a little taller than Jain Zar, though not quite the height of Asurmen. They were dressed in robes of thin material, purple and grey that shimmered as the cloth moved. They wore their hair in similar style, tight braids wound into thicker plaits at the nape of the neck. One of them stepped forward, hands clasped to his chest.

'I am Duruvan, travellers. Welcome to Nir Erva Vanamin.' He bowed, braid falling over his shoulder as his head passed his waist. His three companions bowed less deeply, eyes on the new arrivals.

Jain Zar could see no obvious weapons but they all wore paired rings, one on each index finger, made of silver set with a ruby gem. Quite possibly digital weapons.

'Thank you,' said Asurmen, stepping forward to offer his own bow – a far more dignified nod of the head and slight dip at the waist. 'Your leader, Davainesh, is ready to meet us?'

'He is,' said Duruvan, turning his eyes towards the hub with a placid smile. 'Please follow me.'

When Duruvan turned, Jain Zar noticed that nestled in the braid at the back of his head was a gem, much like the waystones they had gathered from dying worlds. It shone with jade energy, powered from within like the one bound to Jain Zar that she kept on a necklace within her cuirass; Asurmen wore his on a torc beneath the sleeve of his robe.

Duruvan set off and the two outsiders followed. Jain Zar glanced at the three other escorts and noted that they also had stones worn on the back of their head, of slightly different shimmering colours. In all other regards they were identically clad and groomed.

'You all wear the same clothes?' asked Jain Zar. 'Are you a kin group?'

'Please direct all enquiries to Davainesh – he will be happy to explain the ethos of Nir Erva Vanamin.'

They passed beneath a tall arch into the hub tower and found themselves on a broad mezzanine overlooking a looping ramp that led down to the lower levels. Two other portals led to the neighbouring docking spars but the quays were empty, as was the landing inside the terminal. Looking over the rail as Duruvan descended, Jain Zar caught glimpses of other eldar below, wearing similar garb to their escort.

As they descended, their three other escorts trailed a few paces behind, silent but constant shadows.

The station itself was well maintained, suffused with the all-encompassing ambient light Jain Zar remembered from the days before the Fall, as though the air itself was charged with energy so that not a shadow fell anywhere.

The walls themselves were smoothly rendered, slightly stippled with blues and greens, like the pictures of the oceans she had seen in their archive library.

The smell of incense grew stronger as they descended and they started to see more inhabitants – small groups dressed identically, each with a waystone worn on the back of the head.

'No doors,' Jain Zar remarked to Asurmen, nodding towards the open archways either side of the main ramp. Sub-levels and bridges crossed the central opening, the dormitories and other spaces set on the outside of the hub tower.

'Total freedom of movement, no barriers,' Asurmen replied, with what Jain Zar took to be a hint of admiration.

She saw other groups sitting on the floor around circular tables, sharing drinks from silver ewers, passing fruit and other fresh produce to each other on white plates. The sight made her mouth water – it would be some time yet before the garden at Asur would bear fruit.

'Refreshments will be made available, dear traveller,' Duruvan assured her, noticing her gaze lingering on the diners. 'We are fortunate that one of our sister-worlds has recently delivered a cargo of bounty.'

'Sister-world? You have contacts beyond the webway?' Asurmen's gaze was constantly moving, taking in every sight.

'Alas not, traveller,' replied Duruvan. 'I speak of other pocket realms. We are the centre, but two other sister-worlds maintain contact, and through us share their bounty.'

Their journey took them to the middle levels of the hub, broadest of the station. Here the central gap disappeared and a large hall filled the space instead. As elsewhere the walls were breached by many doorways, through which Jain Zar spied more robe-clad eldar seated on a cushioned area of floor at the centre of the hall.

Duruvan stepped up to the nearest arch. He said nothing, but as one the occupants turned their heads in his direction.

'Did you see?' Asurmen whispered.

Jain Zar shook her head.

'Watch his scalp-jewel,' the Hand of Asuryan quietly bid her.

It was subtle, but she saw that the gem light fluctuated; still green, but varying in brightness and shade. The changes settled and Duruvan turned to them.

'Davainesh is pleased to welcome you to the focus, you may enter.' He bowed again, low, a hand sweeping towards the archway.

'Many thanks,' murmured Asurmen. He glanced at Jain Zar and then entered. She followed close behind, but looked back at the others as she stepped across the threshold. They waited in a line, arms hanging limply by their side, eyes turned to each other, their gems faintly pulsing in union.

There were five eldar in the chamber Duruvan had called the focus, older than those Jain Zar had so far seen but dressed and mannered in the same fashion as all the others. They stood together, hands clasped to their chests as Duruvan's had been. They did not wear rings, save for the one that stood at their centre, who bore a red-jewelled band on each thumb.

'Davainesh?' Asurmen nodded to the eldar with the rings. 'Thank you for your hospitality.'

'Asurmen, Jain Zar,' the station's leader smiled at each of

them in turn and then beckoned for them to approach, indicating the cushions before his hand moved to the low table of foodstuffs and sparkling drinks at their centre. 'Please help yourselves. Bounty is for all at Nir Erva Vanamin.'

10

Tongues of lilac power flashed across the hull of the *Swift-river* and left a trailing afterglow in the speeding ship's wake. All semblance of a structural webway had disappeared, the myriad routes of the Gulf of the Hydra finally letting go all pretence of dimension as the underspace and raw warp overlapped. Clouds of boiling auburn swept over the depleted flotilla, spilling past the *Swiftriver* to engulf the *Phoenix Risen*, the *Last Paradise of Vel*, the *Wayward Niece* and the *Starcutter*.

Maensith felt the tremors of power rippling through the ship. Though her psychic senses were dulled, even she could feel wave after wave of malignant intent crashing against the voidscreens of the warship, each tidal wash like a battering ram against the hull. Though there was no physical quality to the attack, quivers of pain and tension throbbed through the *Swiftriver* at each impact. Every spasm sent crew members toppling in the passageways and set the control cradles swaying on the bridge deck.

The former dracon staggered over to Answea, who stood

with a leg entwined around a guideline that ran from floor to ceiling, her gloved hands gripping the cable tightly as another throb of power swayed the ship. Just beyond the captain, Jain Zar stood unaided, riding the buffeting deck without concern, legs bending, body swaying in perfect rhythm with the ship's tortured movements.

'We should have followed the *Windborn Wanderer*,' said the captain. She grimaced as the deck shuddered again. 'The other course was more stable.'

'Only at the mouth of the drop. Trust me, this is the quicker way to the gates.'

Kadoreth, one of the three navigators, turned in his piloting web, face taut with strain. He shook his head, brow furrowed.

'We are blind, captain! All sensor banks have been overwhelmed. No contact from the *Vermillion Errant*. Without the scoutship's signal we have nothing to follow.'

'Turn into the crests of the power surges,' said Maensith.

'We will be broken apart,' argued another pilot, Telekandor, not turning around. Her fingers were set upon two control stones, not moving. Unlike the navigator systems of the kabalite craft, the *Swiftriver* operated entirely under psychic impulse. 'The waves are growing stronger.'

'There's a confluence ahead, bringing in weavestreams from the three gate approaches,' said Maensith. She crossed the floor to stand behind the piloting team. 'We need to breach the largest breakers to get into the docking pools beyond.'

'It cannot be done,' said Kadoreth. 'We have no way to time our approach.'

'You have your wits!' snapped Maensith.

She felt a hand on her shoulder and turned, ready to

strike. She stopped, hand raised against Answea. The captain glared at her, teeth clenched, one hand stretched back to keep hold of the support cable.

'We must find another way. We turn with the next pulse, use that momentum to return to the Coursing Stair. From there we can try the Shadowfall. That's how we escaped last time.'

'And what of the other ships? We've lost them – how will they know to change course too?'

'If we carry on, we will be destroyed,' growled Answea. 'Just admit that you were wrong, let us go back.'

'We continue.' Jain Zar appeared behind them, as solid as a beacon tower amidst the crashing storm. 'Maensith, can you steer this ship?'

Maensith looked at the pilots in their cradles, unsure. Kadoreth, the one that had turned, shrugged out of the mesh with a venomous look, almost falling as the ship lurched beneath another tempestuous strike.

'Feel free to try, Commorraghan,' said the corsair.

Goaded, Maensith fell into the cradle and swung back to the controls. She let her fingers lightly touch the stones as she had seen the other pilots do, feeling a spark of power at the contact.

She was almost swept away by the complexity of the *Swiftriver*, its every system from scanner to skein-powered engine, life supports and communication overlapping into her thoughts like a crowd of clamouring infants demanding attention.

Maensith felt a mental tug, a guiding flicker from one of the other navigators. The other approached, merging thoughts so that the three of them became one. Maensith felt dizzy as she came into contact with the nascent spirit of the ship, to experience first hand the rocking and bucking swells of power that tossed them through the breached webway conduits.

'I can do this,' she muttered, surprised to catch the words echoed back to her from the other two pilots, inside her thoughts as they heard her speak the words.

She could feel their apprehension, increasing with every moment, dubious of her presence. Maensith shared it, doubt forming a knot in her gut even as another tidal surge lashed fresh strokes of lightning against the hull.

Raw stubbornness was her ally. She refused to back down, to be cowed by the flighty craftworlders, to be defeated by the uncaring elemental storm that raged outside the skin of the ship. Urgent and insistent, she thrust her thoughts into the control systems, picturing in her mind's eye the layout of a familiar console, making an imaginary equivalent through which she could communicate with the ship.

Almost immediately the *Swiftriver* settled, like a fractious steed confronted with a stern mistress. Telekandor and Artuis tried soothing and gentle cajoling but Maensith was in no mood to pander to a frightened ship's consciousness.

The ship had been reluctantly following a line of least resistance, almost perpendicular to the course they needed. In the wash of psychic waves the other ships were lost in the crash and mental thunder of collapsing realities and clashing dimensions.

Asserting her authority, she swung the *Swiftriver* into the flowing storm, revelling in the flurry of bolts and sparks that careened off the sleek hull.

'Into the mouth of the abyss!' she cried, fear stripped away by the exultation of confronting the elements.

The other pilots peeled away from her swelling presence, pushed aside by the flood of confidence that poured into the ship's energy and control systems. A mount lashed into sudden activity, the *Swiftriver* dug deep into the aetherscape and leapt into the thickening storm.

Jain Zar watched Maensith, her face reflected in the gems of the control panels in front. Contorted and mirrored in blue and red and green, she looked every bit as daemonic as the realm that raged outside. Eyes wide but seeing nothing inside the ship, lips drawn back in a feral grimace, the Commorraghan's expression was a mix of triumphal elation and abject terror.

The timbre of the ship changed dramatically; its infinity circuit trembled under the unfamiliar influence of Maensith's unfettered passion.

'The waves are parting,' one of the pilots declared breathlessly. 'It's working! We're riding the storm.'

'Broadcast a full beacon, lead the others through,' said Answea. 'We'll be the trailblazer this time.'

The *Swiftriver* continued to buck and roll on immaterial tides but there was none of the shuddering conflict and desperation that had marked its earlier progress. Though a thrill of anxiety accompanied each pulsing assault from the storm, the ship also seemed eager, pulling at the reins.

Answea must have felt it too. She tapped Arathuin on the shoulder.

'Go back in. Try to... take off the rough edges.'

The pilot nodded sombrely and returned to the control gems, leaning further back in the embrace of the cradle.

'The *Phoenix Risen* and the *Last Paradise of Vel* are below us,' announced one of the sensor operators. A little relief softened the tension etched on her face. 'Strong proximity signal.'

'Send them a tether beam. We'll steer this together. Any sign of the *Wayward Niece* or the *Starcutter*?' asked Answea. The crewmember shook her head, her expression hardening. 'Keep looking.'

For a short while relative calm endured. The *Swiftriver* rocked and slipped and fell into troughs of power, but nothing like the raging tempest that had swelled out of the depths at the heart of the Gulf of the Hydra.

The region was well named, an intersection of the warp and webway that continuously spawned new openings and tunnels, leading ships astray with false routes. Dead ends and maelstroms awaited the unwary, and of the rest of the fleet the worst had to be assumed. At best they would have been ejected into the material galaxy with hull breaches and crippling damage. At worst... The naked warp was unkind to all mortal flesh and mind, and for the eldar, becoming immersed in the medium of the Great Enemy would bring about a torment far worse than any physical torture.

It was better to not consider such an end.

It seemed that they had weathered the worst of the storm. The undulations and gyrations of the ship had lessened as Maensith and the pilots rode an easier course through the wells and peaks of psychic wash.

A calm settled on the ship. Wariness replaced alarm. Jain Zar felt the tension in the bridge dissipate a little – Answea left the navigational team and returned to her position overseeing all of the command crew.

'From what Maensith told me, and my own previous adventure here, it should not be long before we reach the gatehead. As long as the *Starcutter* and the *Wayward Niece* stay with us, we should be able to make the final breach back into the mortal universe.'

Jain Zar nodded, only barely listening as Answea continued. Her attention was drawn to one of the pilots, Telekandor. At first she could not tell what had attracted her eye. It was a subtle change in attitude and movement. She had been slightly hunched over her controls, but now she relaxed in the cradle, almost leaning away from the console.

It could have been relief that the tempest was weakening, but the other outcast pilot was still intent upon the gems of his controls. The Phoenix Lord let her spirit flow a little more deeply into the essence of the ship. Nothing seemed amiss. She could feel the bright flares of spirit stones from the crew, the background pulse of souls through the energy matrix, fed by a trickle of power from what remained of the skeinweave around the *Swiftriver*.

While what approximated to her physical senses focused on the reclining pilot, Jain Zar's spiritual awareness drew towards the intermittent flux of energy from the webway – a stuttering connection that ached where it touched the crystalline fabric of the ship's energy grid.

And an echo of an echo, the faintest sensation of mirth, a laugh that she did not quite hear.

She moved, stepping to her left and forwards, keeping her distance from the pilot but able to see her face. Her eyes were closed – not unusual for one in communion with a psychic system – and her face was devoid of expression.

Not quite all expression, Jain Zar concluded. The overwhelming thought that struck her was a look of compliance.

And then she saw the black stain on Telekandor's waystone, as though ink leaked into it from below, dimming the ruby sheen with threads of darkness.

She took a swift step, but the ship felt her intent – and through its system so did the entities that had crept into its systems from the energy exchange. Telekandor spun and pounced from the cradle mesh, face a feral snarl. Eyes of pure black glared as she threw herself at the Phoenix Lord. Weaponless, she was no threat, but her spirit was still connected to the matrix, gently coaxing the ship onto some other course.

Jain Zar slashed off her head with a single stroke of the Zhai Morenn. Kadoreth, the pilot who had been replaced by Maensith, let out a shrill cry of alarm. Jain Zar heard Answea shout and turned in time to see the captain pulling a long-barrelled pistol from its holster at her hip.

'The ship is compromised,' said the Phoenix Lord, taking two more steps towards the other pilot still in his cradle, Arathuin. His stone was untouched. Jain Zar pointed her blade to the blackened stone on the chest of Telekandor's corpse. 'Daemonic intrusion.'

Answea opened her mouth to argue, but before she said anything a sudden surge of power flowed through the ship, bringing with it a tide of malevolent intent that all aboard could feel. The lights dimmed to a hellish purple hue, bathing the bridge in artificial twilight.

'It's closing down the energy filters,' one of the other bridge crew reported. 'We'll be defenceless!'

'Get them back,' snapped Answea. 'Whatever happens, we can't let more of them on board.'

'No, let it fail,' Jain Zar said. 'Open the gates and let them in.'

'Madness,' argued the captain. She pointed to Maensith and directed her next words towards the standing pilot. 'The kabalite is the breach, she has no waystone. Get her out of the matrix.'

Jain Zar threw the Silent Death, its black-flamed blades flashing between Kadoreth and the seated Commorraghan before it returned to her hand, rooting the pilot to the spot.

'Leave her be,' she insisted. 'She is still steering the ship. You have been protected by your waystones your entire lives, but she has fought this sort of intrusion from the day she was born. Let the daemons come. Be a beacon, draw them aboard. We need three ships to open the last gate, better that the daemons are lured away from the others.'

'How do you figure that?' asked the navigator. 'Why would we want them on the *Swiftriver*?'

The door whispered open at Jain Zar's approach, revealing a corridor bathed in the same twilight as the bridge, tinged with a thickening mist from tainted environmental systems.

'Because I'm not on the other ships.'

Maensith was only dimly aware of the conversation around her. Her thoughts were consumed by the need to monitor the energy flow of the webway-warp flood, so it seemed that the real world was one step removed, something on the other side of a pane of frosted glass, muted and indistinct.

She first realised something was wrong when one of the corsair pilots started easing the *Swiftriver* on to a different heading, adjusting their course ever so slightly away from the termination point of the route. She let each breaker of energy push them down a little, deeper into the flux.

Turning her attention to the pilot herself, Maensith found something odd about her psychic signature. She was no expert, but the pilot's presence in the ship matrix had changed, as though the soft caress of her thoughts had become talons clamped into the essence of the ship.

She tried to nudge her free with a thought. At the moment of contact she received a flash of feedback, of something definitely not eldar, not even mortal.

Almost immediately, the pilot disappeared from the array. A flicker of after-pain crackled along the systems, falling silent as the connection was broken. With the pilot's masking thoughts severed, suddenly the corruption of the ship was laid bare. Tendrils of dark ice had infiltrated the power systems and passed into the navigational controls. The presence squatted there, a festering knot of formless malignancy. Like roots splitting stone, its tendrils were slowly breaking apart the psychic filters, corrupting the spirit stone arrays that acted as a buffer between the ship and the power of the warp being channelled through the webway.

'Stay calm.' Arathuin's thoughts betrayed the difficulty with which this statement was issued – barely able to heed his own advice. 'The ship is under daemonic attack. Jain Zar is going to deal with the physical manifestations. We must purge the system of the energy conduit.'

'I don't know how to do that.'

'Firstly, we must isolate ourselves, both in the circuit and our bodies on the bridge. I need your help to project a defensive capsule.'

Guided by the pilot, Maensith tapped into the *Swiftriver*'s psychic reserves and let them flow through her mind. It was an unsettling sensation, like standing beneath a waterfall, gasping at the cold despite its refreshing touch, deafened by the thunderous power, unable to move away from the deluge to relieve the rasping pain.

'Is it… Is it always like this?' she managed to ask. She could feel her physical body shuddering. She wanted to pull out of the system, to let the outcasts deal with the attack.

'You cannot unplug now!' her companion warned. 'You'll dislocate your psyche from your body. Adrift, the daemons will devour you in a moment.'

Maensith resisted the desire to flee and settled her thoughts, numbing herself to the torrent of psychic power churning through her mind.

'And no, what you're feeling is because you have allowed your psychic abilities to atrophy. Like trying to lift a dead weight with an infant's muscles. But you don't have to do anything, just let me use the power.'

She felt a portion of the psychic weight shift. Something touched her thoughts, alien and predatory, momentarily brushing against her mind in the flow of power.

'Think of something else,' the pilot told her. 'Your thoughts will bring them quicker if you focus on their presence.'

The psychic energy bloomed out around them, hardening into a shell around the mind of the pilots, anchored on the strong will of Answea that now formed a lodepoint for the power. It crackled along the psychic circuits, purging the creeping invasion of Chaos energy, creating a cocoon of pulsing fibres through the network. As it closed, Maensith's awareness of the rest of the ship blotted out, hidden from view by the shield.

The spark that had been Jain Zar disappeared and suddenly Maensith was in darkness.

'The only thing we can do to help,' Arathuin assured her, 'is steer the ship to safety. See the beacon?'

Maensith couldn't think of anything but the crushing lightlessness. Formless things thrashed at the boundary now, probing, attacking, trying to break into the mental shield protecting them. She tried not to imagine cracks appearing as in the shell of an egg, fearing that to visualise such a thing might bring it about in this place where thought and dream were reality.

'The beacon! Find the beacon!'

The harsh words were accompanied by a mental slap, jarring Maensith's thoughts. She responded in kind, unable to fight the instinct of a life lived on the precipice of swift death. Her retaliation was a burst of conjured fire, slamming into the mind of the other pilot.

Fortunately it did not damage the shield, and the act distracted her from their predicament. As the imaginary plumes of fire dissipated, Maensith saw a single light in the darkness, impossibly distant and dim, but there, like the lone star in a night sky. She bent all of her will towards it and the spark flared at her attention.

And then she was with the ship again, her thoughts riding upon the waves of the webway, the beacon ahead like a rising sun.

All they had to do was live long enough to reach the horizon.

11

Racing through the passages of the *Swiftriver*, Jain Zar could feel the influx of daemonic energy strengthening. The infinity circuit conduits started to darken and chill, creating ice-covered vein-like structures in the walls that crept along the surface, seeking to enclose everything in their web.

The temperature had dropped drastically – not that she was inconvenienced by such things – so that the mist clung to her armour as she ran, dappling crystals across her cuirass and leaving icicles matting the flowing mane of her helm. Snow crunched underfoot from the haywire environment systems while corsairs loomed out of the freezing fog, shadows that turned into pale, panic-stricken figures.

Many of the outcasts followed her, forming a trail like the tail of a comet, unsure what else to do. Others formed pockets of resistance, drawn together for mutual protection, weapons ready as they eyed the walls with suspicion and spun at every random creak and flicker of shadow.

'Where are you going?' one of the outcasts demanded, stepping out from a chamber in front of her.

'Main energy transfer,' she said as she glided past. 'Cut off the incursion at its source.'

'But that's where they'll be the most powerful!' the corsair called after her.

She reached the main passage down the spine of the ship. Dozens of crew milled to and fro, swords and pistols seeking foes that had not yet manifested. Their breath came in clouds, their limbs quivering with the cold. Some had put on gloves and thick coats, others endured the falling temperature with staunch looks, lips bloodless, eyelashes rimed with ice.

Amidst the bubble and babble of their spirits Jain Zar could feel the burgeoning well of Chaos power engorging the ship's system.

Someone in the crowd called out. 'There!'

She skidded to a halt at the corsair's shout. The outcast pointed back along the arterial route, towards the ceiling. Jain Zar felt the onrush of energy before she saw the visible symptoms. A harsh laugh on the edge of hearing. A growing vortex centred on her.

Answea had been wrong; it had not been Maensith's unprotected mind that had brought them. It was the presence of the Phoenix Lord.

Jain Zar accepted this with some satisfaction. It would make what she had to do easier if the daemons were willing to come to her rather than having to chase them down.

Crystal deposits formed along the veins in the walls, thickening, becoming lines of jagged shards as they raced from the far end of the corridor. They arrowed towards

Jain Zar before exploding into clouds of splinters in the mist-filled air. Accompanied by hideous screeches each shower of pale thorns coalesced into hard-edged figures of diamond, sapphire and ruby. They had wide oval eyes and claws for hands, their legs more like those of a bird than an eldar.

Jain Zar met the first wave of attackers with the Silent Death, black flames melting away the mist, the spinning blades turning crystal bodies to falling clouds of multi-coloured slivers.

More came, shrieking along the walls before bursting into gem-bodied incarnations, falling upon the corsairs as well as the Phoenix Lord. A dozen in the next few heartbeats, wailing and laughing as their claws sheared off limbs and heads. Las-fire sparkled in the fog, reflected from crystal bodies, lighting the vapours with poly-chromatic bursts. The purr of chainswords and hum of power weapons added to the symphony of screams and shouts. The gleam of powered blades and daemon eyes threaded the twilit gloom with tracers of jade and cerulean flashes while scarlet blood splashed the deck and walls.

The Blade of Destruction sang in Jain Zar's hand, shatter-ing a daemon with every touch, splinters crashing against her armour as she danced her way through the throng of daemonic attackers. The Zhai Morenn whistled past her corsair allies, never in danger of harming them despite their proximity and the confusion of battle.

Though the daemons had been initially intent on the Phoenix Lord, the presence of the outcasts distracted them. Baying and whining with desire, they leapt onto the corsairs, pawing at their waystones, trying to pull the gems free from breastplates, necklaces and torcs. They licked and scratched and chewed at the Tears of Isha, desperate to consume the psychic contents.

As more outcasts died, the sparkle of filled spirit stones grew brighter and brighter, a firmament of rainbow colours that littered the floor. Oblivious to the guns and blades of Jain Zar and her allies, the fiends and daemonettes prised the jewels free, cracking them open with powerful jaws, each shattered gem accompanied by sighs and moans of pleasure from the crystal beings.

Disgusted, Jain Zar cut them down with renewed fury, knowing that she could not save the outcasts but driven to try all the same.

Despite her best efforts and their own valiant fight, one by one the corsairs fell to the onslaught as more and more crystal daemonettes and many-limbed fiends materialised out of the sundered infinity circuit, clawed feet trampling bloody remains.

Slicing through another trio of foes Jain Zar realised her first assessment had been wrong. The daemons had been coming for her not because she was the target, but to keep her away. Through the ship's sensors they had tracked her path and divined her plan of action. The daemons were happy to keep her occupied with these fragile mortal shells while their infection of the rest of the ship continued unopposed.

Leaving the last few outcasts to fend for themselves, reasoning that the daemons would concentrate their efforts on her, Jain Zar set off again, slashing a path through the crystal daemonettes. She dared not trust any of the internal mobility systems – grav-transports could easily crush her against the floor or ceiling of their tubes.

It was a long way by foot from the upper decks to the

central energy matrix, every step of the way fought through a sea of leering daemonettes. Yet she battled on, knowing she had no other choice. The corrupted ship had closed in on itself, leaving her with no sensation of its progress or the extent of the contamination. For all that Jain Zar was aware, Maensith and the others had been overwhelmed and the daemons were steering the ship deeper and deeper into the Eye of Terror.

It was not a pleasant thought, that of spending eternity trapped in this battle against an ever-spawning horde of insubstantial adversaries, all the while her rage and desire to live siphoned away for the delight and sustenance of the Great Enemy.

She had no other choice. Victory or defeat, the quest from Asuryan, the future of her people, all came down to occasions like this one. Jain Zar would never give up on that slim hope, would never fall before she could make account in the last battle, the Rhana Dandra.

Fuelled by this idea, she blazed through the daemons. As her fury increased, so did her speed, so that she became a blur of lightning-wreathed energy crashing through the jewelled cohort. Her impetus carried her clear of them, now moving too fast for them to manifest quickly enough to stop her. She easily cut down the few daemonettes that managed to materialise in her path and soon was free of attack altogether.

Jain Zar descended the rampways to the core of the ship. She moved effortlessly through clouds of frost-tinged vapour, still bathed in the half-gleam of purple and gold twilight. The lower she ran the thinner the mists and the brighter the lights, until the ship had almost returned to normal. Only a distant sighing on the artificial breeze told of anything amiss. She felt no other eldar around, no sound or sight or presence on the infinity circuit, and assumed that they had all been slain, their souls taken.

Perhaps it was grief that clouded her thoughts, but it was not until she reached the final passage to the energy core that she realised the daemons had not given up their pursuit without purpose. The whole corridor was filled with apparitions – some crystal, some more flesh-like, others constructed of walking bone or with bodies that appeared to be made of black marble.

The daemons had gathered their strength in defence of their conduit into the ship, mustering all their energy in and around the chamber where the crystal stacks were housed.

Frustration poured into the grief that already fuelled Jain Zar's anger. Born from the knowledge that their salvation was likely beyond her, left to the efforts of Maensith and the pilots, her rage erupted like a volcano. She ran headlong at the daemon host, the scream she emitted resonating not only through the air but also along the psychic conduits of the circuit so that floors, walls and ceiling burned with her incarnate fury.

Like a ship's bow wave the shriek preceded her along the corridor, turning everything it touched into showers of flying particles, atomising the manifestations of the daemons as a blastwave incinerates mortal flesh and bone.

She ran, still screaming, into the chamber itself, her anger a companion that carried her and went before her like a scything blade, tearing apart the last vestiges of the daemons until the circular chamber was clear.

Spent, Jain Zar almost fell, catching her balance at the last moment. The Blade of Destruction in one hand, the Silent Death in the other, she stood before the exposed crystal matrix.

The core shielding had melted away, leaving the sparkling heart of the infinity circuit bare to the world. Lightning of green and white and black flashed across its surface and in its heart other colours merged and split, an entire spectrum of kaleidoscopic hues. And within, she sensed intelligence, something looking back at her.

She was at a loss as to what to do. She could not break the core – even if it were physically possible the ship would be left without power, adrift upon the unfriendly waves and tides of the corrupted webway. Nor could she enter the matrix, not wholly. That part of her still alive, her soul, was not strong enough to face whatever power had invested the crystal structure. All that was left was to hope she could force the daemon to manifest before it took complete control of the ship.

It was claustrophobic in the psychic bubble that protected the navigators. Almost imperceptibly the sanctity space had shrunk, drawing closer and closer to the eldar under the constant pressure of daemonic assault. Maensith knew it had no physical presence, yet still it felt as though she could reach out and touch the shimmering wall of black around them.

But she held back her hand, fearing what contact with the constricting shield might bring.

'What's happening?' she asked.

'We are still pulling in power,' replied Arathuin. 'I think that's a good sign. Your guess is as good as mine on anything else.'

'Reassuring.'

GAV THORPE

'You've been here before, you said. Jain Zar trusted that, brought you along to guide the ships. I haven't seen anything like this in all my time. What else can we expect?'

'I have no idea,' confessed Maensith. 'We do not have spirit stones to channel the skeinpower for our ships. There is no infinity circuit to be corrupted – the wards either keep the daemons out of the ship or they don't. Those in the second situation don't have a chance to pass on their tales…'

'No spirit stones? How do you power the ships? You don't use anything as crude as… fission or plasma?' The words were spoken as if discussing a revolting bodily function.

'Our ships use the same energy as yours – in a way. We just refine the psychic energy slightly differently. Terror, agony, despair. They make soulstuff quite pliable, you know. Expended, unfortunately, but useful for a time.'

'That's barbaric.'

'More barbaric than trapping the essence of our ancestors in ancient circuits and using their spirits to power the lights? Please, don't try to be moral. I accept what I do, and so should you. I even confess that it is not simply cruel necessity, but a source of pleasure. We were created to be dominant, to enslave others. You don't think the empire we lost in the Fall was built on peaceful negotiation, do you? To accept otherwise is to assume the craftworld fallacy of subservience.'

Arathuin said nothing, but his dismay bubbled through the psychic circuitry for some time.

'Did I offend your sensibilities? Little craftworlders, playing away from home, acting the part of pirates and adventurers. Live a little stronger, Arathuin. See the real universe for a change.'

190

'Shut up.'

'Are my words a little–'

'Shut up and focus! The daemons...'

Maensith let her mind project close to the limits of the warding, almost merging with the shield wall around the bridge. It felt stable. Warm.

'They've gone?'

'Maybe Jain Zar has driven them away?' She felt Arathuin start to disengage from the system. The shield quivered as he sought to leave its boundary space. Maensith performed the psychic equivalent of hauling on his collar.

'You are not leaving! It is a trick!'

'But what if we can contact the other ships?'

'It doesn't matter. Either they make it to the gate with us, or they don't. We're either trapped or not.'

'I don't understand what you mean.'

'Part of the corruption in the Gulf of the Hydra has split the gateway into the material universe. It's become tripartite, split between the warp, the realm of mortals and the webway in between. All three parts must be engaged simultaneously for it to open from this side.'

'So if one ship fails, we all fail?'

'To be fair, only we were going to get out. I forgot to mention to Jain Zar that only the lead ship, the one that opens the mortal partition, can actually exit unspace.'

'So, the other ships...?' His horror was palpable, still invigorating despite their predicament.

'To be expended so that I could get the Phoenix Lord to Ulthwé. Ironic if none of us make it, when you think about it.'

'I have to warn the captain.' Again his consciousness sought to exit the psychesphere of the control circuitry.

'There is no other way.' Her insistence was like a slap, forcing Arathuin's thoughts back into the nexus of psychic channels. 'Drop the shield and the daemons will destroy us. And I think brave Answea suspects the truth anyway. If she had really passed the Gulf of the Hydra before, she would have seen what happens.'

His silence was precious, a mixture of sullen indignation and self-loathing born of guilt and impotence. Maensith had never known how exquisite such close contact with another spirit could be when moderated by the power of an infinity circuit. If she had known, she would have made a point of attacking more craftworlder vessels. The ripples of her glee became further fuel for his misery. Though Maensith could not feed on him properly – the guard of his waystone stopped her tapping into his essence just as it did the Great Enemy – she could still enjoy the taste of it.

She let her thoughts drift back to the beacon. They were almost at the breaching point. The rising sun was nearly full across the horizon, impossibly close, its brightness blinding. High tidal surges reeled out from the broken webgate, slowing the ship, pulling at the psychic anchors that held it linked to the skeinway, forcing it off course with each wave.

'Concentrate, Arathuin. I need your help. We must thread a needle here. If we do not pass through the centre of the gate, we'll open one of the secondary partitions – small comfort that perhaps one of the other ships might be lucky enough to escape instead.'

Reluctantly the other pilot meshed his thoughts with her again and together they steered the ship across the scudding energy ripples. She felt his anxiety but her own had passed, washed away by the sensation of the present.

Let Jain Zar worry about prophecies and fates. All that mattered to Maensith were the next few moments. They might be her last so she was determined to enjoy them.

'Of course,' she told the navigator, 'if you really think what we are doing is immoral, you could always steer us astray, purposefully open one of the sub-portals for our companion ships. If you are the self-sacrificing type, that is.'

A surge of self-hate accompanied Arathuin's unspoken admittance of his basic selfishness, sweeter than anything that had come before.

'Do you want me?'

Jain Zar asked the question out loud, addressing the formless shape within the crystal matrix. At the same time she allowed a piece of her consciousness to flare along the uncorrupted pathways of the ship – the few that remained – and saw that the protective cocoon around Maensith was still intact.

'We're going to breach into the mortal realm.' As she spoke, Jain Zar started to circle the column of shimmering crystal. The tip of the Zhai Morenn touched one of the vein conduits running from it, parting the connection with a brief spark of purple energy. 'You cannot stop us. The others have fled, but your hunger is so strong you cannot leave yet. I was wrong, this is about me. You want to taste my soul.'

The colours writhed in the depths, like an iridescent shark through freezing water, flicking and lashing with predatory intent. With a hiss of dissolving crystal and ice, the Blade of Destruction severed another conduit.

'But you are wary. You are not sure. Let me give you a taste.'

193

Jain Zar slipped the roaming part of her thoughts into the connective layers, almost piercing the central energy repository. The crystal core flared white for an instant, a coil of daemonic power snared along the circuit. Jain Zar whipped away the mind fragment just before the daemon could seize upon it.

The blade slit another and then another of the energy tendrils, almost a quarter of the way around the column now.

'You realise that I am going to trap you, don't you? When the gate opens our descent into the mortal realm is inevitable. At that moment, I will sever the last of these connectors and you will be trapped in there. You think you could drag me to the bottom of the abyss? I will see you stranded in the physical realm, abandoned in the coldest void between stars, isolated, devoid of all sensation and stimulus. Nobody will ever find you. And you will never perish, never return to the god-mistress that spawned you.'

The shifting colours darkened and thickened, staining the pillar with smears of purple and vermillion.

'Or you can flee,' Jain Zar continued. 'You can leave now, while the route back through the skeinway exists. I will grant you that mercy, though you do not deserve it.'

The writhing entity pushed itself close to the faceted surface, colours intensifying, as though it looked at her through the glass-like substance. She felt disdain wash through the ship.

'You did not like that? You have one other option. Face me. Exit your prison-to-be and destroy the mortal form of my spirit. Open me up, seize what is inside and drag my screaming soul into the darkness of your master's heart. If you dare. If you think the prize is grand enough.'

Her circumnavigation of the chamber had reached half-way, the black scar left in the wake of the Zhai Morenn describing an almost perfect circle around the core. She paced steadily, confidently, using her rage like a shield to mask her uncertainty.

Without warning, the colours poured from the crystal, seeping across the floor like spilt ink, a rainbow flood. They swirled around Jain Zar, not quite touching her, covering the deck of the inner chamber from wall to wall, and up in threads to the ceiling, bathing the chamber in gently shifting light as though Jain Zar was trapped in a slowly revolving prism.

The shimmering curtain formed into a graceful vortex, a twisting strata of sparkling colour, pulling closer and closer to the Phoenix Lord.

Jain Zar did not stop her purposeful pace and the daemon-colour moved with her, pooling about her steps, forming a second layer just a finger's width from her armour, recoiling from the advance of the blade's tip above. It was trying to stifle her, but she would not allow the proximity of the daemon to stall her despite the knot of unease hidden deep beneath the layer of her anger. Too many lives depended on her. The future of two craftworlds was at stake. Millions of eldar yet to be born would perish if she showed a moment's weakness.

'This is nice,' she said. 'But I prefer a different sort of dance.'

Jain Zar swung the Blade of Destruction two-handed, whipping it down to strike a diagonal rent through the daemoplasm that surrounded her. The colours parted like raw meat beneath a sharp knife, peeling back from the wound.

The daemon convulsed, snapping away from the Phoenix Lord. An instant later it spasmed again, and thorsix crude caricatures of Jain Zar formed from the sliding morass, surrounding her. Rendered in polychromatic vibrancy, each had a flowing mane of lithe serpents and glaive-heads for hands. They were linked by the daemon-pool on the ground, multiple upthrust manifestations of pure Chaos energy with a single sentience guiding them.

Their wail filled the chamber, leaving cracks on the crystal housing of the energy core, stifling Jain Zar's own shout as it rose from the innermost recesses of her spirit. As one the pseudo-warriors attacked, moving across the slick of energy without strides, weaving their blade hands in figures of eight as they advanced.

Jain Zar spun and thrust, parried and ducked, easing her way through the closing ring. Where her blade passed, the daemon was not, slipping like mist through closing fingers.

The two immortals fought like this, neither landing a blow on the other, a blur of speed and motion that complemented rather than clashed. Jain Zar pirouetted, blade aimed for the throat of an apparition. It bent impossibly backwards to avoid the blow, its arm disappearing and materialising beneath her guard to strike azure sparks from her rune-bound armour. A black burn was left in the wake of the blow, no longer than a finger but proof that the daemon possessed the power to breach Jain Zar's plate given sufficient time.

She remembered her original plan and retreated to the core, fending off several blows before striking upwards to sever another energy circuit. The daemon fluctuated, torn between attacking the Phoenix Lord and herding her away from the crystal column through which it still drew its energy.

Leaping over an attack aimed at her legs, Jain Zar stood her ground against the next assault. The Blade of Destruction whined through the air as she wove complex patterns around her, the spinning blade leaving no opening for the daemon to exploit.

Pride would be her downfall if she let it. She did not need to beat the daemon. She had a higher purpose than to rid the universe of the servants of Chaos one at a time. Through her would be brought forth the Rhana Dandra, the Chaosdeath.

With this realisation like a clarion in her thoughts, she slipped further into the trance-like awareness of her battle-state. Nothing else mattered but to keep the daemon occupied until the ship made the breach into the mortal galaxy. Her threats to trap the daemon, they were empty and meaningless. Victory here was survival, nothing more.

And yet that all relied upon Maensith and the others getting them to the gate.

VII

Jain Zar approached and then hesitated, suddenly aware that she carried her polearm, another blade at her belt. The weapons seemed so out of place here, like a blemish on something otherwise perfected. She could not sit without relinquishing her armaments, and was caught between her suspicion and her desire to partake of the welcome being offered.

'Allow me,' said one of Davainesh's companions. She quickly filled a plate with a few choice fruits and brought it to Jain Zar. The warrior held her glaive in the crook of her arm and awkwardly took the plate with a smile of thanks. Another served Asurmen.

'You have many questions,' said Davainesh. 'All that come to Nir Erva Vanamin seek answers, but most do not realise it.'

He sat, cross-legged, and laid one hand in his lap. He reached up to his scalp and pulled free a gem that gave off a golden shimmer on his skin but was itself diamond-clear. His grey eyes reflected the auric gleam.

'The harmony gems,' he said, showing them the jewel on his palm. 'The bounty bestowed to us in the midst of the cleansing. We each have one and through them we are linked, our fates entwined, our goals shared, our doom averted.'

'Doom?' Asurmen asked casually. He popped a small berry in his mouth, chewed it and then continued. 'What doom?'

'Extinction, dear traveller,' replied Davainesh. 'I know that you come from beyond the skein. You have seen what has happened to our worlds. I have seen it too. Nir Erva Vanamin did not exist until we brought the harmony gems. It is they that make us the Harmonious.'

He returned his gem and continued, more animated, hands moving in correspondence to his point with short chopping motions.

'We were a divided people, factionalised. Our individual desires became our personal sins. As a society we fractured, splitting again and again, but instead of a great civilisation being spawned from this cellular growth, we created a nightmare. Bound within our instincts and needs we shunned each other, preyed upon those that were different. We did not court conflict, we sought it. We defined ourselves not by unity but by discord, shaping our identity in opposition to what was around us, not what was within us.'

Jain Zar felt Davainesh's gaze linger on her for a few heartbeats more than was comfortable. She met his stare with a frown and he looked away.

'That which we did not understand caused us fear and from fear came hatred. Violence, bloodshed. These were symptoms of a deep malaise. An absence of love.'

Others had entered the focus, just a few of the

inhabitants, but Jain Zar looked around and saw that more were approaching outside.

'Salandariva,' the leader stroked the arm of one of his companions, 'tell the travellers how we can restore our people to the true wisdom of love.'

'Through understanding and trust, through mutual regard for all that we are,' said the other eldar. Jain Zar could see the lips of the others moving ever so slightly, as if intoning the words themselves. 'Alone we are nothing, together we can be everything again.'

Davainesh indicated another of the group. She stepped closer.

'Allandira is our most proficient harmoniser. She has studied the harmony gems more deeply than any of us. Tell us, Allandira, of their properties.'

'They are a gift!' Her eyes shone with passion as she pulled free her stone and showed it to Asurmen and then Jain Zar. 'Each gem is inert until bound with the spirit of a person. It conjoins with us, becomes part of our essence. Alone it is of little use, but the great Davainesh found a way for us to join not only to one gem, but to link our gems together. Cosmic vibrations can be used to tune one gem to the next, so that we share our thoughts, share our loves and fears. Where there is no division there is only harmony – full understanding of each other.'

'Think of it,' enthused Davainesh. 'Not simply trusting to vague impressions and glimpses of insight, but to know – truly know! – what others are feeling, what they think of us, to share what we think of them. What bonds can be forged when our hearts are entwined in such fashion? Stronger than the forces that hold together the universe. Enmity cannot thrive in such conditions, only unity.'

'Conformity,' continued Allandira, gesturing towards the increasing number of eldar moving into the room, 'reinforces the cosmic structures that link us. Even as we internalise our similarities we remove the external differences that distract us from who we really are.'

'Cosmetic alteration?' suggested Asurmen.

The moment he said the words Jain Zar realised what had been unsettling her. It was not the hair or the clothes, it was the uniformity of everyone's features – height, shape of their faces, proportion of limbs. There was variation between the inhabitants of Nir Erva Vanamin, but far less than one would expect.

'Physical assimilation,' replied another member of Davainesh's inner group. 'How often have we judged based on looks? What assumptions do we make based on the smallest surface detail?'

Jain Zar felt a stab of guilt, reminded of her words concerning Mahagrati and her scar. Something in her face betrayed her, as the Harmonious eldar rounded on her with an expression of delight.

'You know of what we speak. So much was made of our bodies that we sacrificed our spirits. Think of the excesses the desire for physical difference brought to our people. Body-modifiers that craved animal claws and bird's wings. Exotic dancers with extra limbs and courtesans with augmented sexual attributes. And those that went further, merged with the web-weave to become something else again.'

'We were disparate folk,' Davainesh intervened before Jain Zar could reply. 'All of us came here seeking something different, be it to get lost in our own thoughts, to find sanctuary or simply craving company. All that come find harmony and it answers all questions and quells all doubts. With harmony, with our people as one, we can restore our place in the galaxy.'

Several dozen eldar had joined them, forming a crowd around the entrances, silently watching the proceedings with half-vacant eyes. Glimmers of coloured light around them dappled the air.

'You can communicate through the harmony gems,' said Jain Zar. 'Like the webway communicator?'

'Of sorts,' said Allandira. 'The principles are similar but the execution different. When we are in each other's minds there is only harmony, the constant flow of contact and communion.'

'What if you want some privacy?' asked Jain Zar.

'Privacy is destructive, traveller,' said the Harmonious that had confronted her earlier. 'Privacy is only useful for secrets, to harbour antithetical thoughts and foster division. When none will judge you, when all feel as you feel, what is the point of secrecy?'

'What you have here is remarkable,' said Asurmen. He indicated the nearby eldar, who had finished eating and watched them in rapt silence. 'To bring forth such society from the ashes of our broken worlds is an achievement of grand proportion. That you have reached out to other places, even more noteworthy perhaps. But I fear for you, Davainesh. Others will come, coveting what you have created, thinking to take it from you.'

'They tried,' said Davainesh. 'They came bringing war and they found harmony instead.'

'When they see what we offer, peacefully and without price, they all accept,' said Allandira.

'You do not fight them?' Jain Zar thought it impossible.

Some of the depraved pirates they had already encountered would raze such a place simply for existing, never mind to take slaves and captives. 'What happens with those that give you no opportunity to show them your new way of life?'

Davainesh looked at her for some time, perhaps weighing up his answer, or weighing up her potential response. He then addressed his reply to Asurmen.

'You know something of what I speak, traveller. You have a mission, I see it in your demeanour. You have been touched by powers we do not understand, as have I. I was led here, to build a new paradise for our people, free of rift and curse. I think we might make common cause. Tell me of your philosophy, Hand of Asuryan.'

'It would take a long time in the teaching,' Asurmen said. 'Suffice to say that I think we each must find our way to salvation. I think it impossible to divest ourselves of our curses and urges, but possible to overcome them. We must embrace that which destroyed us and turn it to our advantage, weakness to strength, entrapment to freedom.'

'You did not answer my question,' Jain Zar said to Davainesh. 'Some of our former kind are bent on destruction and nothing more. What will you do when they come?'

Davainesh laughed, a lilting sound without care.

'They have come already and they are no threat.' He laid a hand on the shoulder of Allandira. 'We call the harmony gems a gift because they were not delivered to us by chance. They had a creator.'

Asurmen shifted his weight. It looked as if he simply moved from one foot to the next but Jain Zar could see that he had created a little more space between himself and the nearest of the Harmonious. The new stance presented the hilt of his sword more easily to draw.

'Thank you,' she said to the Harmonious who had served her. She passed her back the plate and thus freed her hand to renew her proper grip on the haft of her glaive. 'You have been generous.'

'You must have felt her, our new saviour,' Davainesh continued. 'She has laid her blessing upon all of us, clearing away the unworthy so those that remain can flourish.'

Jain Zar knew of what he spoke, but she did not think the overwhelming presence that loomed large over the eldar was a saviour. There was malignancy, hunger in its presence. The merest thought of it caused her gut to twist in anxiety. She held her tongue, allowing Davainesh opportunity to expound his belief.

'We become one under her eternal gaze. The Harmonious are equal, none greater than the other, but we all exist to spread the word of the saviour's power. It is our duty to take this enlightenment to the rest of our people. Slowly, carefully, so that this new civilisation can be nurtured to full prosperity beneath her temperate guidance.'

A movement at Jain Zar's elbow caused her to turn quickly. A young eldar – as far as she could tell through the effect of the cosmetic restructuring – stood just to one side with a dormant waystone in hand. Another approached Asurmen.

'If you but glimpse what we share together, I am convinced you will see the wisdom behind it,' Davainesh assured them. He opened a hand towards one of the stones. 'Please, simply pick up a harmony gem.'

Jain Zar hesitated, seeking guidance from Asurmen. He regarded Davainesh and then the stone for a considerable time. Eventually her mentor gave a reluctant shake of the head.

'I do not think I am destined for a life of conformity. We must all be pieces together, you are right, but not like this. We must find the ways our jagged edges can match, not smooth them away entirely.'

'Disappointing,' said Davainesh. He nodded to the Harmonious next to Jain Zar. The eldar suddenly thrust forward the stone, pressing it against the flesh of her cheek.

Jain Zar slapped the hand away with a blow to the wrist, the gem falling from deadened fingers, and only just held back another blow that would have crushed the Harmonious' windpipe. He scuttled away with a yelp of fright, holding his damaged arm. The Harmonious next to Asurmen dropped her waystone and rapidly backed away, fear in her eyes.

'What are you doing?' Jain Zar snapped.

Davainesh looked on with shock, staring at Jain Zar before turning his attention to the fallen gem with a frown.

'How...?'

She pulled out the gleaming waystone from within her breastplate.

'Perhaps this has something to do with it,' Jain Zar snapped. She kicked away the other gem and stepped towards the Harmonious' leader.

'We are leaving now,' Asurmen said softly. His calms words doused the flame of anger that burned inside Jain Zar. His hand moved to the hilt of his sword. 'Do not attempt to stop us.'

Davainesh said nothing but his harmony gem glowed and the crowd around them parted, forming a path towards the arch by which they had entered.

'You are already lost to us,' he said, with what appeared to be genuine sadness. 'Farewell, travellers.'

'One last thing,' said Jain Zar before she turned to leave. 'Why do you keep calling us "travellers"?'

'Because you are still in motion,' the other eldar replied. 'We have come to a stop and found peace, but in seeking it you continue to move, looking in all of the wrong places. You will not find the future out there, but inside yourself. Why hunt after something that you already carry with you?'

The Harmonious followed their progress out of the focus with passive stares, the flicker of harmony gems betraying a discourse only they could hear. No attempt was made to bar their passage out onto the main floor and Jain Zar relaxed a little as they ascended the great ramp back towards the docking bridge.

She glanced over the edge towards the focus and saw the crowd dispersing, scattering back to whatever distractions and pursuits occupied these strange folk.

'At least they didn't try to kill us,' she said to Asurmen.

'I'm making no wagers on that account,' he replied, flicking his gaze to the upper levels.

Jain Zar darted a look and saw a handful of Harmonious eldar looking down at them from the highest turn of the ramp. Though it was impossible to be certain – the uniformity of the Harmonious made identifying any individual problematic – she thought she recognised Duruvan.

'Perhaps they are not so happy for us to leave after all.'

'Indeed. I would think that knowledge of this place must be carefully controlled. Davainesh cannot simply let us go.'

They continued at an even pace, not showing alarm or haste lest it provoke swift intervention from Davainesh's enforcers.

'Do you have a plan?' Jain Zar asked her teacher, very much hoping he did.

'Kill them and get to the ship, fly from here as quickly as possible and avoid any pursuit.'

'That doesn't sound like a plan, more a list of objectives.'

'I am hoping that inspiration will occur before we reach them.' He looked at Jain Zar and smiled. 'Suggestions would be welcomed.'

The scattered groups of Harmonious thinned and then were gone as they neared their destination, perhaps deliberately cleared from their vicinity.

'How fast can you run?' Asurmen asked.

As he spoke, he slowed a little, so that Jain Zar was between him and the waiting enforcers spread along the loop of ramp above. Concealed from their view, he slid back a sleeve to reveal a thick bracelet. Jain Zar did not recognise it at first, but as Asurmen turned his arm she realised he wore a stripped-down shuriken gauntlet beneath the voluminous cuff. A glance confirmed he had another on the opposite wrist too.

'A plan?'

'I shoot, draw such fire they might have, you get close and attack, and then I join you and we finish them off together.'

'Better than anything I've thought of,' confessed Jain Zar.

As they moved around the final bend, Duruvan and his companions came together, barring their passage towards the arch that led to *Stormlance*.

'Allandira would like to study your harmony gems,' he announced. 'She very much would prefer to do so while you live, with the psychic bond intact. If you cooperate it needn't be painful.'

'We would prefer it if nobody was harmed,' said one of the others. He raised a fist, the ring on his finger glinting with scarlet energy confirming Jain Zar's earlier suspicion of a digital weapon. 'Nerve-flares. Not lethal but they will hurt a lot.'

'Stop where you are and put down your weapons,' said Duruvan. 'Now.'

Asurmen lifted his hands, as though keeping them away from the sword at his waist. He took two more steps and stopped. Jain Zar carried on a few paces more, watching as two of the enforcers tracked her with their nerve-flares while Duruvan and two others watched Asurmen.

A whisper of sliced air, a faint blur and the closest Harmonious fell back with a gargling shriek, throat spraying arterial fluid.

Jain Zar broke into a sprint, trusting that Asurmen was already taking evasive action. As he had predicted, the enforcers immediately turned their fire on him, flashes of scarlet whipping down the ramp with a hiss of energised particles.

Jain Zar did not look back, did nothing but fix her attention on the enemies in front, every muscle and nerve directed towards closing the distance to her foes. As she sprinted with light steps she felt the anger rippling up from within, fuelled by her distaste of what the Harmonious had done to themselves; of what they had tried to force upon her.

To become one with them, to be subsumed into a

group-thought that allowed no individuality or deviation, to conform physically and spiritually to the mediocre
demands of others. To be subject to the will of everything,
nothing more than one piece of the whole, interchange-
able and ultimately unimportant.

More than that, she knew that they did not serve the
eldar people. The saviour of which Davainesh spoke was no
such thing. Even through the flames of ire that rippled up
through her body Jain Zar could still feel that ever-present
malevolence intent upon her every thought and deed, hungering after her body and soul. The Harmonious were not
free, they were slaves, whether willing or enforced, trading a meaningless existence to the all-devouring deity that
had been spawned from the hubris of the eldar.

The rage became a pinpoint of energy balling up in
her chest.

She was herself, nothing more or less. The thought that
they would steal that from her burned like a fire, setting
her aflame with indignant rage.

She was still at least ten strides from the closest Harmonious when he turned to face her, both fists lifted towards
her, nerve-flares sparkling.

Jain Zar screamed.

The anger burst from her not just as sound but as a wave
of pure rage, channelling the power of her mind into a
near-physical attack.

Hit by the psychosonic blast the Harmonious went rigid
for a moment, eyes rolling up, before he fell backwards,
limbs flailing, head cracking heavily on the floor. The
eldar next to him was caught on the edge of the furious
wail and staggered back, flinching as if struck in the face.

Though shocked by her own power Jain Zar did not

miss a stride. She leapt at the stumbling Harmonious and lashed her glaive into his chest, opening ribs and organs with one sweep of the energised blade. She spun as she moved past, neatly sweeping the head from the eldar that had fallen.

She turned on the others slowly reacting to her charge, and screamed again. Duruvan caught the full force of her hate-filled cry, falling to one knee, hands to his face as blood streamed from his nose and eyes.

A hail of shurikens cut him down in a welter of slashing wounds, leaving the last Harmonious to fall to the thrust of Jain Zar.

She pulled the point of her blade free and saw Asurmen running up the ramp, limping slightly.

'I caught a nerve-flare in the hip,' he explained through gritted teeth. He put his arm across her shoulder and almost fell into her with a moan. 'Can barely feel my leg.'

Panicked cries and angered shouts echoed up from the lower levels. Together they hurried as quickly as possible through the arch and onto the quay. Much to Jain Zar's relief *Stormlance* waited for them still – she had harboured a fear that the Harmonious would have found some way to spirit away their ship.

The lens door opened as *Stormlance* detected their approach, projecting a boarding step for them. Asurmen pulled himself from Jain Zar's grip and slumped into the piloting cradle as they reached the control chamber. He thrust his hand onto the steering gems and she felt a pulse of his urgent thoughts, commanding the ship to power up and take off.

Settling into her position, Jain Zar touched the stones that controlled the scanning array. A vision of the hub and

surroundings sprang into view. Evidently the communication between the harmony gems had limited range; the
patrolling ships seemed unaware of their escape attempt,
there being no obvious redirection towards them.

Turning as it rose away from the platform, *Stormlance*
accelerated, gaining speed as it circled the hub, heading
back along the course by which it had arrived, guided by
the piloting system. Driven on by Asurmen's agitation
and urgency the ship continued to gather momentum,
flashing into the access strand of the webway like a projectile from a gun.

Jain Zar studied the scan image. Only now did some of
the Harmonious craft react, too late to catch them. She
sighed and settled back in the cradle.

'That cannot be our future, can it? Submit to the monstrous thing we have created, or be consumed by it?'

'It is our doom, of our own making,' Asurmen replied.
He settled his thoughts and in response *Stormlance* slowed
its headlong dash through the winding immaterial tunnels. 'If we can survive for a while there may be hope. We
must show that there is another way. There will be others,
that much the Harmonious have proven even if they are
lost to the Great Enemy that stalks us. Not all of our people have fallen to depravity. We will find them and spread
the word of the Path.'

12

The Phoenix Lord's concentration faltered, a moment of doubt disturbing her equilibrium. A daemonblade scored a deep mark across the side of her mask, leaving a welt from the angled cheek to the bridge of the sharp nose. Taken aback, she retreated a step, hurriedly fending off the next flurry of attacks.

A pain in her ankle told her that another blow had landed, unseen by her. The pain was not so great that she could not stand, but it was a dull ache, her armour as much part of her as the flesh of a mortal.

She felt the wall at her back, surprised that she had withdrawn so far, consumed by the need to defend against fourteen singing swords. Singing, yes, the chamber filled with a keening delight, the daemon invigorated by the taste of her spirit leaking from the hairline wounds in her plate.

Something lanced into her side, piercing the cuirass where her ribs would have been. She slashed her blade through the daemon construct attached to the blade, but it simply fell away from the blow, sliding its weapon from the breach in her armour.

Her essence leaked out, star-like particles falling from the wound. The daemon lapped at the fountain of psychic power with the serpent tongues, quivering with sensation.

As suddenly as it had burst from the crystal, the daemon collapsed, forming into a single entity that towered over Jain Zar.

Four-armed, two ending in elongated, serrated crab claws, the others wielding elegantly curved golden swords. Upon a tapering neck its head was slender, elongated, muzzle flanked by flaring nostrils. Six horns crowned its head amidst a mane of white fire. Compound eyes glittered with cerulean power as they regarded the Phoenix Lord in triumph. Black armour grew in plates from its pinkish flesh.

'Bow, Jain Zar,' the creature demanded, pointing its blades towards the floor. 'Accept me as your master and become one with perfection.'

She looked up into the gleaming eyes and shuddered. She could not defeat the Keeper of Secrets, not here in this place crushed between the realms of mortals and immortals. While the crystal matrix sustained it, even fully manifested the daemon was invulnerable to her physical attacks.

And so there was only one thing to do.

She pushed back her rage and fear and hate. All that she was and had become she surrendered to fate. Khaine had made her, but it was Asuryan that had brought her to this place, his long-dead hand guiding her to this point on the skein of the future.

She lowered the Zhai Morenn and bowed her head.

'Kneel before your mistress.'

Hesitation would only bring attack. She was beaten. It mattered nothing to be humbled. If she failed here all was lost. Humiliation was the smallest wound she would suffer.

She knelt before the daemon, both knees on the floor, hands held out in supplication, the Blade of Destruction in one hand, the Silent Death in the other.

'I expected better. A long time I have spent looking for you, Jain Zar. Did you think you could slight me and escape retribution?'

It was hard to let go her instinct to strike. In a single movement she could be upon the Keeper of Secrets, its immaterial throat pierced by her blade.

And it would avail her nothing in the current situation except to bring about her demise.

'I have given my soul to only one,' she said. 'It is not you or your creator.'

'Asuryan? Khaine? Figments of memory, long since dust in the wind.'

'Not a god. A mortal.'

'Jain Zar bows before no mortal.'

'I did not say I bowed. He would not have it.'

'Asurmen, the Denier.' Its mouth approximated a sneering smile. 'He is not worthy of you. He did not teach you well enough. I have defeated you.'

'You are superior in combat, that cannot be denied.'

Jain Zar felt the touch of twin blades either side of her neck. In moments she would be broken open, her soul exposed, like the souls of the outcasts prised from their spirit stones.

The banshee wanted to shout. The gift of Khaine boiled

her blood. All that she was screamed to fight, not to suffer this doom meekly.

'Asurmen taught me the most valuable lesson.'

'Really? I am intrigued.'

'The greatest victories are achieved when we do not fight.'

With a twitch of the wrist, Jain Zar sent the Jainas Mor spinning towards the ceiling. Black flame left a dark furrow in its wake, severing the last of the circuit lines.

She rolled backwards as the triskele left her hand, turning the haft of the Zhai Morenn to catch the two blades as the daemon slashed down out of reflex.

In the space of a heartbeat the infinity circuit collapsed, plunging the chamber – the whole ship – into freezing blackness.

A great calamity tortured the skein. The runes that spun and circled about the young seer's outstretched hands created ever more complex patterns, twice almost colliding as catastrophic futures unveiled themselves.

Along with his fellow seers, close to the heart of Ulthwé, the one they already called Ulthai-das – the Eye of Fates Unseen – tapped into the core of the infinity circuit, trying to divine the nature of the perturbations that had vexed their scrying of late. He was dressed in only his basic regalia, a loose robe of purple and a headband of gold set with an oval topaz. His gloves were black, close-fitting, his hands like shadows as he tried to conjure some semblance of order out of the runes that danced madly about him.

The rune of Khaine and that of Ulthwé nearly touched, pirouetting around each other while the Hawk and the Dove chased one another through eccentric orbits. The Crow, messenger of Morai Heg the Crone, darted to and fro, incapable of settling, zipping first one way and then another.

Beyond the runes, the skein itself was a buckled sheet, a tangle of so many threads it was impossible to pick out a single strand of fate. Something knotted the future, turning the paths of millions of eldar into an incomprehensible anarchy of death and ruin.

The scope of it froze Ulthai-das' heart. Destruction on an unprecedented scale.

Another rune fluttered from his open palm, rotating slowly, drawing the others about it. Asur, the purity, the word, the guiding light. The other runes fell into immediate subservience, but rather than taking up established orbits they clustered about the master rune, vibrating wildly, giving no clue as to their future course or purpose.

Khaine's rune turned to a bone sheen, paired with Morai Heg's sigil. The two danced, quivering with power, emitting a whining noise that struck into Ulthai-das' thoughts as much as it cut into his ear.

There could be only one signifier of such union, the metaphor from ancient myth clear.

The banshee.

He turned to the other seers in the pastel-blue chamber, each of the eight wrestling with their own runes, trying to discern patterns from the anarchy that wrought impossible convexes and curves on the weave of future lives.

'I need a ship,' Ulthai-das declared. 'Quickly.'

Daensyrith looked across the chamber at the younger seer, frowning, perhaps offended by his demanding tone. Her runes hung docile in the air as she turned her attention to Ulthai-das.

'A ship?'

Ulthai-das indicated the pattern of his runes – the looping path of the banshee and Ulthwé runes.

'She is coming. The Storm of Silence.'

'Where?' Daensyrith directed her gaze to the rest of the council. 'Find her.'

All minds turned to this singular purpose, flooding into the infinity circuit and out into the webway beyond the craftworld, seeking a sign of the banshee. Ulthai-das had another instinct. He let all but the banshee rune fly back to their pouches at his belt, and focused all of his powers of farseeing onto the solitary rune.

Unbidden, the World Serpent flashed from its pouch, bathing the Banshee in an auric glow. The two hung together for several heartbeats, immobile, as though watching each other.

They clashed. With a crack like distant thunder the World Serpent split, forming six splinters that raced around his head before falling to the floor. Where they fell a dark rune was marked in ash on the ground. A rune of the Great Enemy.

Ulthai-das swiftly erased the trail with the toe of his black boot and turned to the others, trying to stop his heart hammering in his chest.

'The sundered dragon,' he told the council. 'She comes through the Gulf of the Hydra.'

'Madness,' muttered Charythas with a shake of the head.

'She is beset,' Ulthai-das continued. 'In need of aid.'

'She is an agent of Khaine,' countered Licentas. 'Let the Bloody-Handed One save her.'

'Not idly does the rune of the banshee come into our lives,' said Daensyrith. 'Whether she arrives or not, we have heard the call of Morai Heg's daughter. The doom has been laid upon us already.'

Ulthai-das felt the pulse of the senior farseer's thoughts speed through the infinity circuit. They paused briefly at the docks by the Bridge of Sighing Clouds and then returned to the council.

'The *Dawnsail* is waiting for you, Ulthai-das. Go now. Bring the banshee back to us.' As she spoke the words something trembled through the infinity circuit, a bass throb that set fire to Ulthai-das' thoughts and coursed through the minds of every eldar on Ulthwé. It left the taste of bloody iron in his mouth and a prickle of heat on his flesh. 'Swiftly now. The Avatar of Khaela Mensha Khaine is awakening. It calls the exarchs, soon we will be at war!'

The star of the webgate was so close Maensith wanted to throw herself forward into its shining light. It encompassed the entire horizon, save for the blot of darkness that remained of the protective shell around the bridge. There had been no further assault from the daemons but, as she had warned Arathuin, the peace could be subterfuge. For all that Maensith knew she and the other pilot were alone on the *Swiftriver*.

The lift she had gained from tormenting her companion faded, leaving her anxious. His thoughts were closed to her, guarded beneath a layer of sullen antipathy. The effect was a weight dragging at her consciousness rather than a heat that raised her up. She shunned any contact more than required mutually to steer the ship through the buffeting energy flows.

This close to the gate the webway became a maelstrom, whirling tighter and faster around the portal, so that they had to steer into the current to stop themselves being funnelled into the formless warp that lay beneath the skeintunnel.

It would be a matter of luck whether they hit the gate correctly, and even then safety was still a long way away.

Too much depended on circumstances beyond her control. It was very likely the other ships were destroyed already. They would pass into the gate and be rejected, sent flailing down into the abyss of eternal damnation.

With such doubts in her mind, her concentration wavered. The ship bucked across a harsh pulse of energy, jolting her out of her bleak contemplation.

'Not much further,' insisted Arathuin. 'I see it now. The eye of the gate just ahead.'

Maensith could not find it, but trusted to the pilot, who was far more experienced with the ship's psychic systems than she was.

Determination replaced melancholy. If she was to be doomed to an existence of torture within the bowels of the Great Enemy it would be through no fault of hers. All of her life she had railed against the fate set for her and all of the eldar since the time of the Fall. She was Commorraghan and would not meekly accept anything but complete and total satisfaction of her slightest desires and wishes. To suffer anything less was to court failure, death and the ultimate loss of all self and dignity. In this place of all realms arrogance was a sword to be wielded freely.

Maensith gritted her teeth and helped drag the *Swiftriver* back on track. As they manoeuvred she thought for an instant she spied one of the other ships below, a moment of tangible connection through the tether beam they had sent before the daemonic attack.

'I think it's the *Wayward Niece*,' declared Arathuin. His

JAIN ZAR: THE STORM OF SILENCE

happiness was tempered, as was Maensith's relief. 'We might just make it.'

Maensith felt inclined to agree even though the presence of the other ship made no difference if the third had been lost – it was better they had some hope than none even if born of delusion.

'While I'm not convinced I appreciate being this close to ruin and eternal torture, this has been quite an experience,' admitted Arathuin. 'Certainly more compelling than raiding human freighters.'

'We'll make a proper pirate out of you yet,' said Maensith. A thought occurred to her. 'I am outcast too. I cannot return to Commorragh, not even to one of the outer sphere settlements or border citadels. My kabal will disown me, my enemies within still seek me. Vect would happily see me returned to his haemonculi. I think I could make a life out here instead.'

'With little craftworlders playing at corsairs?' His scorn left a welt in Maensith's thoughts.

'I stand by my judgement, but you aren't without your interests and skills,' the former dracon admitted. 'Perhaps the right kind of leadership...'

He said nothing but the close proximity of their thoughts betrayed his interest.

'You realise that even if we escape this we are going to be trapped with Ulthwé in the outer fringes of the Abyssal Storm.' Maensith thought the words almost casually, though the realisation formed a knot in her gut. 'Getting in is difficult. Getting out will be just as hard.'

'Surely the ships of Ulthwé have a safe route.'

'And do you think they will let us use it?'

'It's got to be worth–'

Everything went silent and black. In a heartbeat all reality outside of Maensith's head disappeared. The sun-gate, the ship, Arathuin. She was suddenly and utterly alone.

Cold filled her, a void of emptiness even more terrible than the ache of breaking into the real universe from the webway.

The ship was dead.

This realisation was quickly followed by another.

The blackness was not of the sanctuary cocoon but of raw warp energy seething around her, too alien, too anarchic for her senses to process.

She was literally alone in the heart of the Great Enemy.

Terror consumed her, blanketing all other thought. Primal dread, the fear that had stalked her from the moment she had been self-aware, suddenly became reality.

No waystone. No souls to bargain. No pain and fear to mask herself against the all-devouring presence of She Who Thirsts.

Just as she thought she could take no more, as the crushing despair and frustration and fear was about to tear her apart, something glimmered in the bitter void.

It was a ghostly silver hand, as though made of a thousand threads, reaching out to her from the impossible abyss.

Even if it was some lure of the Great Enemy it mattered not, she was doomed either way, and so seized hold of the thin fingers, feeling psychic energy surge through her.

The hand formed an arm, and then a body, legs, head. A smiling face, of an eldar a little younger than her, concern warring with relief in his eyes.

The figure became the shimmering gate, and exploded

into a hundred thousand suns. The fire of the detonation consumed her.

The sky unfolded.

Jain Zar felt the instant of connection like a universe being born. From nothing sprang everything, a timeless loop of existence that spiralled away to the dawn of the cosmos and into the cold everdeath. All that was, is and would be sketched across the skein in broad strokes. Stars and worlds emerged and died. Civilisations of a thousand lifetimes came and went in a blink of an eye. Systems whirled and danced together to the choreography of gravity and nuclear forces, birthing nebulae, black holes and maelstroms.

And she was one with it all. The secrets hidden within the interconnectedness of matter and energy that defined the universes – both mortal and immortal – entwined through the stones upon her armour.

For an infinitesimal moment something touched her – the last clawing grasp of the daemon before it was scattered back to the ebb and flow of immaterial energy beneath the world unravelling around her.

Another presence replaced it, amorphous at first but growing more distinct with each passing moment, as though emerging like another of the celestial phenomena. Jain Zar let her consciousness settle into the filaments of space and time weaving out of the insubstance of the webway, gaining form once more.

With a flicker, the ship lights returned, a steady glow of reassuring ochre. The crystal core hissed and crackled, sparks spat from the fractures on its surface. The severed conduits leaked light like blood, droplets of effervescent power dripping to the floor.

Of the daemon there was no sign.

'Touch my hand.'

She turned at the words to find an indistinct apparition of a farseer clad in purple, his features hidden, projected from the ruin of the core. He raised his left hand towards her, flickering with flecks of white static.

'Swiftly,' he continued. 'I am powering your ship for the moment. I need you to take over.'

'You are powering the *Swiftriver* with your mind?' It was a stunning feat of mental prowess.

'I am quite puissant,' said the farseer. 'Touch my hand to form a connection between your spirit circuit and the ship. Your energy will sustain the ship until we reach you. Quickly, please. We detect life signs on your ship – some of your crew need the support systems to live.'

Jain Zar remembered Maensith and the others and lifted her fingers towards the juddering image. It looked two-dimensional, as if seen in a pane of glass with darkness behind it. Her gauntlet disappeared into the aura of the projection.

The *Swiftriver* latched onto the power of her soul, starving and desperate. Jain Zar shuddered as she felt her essence drawn into the ship, flooding the conduits and channels with her naked power.

'Who are you?'

'One of the farseers of Ulthwé. My peers call me the Eye of Fates Unseen, but my name is Eldrad Nuirasha.'

13

Maensith looked down at the bowl of sweet soup and then back to the porthole, taking in the confines of the small chamber. There was a memetic chair that became a cot if she desired, a crystal reader and several treatises by Ulthwé philosophers, and the stars beyond the window. A grass-like carpet grew from the floor in subtle shades of grey and red.

She had not tried the door to see if it was locked, because she was unsure what she would do if she discovered it wasn't.

Nothing had been said, not directly, but it was clear the craftworlders had singled her out, escorting her away from Jain Zar and the outcasts to this well-appointed cell. It was easier to remain here, away from the hostile stares and condescending looks. She had never much thought ahead, other than the residual planning and plotting that occupied all kabalites who wanted to survive and succeed. Alone with nothing but her thoughts she was left to ponder the next stage of her life.

Confronted with the yawning chasm that was her future, she put the dish aside and moved to the window, seeking to distract herself. And distraction she found.

The craftworlder ship had turned, its new course now revealing Ulthwé. Maensith had never seen a craftworld before and she drank in the amazing structure lit by starlight against the seething purple and blue storm that was the Eye of Terror.

Its centre was not so different from the towers of Commorragh, as equally steep and tall, clustered with smaller turrets and an arc of docking spines. Impossibly vast solar sails lifted from the pinnacles, golden and silver pennant waves that drew in the scant photons from a dying star barely visible within the fluctuating boundary energies of the Great Abyss.

A profusion of hundreds of skybridges and slender tunnelways curved down to the main plates of Ulthwé, linking the citadels to mountain ranges and seas, deserts and river valleys. Beneath a shimmering field of reflected stars, under a trapped atmosphere that cast a blue haze over everything, a mass the size of several continents hung in the void. It was nearly as vast as Commorragh, made all the more remarkable by the fact that it existed in the realm of the physical, not the more malleable nature of the webway.

As the ship moved closer Maensith could see beneath the craftworld to where huge crystalline structures grew, many-faceted foundations burgeoning from the central core, the substrata of all that was set above. Much was dark, inert, but closer to the hub she saw a magnificent tracery of light, veins of yellow and white and pale green; the glimmer of the famous infinity circuit.

The thought of so many spirits caught within that crystal web made Maensith's heart ache. It reminded her of the void in her own soul, the hunger that gnawed at her essence during every waking moment.

What a prize it would be to break open the soul-vault, to torment the spirits within to the highest peaks of terror and pain, and then to drain them of their vitality. A whole kabal could exist for eternity on such a feast.

Yet a dream it would remain. There would be no return to Commorragh with such wild schemes. Even if she were to return in favour there was not a fleet that could challenge such a foe. From the porthole Maensith easily counted thirty warships, not to mention the plethora of smaller trading and scout vessels that plied journeys to and from the swirling nebula of a huge webway gate that trailed after the craftworld.

It was impossible to make out where the original trading ship stopped and the craftworld began. Over the course of the generation following the Fall, the self-sustained ecology of the long-range vessel had become something far grander – a refuge for millions. A world not just in name but size and population, still growing as fresh landscapes were sculpted out of the base material – forests of saplings and the foothills of mountains yet to be raised.

It was, Maensith considered, a glorious prison, but she would rather die and be taken by She Who Thirsts than have her spirit end its days trapped in the crystal maze of the craftworld's heart. Whatever the future held, it would not be a quiet decline.

The infinity circuit was alive with the preparations for war. Eldrad felt the ebb and peak of the surges, each mounting wave from the wakening Avatar of Khaine a little stronger than the last. In the Chamber of All Futures the effect was diminished, muffled by wards and runes to allow the seers to ply their courses upon the future strands without undue deviation. Even so, the effect was quite beguiling, tugging at his martial pride, trying to release the blood-thirsty spirit, the primal desire for conflict and dominance that existed in all eldar.

There was another presence, not as strong but sharper due to proximity. While the Avatar was a building hurri-cane, the Storm of Silence was a counter-cyclone, an absence of anger that left a keen-edged chill in the soul. She was the doom-maiden, herald of death, the caller of the damned.

When she had last come to Ulthwé Eldrad had at that time stepped from the Path of the Seer, his psychic acu-ity dulled while he pursued other ends. Now that he had returned, indeed now that it seemed his obsession with unfolding the secrets of the future would not allow him to pass onto a new Path, her presence was wholly more unsettling.

The seer council stood in a circle, Jain Zar to one side, present but slightly excluded. The seers addressed each other knowing that their words carried to her. It was not meant as insult but as a precaution. As they communed, their minds intermittently touched, sharing nuances and glimpses of their otherworld visions and paths along the potentialities of the skein. The interjection of the Phoenix Lord would disrupt the harmony required for the seers to form this delicate mental balancing act.

Yet for all that they delved every route and fate, nothing more could be found of the destiny that had brought Jain

Zar to their craftworld. Given the extraordinary lengths she had gone to in order to navigate to Ulthwé, the Phoenix Lord was driven indeed. On the journey back from rescuing her ship from the broken void she had insisted that the craftworld was in great peril, but nothing of it could be seen on the skein. Indeed, Ulthwé had dared the outer stretches of the Eye of Terror precisely to avoid attack.

Evasion had not been the only course of action, but one that Eldrad had successfully argued for with his seniors. Their presence this close to the Abyssal Heart not only afforded protection but opportunity – to delve into the mysteries of the monster the hubris of the eldar had spawned.

'We can find no fulminous disaster,' declared Astrothia, breaking away from her place in the psychic commune. 'Not for a thousand cycles does any foe threaten Ulthwé.'

'I see nothing,' agreed Eldrad.

Others murmured their assent, but Daensyrith held them together, her mind not relinquishing the parts of their spirits they had lent to her scrying.

The head of the council turned to Jain Zar.

'Speak. Tell us again of your mission. Perhaps some detail has been lost, some clue as to the fate we seek to avert.'

'You will not see it,' the Storm of Silence told them. Her voice was quiet but filled the chamber, echoing with its own power in this place of spirits and the dead. Souls in the matrix whispered her words in return, unheard but for a susurrant ripple through the circuits that grew through Ulthwé's wraithbone foundations. 'Keen is the eye of dead Asuryan. Keener even than the seers of Ulthwé. If mortal mind could predict this future why send me to guide your hand?'

'Do not treat us like children,' said Eldrad. 'Tell us plainly the nature of the threat.'

'You have been despatched to send warning,' added Licentas. 'Deliver it and then take your doom to some other unfortunates.'

'Let me show you,' said Jain Zar. The Phoenix Lord strode into the circle of seers and drove the point of her blade into the floor, earthing her power into the circuitry of the craftworld.

The banshee scream filled Eldrad's head, coursed along every nerve of his body, electrifying and invigorating and overwhelming. For a moment he was nothing, a sineform within the scream and nothing more.

Vision returned, flooded with images of black-clad guardians and bright-armoured Aspect Warriors dying as the halls and domes of a craftworld crashed around them. White fire raged from fracturing geoplates to engulf thousands in their city towers, sweeping across forests and hills and mountains to turn all life to ash.

The dead erupted from the broken infinity circuit, a wailing army of disembodied souls, shrieking wraiths that flitted to and fro through the destruction, given voice through the wail of the banshee.

The Avatar of Khaine stood at the heart of the destruction, gigantic spear raised in one hand, blood-drenched fist held before it in triumph. Yet this was not victory for Ulthwé, but a revelling in the blood and ruin of the eldar themselves. The colours of the armour changed, to the red of Saim Hann, then the blue of Alaitoc and others, but the ruin remained constant.

Symbolic of every craftworld, of an entire society once again annihilated.

And Khaine split asunder, his fire-and-iron form consumed from within by a lithe, androgynous, malevolent figure that could not quite be seen. Eldrad recoiled in terror from the incarnation of the Great Enemy, but wherever he sought to flee the maiden-king was already waiting, gloating and lustful, golden eyes seeking him out in every shadow and nook in which he tried to hide.

The shriek of the banshee turned into a lilting laugh, became a guttural roar. A clawed green hand closed about the crumbling craftworld, crushing it in its fist. Where splintered pieces of the world-ship fell from its grasp, green figures cavorted, smashing and burning, ripping with their hands and tearing with their teeth until it felt like they devoured the body of Eldrad.

Gasping, he hurled himself from the skein. His body collapsed like an empty sack as his tumultuous thoughts reconnected with his body. The other seers were stunned as well; their thoughts whirled around the chamber like chittering birds, questioning, frightened, damning the Phoenix Lord. Yet he had felt it more strongly than any of them, so enmeshed with the skein were his thoughts. He could barely breathe and his heart beat fit to burst. Legs and arms trembling, he stood, using his seer staff for physical rather than psychic support.

Jain Zar stood in the midst of their clamour unmoving. Truly she was the Storm of Silence and as the psychic clutter died away, she turned her head to look at Daensyrith.

'Now you have seen.'

'What must we do?' asked the head of the council.

'The orks cannot destroy us,' said Eldrad, regaining his composure. 'What little remains of them after the failed conquests of the humans is no threat.'

'The orks are the beginning, not the end,' said Jain Zar.

'Did you not see?' replied Daensyrith. She looked at Charythas, then Licentas, who had voiced doubts earlier, and her grey eyes settled on Eldrad. 'The world that fell was not this world, but the one we shall build. How many lifetimes until this comes to pass? Not even the greatest of us could see such an outcome from the smallest actions of today.'

'I saw something else.' Eldrad directed his words to the other seers even though he met the stare of his superior. 'I saw Ulthwé as a great power. I saw vindication, that what we have started to build will see us safe for many lifetimes. And I saw several possible dooms. We do not need the word of a witch-herald to warn us of these perils. They are everywhere. We will train our minds, we will continue to study these new warp tides and we will see further and more sharply than ever before.'

'Your quest is folly,' said Daensyrith. 'You have immense potential, Eldrad, but do not think you can pierce all time to the Rhana Dandra.'

Eldrad said nothing, and simply bowed his head in acquiescence. He moved his attention to Jain Zar.

'I trust that you bring not only doom but hope, Storm of Silence?'

'Show some respect,' snapped Elinadathin. 'You address one of the Phoenix Lords. Without them we would not have survived the consequences of the Fall.'

Eldrad bowed again, head cocked at a slight angle that lent it a literal ironic twist.

'My apologies, Jain Zar, but I have cold welcome for those who bear ill news without solutions.'

'Then your welcome should be warmer, Eldrad of

Ulthwé. There is time to act. The Avatar stirs, but war can be averted. I need a small force, easily and rapidly despatched through the webway. I have been shown the leader of this green horde. A small change to the course of its destiny will avert the disaster that will engulf our people.'

'"Our people?" The orks will not attack Ulthwé?' said Eldrad.

'Enough!' Daensyrith brandished her rod at Eldrad, its crystal tip gleaming scarlet with her frustration. 'Be silent. Jain Zar, tell us more of this plan.'

Eldrad listened attentively, but even as the others started to explore the skein with Jain Zar's direction he let a little of his consciousness drift into less-travelled paths, skirting the soul-vacuum of She Who Thirsts for glimpses of the most powerful prophecies. His runes burned cold but he took with him the spirits of the dead, harnessing Ulthwé's growing infinity circuit to cloud his presence from the penetrating gaze of the Great Enemy. He had seen the same vision as the others but it was not orks that would deliver the fatal blow. From Chaos came the greater threat. There was a longer game afoot in this matter than Jain Zar was willing to admit.

He did not trust the Phoenix Lord, even if the warning seemed sincere. Vague were the ways of the immortals. The destiny of Ulthwé would be determined by those that treasured its survival above all else.

VIII

The archives of *Stormlance* contained over four thousand locations of interest, and Asurmen was determined to investigate them all if need be. Several hundred had already been ruled out from his schemes by breaks they had found in the webway – reachable only through the raw immaterium or the vast tracts of the material universe.

Others were equally inaccessible due to the presence of marauders and nascent dark empires, knots of predatory eldar that had grown swiftly after the collapse of the stellar empire. Neither Asurmen nor Jain Zar were skilled enough navigators or pilots to dare the routes that passed close to the pirate lairs.

A few dozen locations had proven abandoned, as they suspected most would be, and some had proven hostile to all approach despite Asurmen's assurances of peaceful intent. Trust was a commodity rarer than stardust in those dark times.

Even so, nearly three thousand sites remained to be explored, a daunting task that Asurmen put into some perspective as he guided them along winding webway tunnels on another expedition.

'Our navigational charts only include those systems easily reachable for an idling tourist or casual explorer,' he said, reminding her that *Stormlance* had once been a pleasure yacht, not a vessel for daring blockades and delving into enemy-infested worlds. 'How many worlds did we settle before the Fall? How far did the webway spread?'

'I don't know, hundreds of thousands? Across the galaxy?'

'I know not either,' said the Hand of Asuryan. 'We have seen but a small part of the civilisation that was. How small our own part now seems, when we thought before that we were the centre of the universe.'

'Where are we heading now?'

'A library, of sorts. From what research I have done, I have discovered that Biel-Tanigh was an institution of learning, a great archive and centre of art and philosophy. If anywhere retains civilisation and culture it must be there.'

'I have no experience of such places but I know that before the Fall the learned were equally as welcome in the blood-dance arena as the ignorant. Education does not equate to moral strength.'

'If nothing else, we might find records that will aid us further.'

This Jain Zar accepted with a nod.

The journey took some time, several cycles of artificial day and night aboard *Stormlance* during which they read what few materials they could access and trained their minds and bodies through the rituals that Asurmen had been developing.

Jain Zar sat alone in her chamber, in darkness save for the gleam of her waystone held in her hands. It helped still her thoughts, an anchor that tied her to a single moment and place amongst a whirl of emotions that constantly assailed her.

'I walk the Path,' she said, taking a long breath.

As Asurmen had taught her, she found that if she concentrated she could isolate specific emotions and thoughts, finding the memories that triggered them. Many were in the arena or below it; near-death experiences, moments of ecstatic victory, witnessing companions dying upon the healer's slabs. The roar of bloodthirsty crowds, the whimper of a dying foe, the silent shadow that watched all proceedings.

In knowing the source of these fears and desires she was able to control them. She considered each with a dispassionate eye, turning them on and off as one might activate and deactivate a light, slowly shutting down her memories like someone closing down their dwelling for the night.

She continued, the glow of her stone suffusing everything, all other stimuli pushed away, until she found the space where existed only her fear.

She did not see a warm oval gem in her palms, but her hands cupping blood, the thick liquid trickling through her fingers, staining the floor, leaving gore beneath her fingernails. In the crimson fluid she could see her reflection but she knew it was a mask. The face looked serene but beneath was a snarling beast, a shrieking, gore-ridden wraith that demanded blood.

'I am not you.'

She did not say the words, they barely registered as thought, but they formed the essence of her.

A lie.

In denying this part of her, Asurmen had said, she was unable to confront the consequences of its existence.

'I am you,' she forced herself to admit.

The apparition smiled, its true visage melting through the mask, grinning with blood-flecked fangs amid a mane of serpentine hair matted with dregs of gore.

'I am the terror.'

The creature nodded, scarlet eyes bright and wide.

'I will become more.'

The ghastly face frowned and snarled.

'I am becoming greater than you.'

It started to thrash as though bound, baring sharp teeth, spitting silent hate.

'I am the mistress, not the slave.'

For a moment the apparition submitted, closing its eyes, face demurely bowed. Peace. For a few heartbeats all was still.

With a shriek only Jain Zar could hear, the killer awoke, snapping her out of her trance, bringing her back to the room, staring at the stone in her hands.

'I walk the Path,' she whispered.

Jain Zar felt the change in the webway before they disembarked. There was a chill in her spirit, an emptiness as though her energy was being leached from without. Stepping out onto the ramp, the sensation grew stronger.

Here the webway manifested itself with great antiquity, interacting with mortal senses in a way that conveyed its atmosphere and age. Winding tunnels of rainbow hues had vanished, no more high-vaulted corridors of colour and light. Before Jain Zar spread a dilapidated township, in a ruddy twilight that seeped through abandoned streets beneath a starless sky.

Asurmen led them away from the dead parkland where they had landed, wading through the cracking stems of tall grass, dead-bloomed bushes delineating where gardens had once been formed. The moss-covered walls to either side that guided their course were crumbling, and thorny vines that slowly moved with a life of their own wreathed the faux-masonry.

The air was dry like a millennia-old tomb; Jain Zar breathed fine dust as if from a desert wind. Debris drifted against the sagging walls and filled the nooks between worn stones. Arched courtyards sighed despairingly with the breeze, their echoes lingering in the mind long after the sound had gone. Through the gaps in the half-broken walls, Jain Zar caught glimpses of decaying villas and overgrown estates.

Despondent voices carried on the wind. Each rasping breath set the thorn-vines rattling and scratching, the noise adding to the susurrant language on the edge of hearing.

'Whisperthorns,' said Asurmen. 'I used to listen to them in the Gardens of Ashio. Summer nights touched with praise and love.'

'Not anymore,' said Jain Zar. 'No warmth in this place.'

She stopped to listen. The whisperthorns chattered of lost glories. We are dead, dead by our own folly, whispered the spirits of the thorns. Let the living learn from dry Biel-Tanigh, for we can learn no more for ourselves.

The intrusive fingers of the dead spirits sought to claw into her thoughts with their freezing touch, prising at fault lines of pity and compassion, trying to worm their way through hesitation and doubt.

'Stay dead,' hissed Jain Zar.

Suppressing a cold dread, she hurried to catch up with Asurmen, who had turned down a broad boulevard.

'We are going in circles,' she said. 'The park is just beyond…'

She fell silent as they came around a corner and found a plaza some distance across, fronted by a huge columned forum several storeys high, stretching from one side of the square to the other. Twin towers that pierced a now-crimson sky rose at each end of the immense edifice, one silhouetted against a silver sun.

'This is the webway – not all places can be reached from every direction,' said Asurmen. 'One only gains entry from within the town.'

They stood before an impressive gateway. To the casual onlooker it was wrought of iron and gold, its main structure a dark, forbidding metal decorated by curling eldar runes in glittering yellow that declared its name: Biel-Tanigh. Within the bars of the gate Jain Zar could see a complex interweaving arrangement of bars and levers, parts of an ornate silver locking mechanism covered with the faintest, tiniest lines of inscribed runes.

The gate hung from a no-less-imposing pair of pillars, of red-veined marble carved with dire warnings and warding glyphs. The red was the colour of blood and seemed to throb as if fluid passed along it.

'How do we enter?' Jain Zar stepped closer. The bars were too close for her hand to pass through and there was no obvious keyhole for the mechanism. Peering closer she could see shapes in the grounds beyond – angular figures, either tall or standing on pedestals she could not make out.

The wall to either side was thrice her height, the stones so smoothly jointed that she could barely find where one met the other.

'It is no physical lock,' said Asurmen, examining the gate. The Hand of Asuryan followed her gaze to the wall. 'And that is no ordinary barrier. Like Asur, this is a pocket-realm of the webway, not a place within the material universe. The wall is just a representation, it cannot be scaled or penetrated.'

He raised a hand to where the two gates met. His forearms were encased in newly fashioned vambraces, each containing a full-size shuriken catapult, far longer-ranged and more accurate than the concealed wrist-launchers he had worn previously.

Jain Zar had also used the forge facilities to make improvements to her own panoply. Her glaive now contained a powerfield generator to supplement the monomolecular-edged blade, as did the throwing triskele at her hip. She had extended her armour with reactive plates that covered her midriff, thighs and upper arms; Asurmen had forgone robes for more armour also. Each cycle they became more like true warriors than armed wanderers.

'A psychic lock?' Jain Zar had heard the Master of the Blood-dance had such things for his lowest vaults but had not seen such a thing. 'What manner of scholars live here?'

Her question was answered by a sigh from the gate mechanism. With only the faintest sound of metal gliding against metal the lock twisted and turned, peeling apart to form a different rune on the other side of the gate – one of welcome.

Jain Zar stepped back, whipping her triskele from her

belt, eyes scanning the shadows. Asurmen responded by stepping forward, hand outstretched, but the gates opened before he laid his touch upon them, effortlessly swinging inwards to reveal a white-stoned path.

The figures that Jain Zar had seen earlier were revealed to be slender statues, each half again as tall as Asurmen, of smoke-grey metal. They were featureless, their faces slender inverted triangles with shallow depressions to denote where eyes would be. Their hands and feet were pointed blades that sparkled in the silvery light. All seemed to be looking at the new arrivals.

The grounds stretched to either side of the path, apparently without end, unkempt lawns and hedges and more of the silver figures until concealed by the haze of distance.

The stones crunched underfoot as they walked, loud in the silence that blanketed the library. Breath formed mist in the cold, lips and fingertips tingled with chill.

They came to the first pair of figurines, flanking the path not quite directly opposite each other. There were no plinths, the statues impossibly balanced on bladed limbs. Though the pair had covered some distance, the twin statues still looked directly at them, as did the others across the gardens.

'Guardians,' whispered Jain Zar, afraid to break the grave-silence by speaking any louder.

'Content to let us pass,' replied Asurmen, equally subdued. 'For now.'

The path was long, far longer than had seemed from the gate, and they continued on, walking in silence until they came to the steps of a great portico, itself topped by two towers at each end, a smaller-scale representation of the whole building.

The colonnaded porch had no gate or doors but simply opened into the interior. A semicircular chamber adjoined the entrance, tiled in grey and black, the curving walls a lighter shade. The only light came from outside through narrow, grimed windows that lined the top of the walls. Asurmen did not hesitate, but Jain Zar lingered for a moment on the threshold. The quiet was like a shroud, the old stones heavy with the weight of prehistory. It was worse than the whispers beyond the walls, and she wondered what kept the ghosts at bay, and if she desired to meet that power.

'Come on.' Asurmen's voice was as deadened as the air, flat as it reached her ears. 'There is nothing to fear in this place.'

'A bold statement.'

The voice rang across the entrance hall from a doorway on the left. A figure stood against a flickering light beyond. Broader than Jain Zar but no taller, the details of the figure-hugging bodysuit lost in silhouette.

The stranger came closer, hands held away from the body to avoid any hint of threat. His suit was dark blue, of one piece, just the faintest shimmer as though catching starlight. His hands were empty and as he approached the dim light revealed a gaunt face, dark hooded eyes, black hair held back with a silver band. Despite the skull-like appearance, he was young, probably an adolescent when the Fall had swept the eldar from the galaxy.

'But, for the most part, true enough.' He regarded Jain Zar first for some time and then Asurmen, eyes moving between their faces and weapons and back to their faces. 'We do not get many visitors here at the Library of Biel-Tanigh. In fact, you are the first we have had since the arrival of She Who Thirsts.'

'She Who Thirsts?' asked Asurmen.

'We shall talk about that soon enough, I am sure.' The eldar clasped his fingers together and held his hands at his waist. 'I'll not ask for your weapons, as I know you have no intent to use them here, and there is nothing against which you would wish to raise them.'

'You are sure?' said Jain Zar.

'About the second, absolutely.' He regarded her with an almost lazy look. 'On the first account I trust to the guards to have detected any malicious intent. If they have allowed you to pass, I do not think I have anything to fear from you.'

'What do you do here?' asked Asurmen. 'Are you one of the keepers?'

'I attend them, such as remain. I used to catalogue, serve food, organise things. Now I have taken on a more important duty.' He looked at them both again, solemn. 'I am Maugan Ra.'

The Harvester of Souls.

14

Waiting with the other exarchs, Danaesh felt an improbable calm. For anyone that had not walked the Path of the Warrior the prospect of his immediate future – and its inevitable and abrupt end – would have been a cause for terror. To the Young King it was simply a passage to the next step of existence.

With the aid of the farseers he had been chosen to serve as Young King for a pass and a cycle, to stand ready for the awakening of Khaela Mensha Khaine's avatar. It was not a lottery, but fate that had placed him in this position, and to rail against the vicissitudes of fate was as pointless as arguing against the turning of the galaxy. Both had a momentum that could not be overcome.

As exarch he had no future but a bloody death – this physical incarnation would not last forever. He also had no past. Such recollections as he had did not move beyond his war mask. He could not even recall how it was that he had come to be trapped in this stage of his life, nor what fears and tremors of mood had taken him to the Shrine of the Howling Banshee.

With him were nine others, drawn from across the shrines, representing different aspects of Khaine.

'You have been chosen, Young King elect, to become the blade.' Napheriuth, one of the three Dire Avengers, spoke the words quietly, with respect for the occasion. 'The banshee scream calls us, war for Ulthwé, a foe to be slain. Are you ready, Howling Banshee, to be awoken?'

Danaesh nodded his acceptance. Six of those that attended came forth, each the oldest of their shrine. They conducted the Young King into the chamber that neighboured the throne room of Khaela Mensha Khaine.

Danaesh felt excited as they passed into the Bloodied Way leading to their sanctum. Painted scenes from the battles of Khaine illuminated the walls, representing the Bloody-Handed God as Destroyer, Avenger, Cleanser and other aspects embodied in their ranks.

Eventually it brought them to the antechamber of the Avatar's throne room. The great bronze doors were closed but ruddy light crept from beneath the immense portal.

The Young King felt the brooding strength of the Avatar like heat on his body and in his mind. It called to the anger that had trapped him upon the Path of the Warrior, celebrating his bloody life.

Warlocks in robes and masks entered after the exarchs. Psykers that had passed through the shrines, they also felt the pull of Khaine. With them they brought a long cloak of red and a golden pin fashioned in the shape of a dagger. They stopped before Danaesh while the exarchs slowly removed his armour. With reverent bows they passed their accoutrements to the priests of the Bloody-Handed One. Naked, Danaesh took the dagger-pin in his left hand.

When Khaine had slain the eldar hero Eldanesh his blood had been caught in seven cups. Though the Bloody-Handed God had waged war to seize back the life and spirit of his victim, the folk of Eldanesh saved his soul and in doing so guaranteed the longevity of the eldar people. One of the warlocks brought forth a grail in memory of the foul deed – the Cup of Criel.

Standing behind the Young King, one of the other exarchs took the cloak pin and with it scored the rune of the Dire Avenger into Danaesh's left shoulder. Skin and flesh parted without effort before the cut of the enchanted dagger; Danaesh felt his blood running from the wound, caressing his back and thigh before he heard the drip of it falling into the Cup of Criel.

Each exarch took up the dagger-pin and cut their own rune, moving across Danaesh's flesh to cover him with their marks, blood streaming from the incisions.

He stood in silence, the pain almost something of memory rather than reality, detached from the incisions made upon his body. He stared mesmerised by the doors beyond which waited the Avatar. He had been the knife-wielder before, and knew what fate lurked beyond the portal of bronze. It did not worry him, it was the apotheosis of his being, the pinnacle to which a dedicated warrior of Khaine could aspire. In his death he would bring life to his god's mortal incarnation.

Carrying his spirit stone, a warlock approached with slow strides and placed the gem into a necklace that she hung around the Young King's neck. Armed with the dagger-pin she then gently cut the rune of the Avatar into his forehead. Crimson poured down his face but he stared through the sting, ecstasy building, the room fading, colour and sound washing away towards greyness and a slow pulsing beat.

Its first purpose fulfilled, the dagger was used to pin the cloth of the cloak. The cape was vast, wrapped twice about him as a toga and still long enough to trail on the floor. It soaked in the blood from his injuries, red fibres darkened with life fluid.

Then came the Wailing Doom, the great spear known as the Suin Daellae. He took it in his right hand and the Cup of Criel filled with his blood in the left. It took all of his focus to remain steady, limbs quivering with agitation.

Exarch and warlock alike lifted up their voices in a cruel hymn of appeasement, calling forth Khaine's spirit to answer them. Danaesh felt something flicker through his spirit, surging along the bloodied veins of the craft-world beneath his feet, seeking him, predatory and dark.

As still as a statue, Danaesh waited, struck immobile by the power that coursed through him. He felt again the pound of a tremendous heartbeat, his own pulse thundering in time with it.

A furnace unveiled, the immense doors crashed open to unleash their heat. It poured over Danaesh, bathing skin and flesh in the blessings of the Bloody-Handed One, forcing his blood through his veins like water out of a broken dam.

Firelight filled his vision, his entire world, save for a dark figure on a throne in the heart of the inferno, an ember from which the flames burned.

He heard a command in his spirit and paced forward, unable to resist even as terror burst free from the mental vault to which it had been long consigned. Staring into the face of his god the exarch knew a profound dread even as the doors slammed behind him, cutting off all other sound and sight.

The eyes of the Avatar opened, pits of darkness that consumed him. Its iron mouth twisted in a cruel smile.

Sitting cross-legged in the darkness of a hidden chamber beneath that of the Avatar, Jain Zar felt the awakening of the Bloody-Handed One like a blade in her head, its howl of joy and rage coursing through every part of her immortal being.

Its power choked her, threatening to overwhelm her soul with its bloodlust and anger.

A roar reverberated across the infinity circuit, echoed by the throats of a thousand Aspect Warriors.

She tried to resist but was as powerless to stop its flow as a leaf to hold back a conflagration. Khaine's gift flared within Jain Zar and forced its way from her lips as an ululating scream of hate.

Thrice heavy fists drummed on the door and stopped. The chamber was pregnant with energy, as though all air was sucked from it, the heat that shimmered from the great portals filling the space in its absence.

The pause was dreadful, full of lethal potential, the last echoes of the resounding crash, the last ring of the impact vanishing at the same moment that the next trio of deepening pounds began.

And as before a near-silence was allowed to fall, the reverberations almost lost in the hammer of heartbeats and the pulse of blood through burning veins. The gleam beneath and between the two doors was white-hot, the crackle of flames and the creak of expanding metal not quite muted by the heavy portal.

A third time something immeasurably strong smote the metal and on the ninth stroke, thrice times three blows, the doors flew open in a wash of furious light and heat.

Smoke issuing from its burning iron body, the Avatar of Khaine stood at the threshold of its throne room and lifted a hand. Boiling blood slicked the fingers and up to the elbow, dripping constantly to the floor to leave a pool of steaming crimson. In its other hand it held the Wailing Doom, grown in proportion to its wielder, now thrice the height of the exarchs that welcomed the avatar of their bloodthirsty god. From its back hung the long red cloak, blood-soaked, steaming where it touched the heated metal flesh of the immortal.

Eyes of burning embers flashed, and a wave of murderous intent flooded the chamber as the Avatar glared at the exarchs that had awoken it.

They fell to their knees, cowed by the presence of their master incarnate.

Its step into the main chamber was accompanied by the crash of metal. Molten droplets hissed in its wake as it advanced another stride, accompanying the groan of tortured metal as it turned its head one way and then the other, regarding the exarchs with baleful hate. A lipless mouth twisted into a sneering smile.

A whisper of a chill breeze entered the room, fluttering the crests and cloaks of the kneeling exarchs. They looked up, surprised by this unprecedented occurrence. The Avatar glared across them, towards the doors of the chamber, its iron smile becoming a grimace of anger. They turned to find the object of its scorn.

At the door Jain Zar waited with the Silent Death and the Blade of Destruction held across her chest. A cold wind flowed from her, dispelling the fume of the Avatar's awakening. Unsure what this interruption portended, they looked from the Phoenix Lord to the Bloody-Handed One and back again.

A pulse of displeasure from their god's avatar brought the exarchs to their feet, instinctively bearing their weapons against the intruder. Jain Zar did not move, the gaze of her screaming mask fixed upon the incarnation of Khaela Mensha Khaine.

Sensing that this was no place for mortals, no matter how changed by their circumstance, the exarchs filed from the chamber, giving the Phoenix Lord a wide berth. The door closed behind her as the last of them left.

15

Letting out a roar, the Avatar charged, trailing fire and blood as it swung the Suin Daellae at Jain Zar's head. Still as a statue she let the lethal blade slice a hair's breadth from her face. The Avatar stopped, with a screech from the floor as its metal feet skidded across the bare stone. It towered over the Phoenix Lord, bending to thrust its face towards her, sparks falling from its eyes such was its rage at her defiance.

Daughter. The word was formed of thought, not sound waves, but still the chamber shook with their volume. *Why do you disrespect us in this way?*

'You have taken one of mine already, you will take no more, spawn of Khaine.'

We are Khaela Mensha Khaine! We take what we please. The children of Ulthwé have awoken us, their fate is bound to ours. The sacrifice was but a taste. Great will be the bloodshed ere we rest again, daughter.

'I will end the war before it begins. Already your grip is tight around the throats of too many of my people. I will not let you burn more in your fire of rage.'

You cannot stop us, daughter. They have called and we have answered. The Avatar straightened, flames and sparks flaring along its arms like hot steel smote by the foundry hammer. *Your people are weak. They need us to survive. What does it matter the cost of some to protect the others? They gave themselves to us willingly, took up the mantle we gave them. The gift we set into the heart of each of them burns brighter with our return.*

'And yet here you slumbered when they did not need you. The lessons we taught them, the path on which we set them, keeps you in check, even as it holds back the appetite of the Great Enemy.'

They will drown in blood before we are sated. You cannot defy our will, you are our daughter.

'I will not serve you. Some are trapped in your wrath, but we save more. You shall not be our ruin.'

You cannot live without us. Our fate and yours is the same.

'You were my father but my mother was Morai Heg, the mistress of fate itself. By Asuryan's hand we are not bound by the fortunes of mortals anymore. We are not beholden to your demands. We were delivered from you, released from the iron fortress you raised around our minds.'

And you threw away the greatest weapons we gave you! Look at them now, cowering in the shadows, flinching at the movements in the darkness. There is no greatness left in these people. They are not worthy of your protection. Give them to us, my daughter. Bring us together and let us feast on them until we are strong and whole again. We will free you from the domination of the one that sundered us.

'No! We shall not be enslaved by gods or ourselves again.'

And so you will imprison yourselves instead. You will gutter and die like candles rather than burn bright like pyres.

'Better that than servitude to the kinslayer. There is nothing you will not bend to your will, and you will use us and destroy us in that purpose. Eldanesh refused you with good reason, breaker of oaths.'

You would not exist without us, daughter. You speak of the mistress of fates, but forget that it was she that begged us for the knowledge of her own blood. Blood! In all it is the deciding player, calling us to war, sending us to the tomb. Who knows blood better than we do, daughter?

'And yet it was the banshees that tormented you, your own daughters so vilely sired sent back to hound you with our laments. We told you that even the mighty Khaela Mensha Khaine would fall. Did you hear your own doom in our cries?'

We cut off your mother's hand to rid ourselves of this harping, yet you are here, wailing in our ear, witch of Morai Heg. What must we do to rid ourselves of your tyranny?

'Let them go. Take your blade from their hearts and let them know peace.'

The Avatar kneeled, the molten fire in its body dimming to leave cracked, creaking metal. It reached out its bloody hand and placed it upon her shoulder, matting her crest with the gore that seeped from the articulated digits.

You are our daughter and we would not deny you, but we cannot do this. You would cast us into the abyss, forgotten and impotent, when we should be raised upon thrones of gold and feted as the lords of the eldar.

Jain Zar bowed into its immense frame, letting her forehead touch the hot metal of its chest. She could feel the steady thump of a heart, though she knew it physically possessed no such thing.

The universe does not know peace. They will all die without us.

'Then let us die!'

That will not save you.

She pulled back, wrenching herself from the Avatar's grip. It stood as she straightened, the fires of its inner being crackling into life again to bathe her with their ruddy glow.

'We will not return to those bloody days when craftworlds tore themselves apart at your command. We have the Path to curb those excesses. You are contained now, a weapon to be unsheathed but nothing more.'

Take care of the blade, for it can still slip unbidden from its scabbard and cut you.

'Not while I am here. We will resist you and keep you chained as you chained Vaul, and come the Rhana Dandra you will serve your purpose and die with the rest of us.'

The Rhana Dandra is an age away, daughter. There are others that lack your patience.

'What does that mean? What others?'

The Avatar bared serrated teeth in its grin.

When you run the errands of gods, be sure which ones you serve, daughter. You are the daughter of Khaela Mensha Khaine and Morai Heg, yet you are the bride of Death.

'There is no death, only a return to the state of formlessness. I know, I have travelled that road.'

Heaven has fallen and your mortal paradise is lost, but this new age is still young. Ask us how powers may rise and fall in the turning of an aeon, daughter. Heed our stories of the folly of mortal impatience and the rise of the dead ones.

The Avatar lifted its spear, the Suin Daellae, and a loud keening screeched from it, echoing around the chamber, rising and falling in pitch until everything resounded with its numbing cacophony. Jain Zar listened and heard the melodies within, and knew that she listened in part to her own voice. Confronted with the incarnation of Khaine, it was impossible not to reflect on its weapon, the Wailing Doom, the aspect of which she had taken into herself to become the Howling Banshee. Was that all she was, when all other fates had been laid bare? A weapon?

Not yet. The people of Ulthwé needed an alternative to the war of Khaine. That was why Asuryan had sent her. Faced with the burning will of Khaine, the thirst for bloodshed barely suppressed, she recalled the lure of violence within all eldar that the Path had been created to overcome – be it for revenge or justice, art or survival.

This was her mission. To change the direction of the war with the orks and save her people.

She raised the Zhai Morenn, its silver blade catching the light from the fire of the Avatar's weapon, the chill absorbing the heat, the void that swallows the energy of stars.

'I have spent enough time indulging your arrogance, hollow thing. Now I go to fight to save your people.'

And when you win, remember to thank us, daughter.

Without Danaesh the shrine seemed larger, less oppressive. Like the other temples to Khaine where the Aspect Warriors trained, the Shrine of the Howling Banshee, known to those who passed through its tapered bone-white doors as the Shrine of the Last Heard, it was located close to the chamber of the Avatar of Khaine. Here the structure of the craftworld was not laced with the crystal pathways of the infinity circuit;

instead the pulse of the Avatar's heart throbbed along spurs of bone and thrummed on weaves of sinew.

The shrine sat at the edge of the campus of Khainite temples, reached by a solitary narrow causeway of black stones to the centre of a frozen lake. The temple thrust from waters caught in icy stasis like a stalagmite of white rock, without windows, the single door the first and last portal into the realm of the Howling Banshees.

Within the lower floors was a complex of training chambers, meditation halls and armoury ranged about a spiral stair that led into the sanctum pinnacle. Viewed from the pointed arch of the entrance, the circular shrine was dominated by the design decorating the floor in monochrome mosaic – white and pale blue depicting the screaming face of the banshee, her forehead marked with the Khainites' rune of their aspect. So cleverly arranged were the thousands of tiny tiles that in the flicker of the black candles that provided the shrine's only light it seemed as though the face appeared at times to change, taking on the appearance of Khaela Mensha Khaine, mouth agape to stream fire and blood, eyes ablaze.

The seven remaining followers of Danaesh sat facing inwards, legs crossed, armoured but for their ornately maned helms, which were set upon the floor in front of each of them.

It was the first time Tallithea had felt the touch of the Avatar after learning how to create the war mask that disassociated her warrior-self from the rest of her personality. Before she had come to the Shrine of the Last Heard and absorbed the teachings of Danaesh the call of Khaine had been ill-heard, an unease that made her short-tempered, uncomfortable with others.

Now that she had learnt how to tap into the part of herself that desired death, that thrived on conflict and the thrill of confrontation, the Avatar's awakening was a constant martial drumbeat that matched the throb in her chest. Even before she had joined the others Tallithea had felt the urge to begin the mantras that would slide her war mask into place, but knew that it was only safe to do so in the sanctuary of the shrine.

She had been breathlessly eager ascending the stair to the sanctum, and the absence of Danaesh had hit her like a hammerblow when she had found the exarch's armour empty on its rack in the arming chamber below the sanctum.

'I never quite realised what being the Young King meant,' she confessed to the others.

They nodded their understanding, measuring their movements even though each was obviously on edge, invigorated by the wakening power of their bloody master's mortal incarnation.

'We know the rituals,' said Anothesia, flicking blonde strands of hair from her face. She looked at the silver grail and curved knife that stood on a plinth where Danaesh had previously led the ceremonies. Each had already spilled their blood into the cup as part of the ritual of entering. 'One of us should lead.'

'Not I,' Nadomesh said quickly. He averted his gaze at the sharp looks from the others. 'I… I think it a step towards becoming trapped. Can you not hear it already?'

Tallithea knew of what he spoke. A whispered lament from the chamber below, where Danaesh's empty armour sang psychically in yearning for its lost soul. In the melancholic dirge was also an invitation, a note of hope to

259

be reborn, offering immortality to the one that dared take Danaesh's place.

'We know the consequences,' said Anothesia. 'Yet it must be done. Khaine's spirit would take any that does not wear their mask properly. Do any of you trust that the mask will not slip in battle, that these eyes you have now will not see the depravity that will take us?'

'I do not know what I have done as the Howling Banshee and I do not want to remember,' Kathllain said vehemently. Her eyes flicked to the accoutrements of Khaine's priestess but she did not volunteer to take them up.

Tallithea swallowed hard, caught between her desire to see the ceremony under way and her fear of doing so. The scream of the banshee was gaining strength inside her, rising in volume, demanding to be let free. She feared that if she did not don her war mask soon it would erupt anyway, with who could say what disastrous consequences?

She was about to rise, tensing the muscles of her legs to stand, when a freezing wind rose up from the stairwell to tousle the crests of their helms, leaving a chill touch on the exposed skin of their faces. The wind snuffed out the candles, plunging them into utter blackness. Tallithea stifled a cry and felt the unease of the others, heard the whisper of armour as some of them stood.

The air drew out of the chamber and from the stair came a pale light, barely enough to illuminate the floor for a few paces. They turned to see who had entered. The slow, measured ring of boots on stone heralded the step of the new arrival, louder and louder as they ascended, each footfall becoming the crack of a tomb lid closing. With their approach the illumination brightened, still a wan corpse-light but spreading to the further reaches of the shrine.

Tallithea could not stop the gasp that escaped her when she looked down to see that the face of the banshee on the floor had changed again. In the paleness it seemed as though the daughter of Khaine and Morai Heg closed her mouth, her mane a nest of serpents coiling about her head.

From the stair emerged their god-maiden given form. Clad in black-and-bone, she stood a head taller than any of them, her mane of sable black hanging to the floor. The light came from the blade of the glaive in one hand, while shadows danced from the black flame that burned along the three arms of the triskele in the other.

Tallithea had heard rumours that the Storm of Silence had come to Ulthwé, but to see her in person, for Jain Zar to come to the Shrine of the Last Heard, was overwhelming. Tears running down her face, she stood trembling with shock as the Phoenix Lord strode slowly across the floor, the mosaic beneath snarling and grimacing in the changing light.

'Your exarch has been taken,' Jain Zar said quietly. Her voice was soft, almost impossible to match to the lips that had taught the Scream that Steals. She placed the haft of the Blade of Destruction against the grail stand and the cup burst into black fire, becoming a brazier. The Silent Death she hung from the frame, as if it had always belonged.

She dipped a gauntleted finger into the flame and drew it out, burning blood hissing on the tip.

'For this battle, you shall dance beside me.'

* * *

Nothing had changed, except the faces.

Jain Zar could remember standing in front of the first warriors of Ulthwé. Danaesh had always been the most fervent, and though it disappointed her that he had succumbed to the traps of Khaine, he had led well. He was gone now, his spirit saved from She Who Thirsts at the expense of being consumed by Khaela Mensha Khaine's physical avatar. How many had followed Danaesh into that dead end? Which of these would succumb?

Not one of them flinched as she moved about the circle, painting the rune of the Banshee upon their foreheads in hissing blood. Their adoration shone in their eyes, uncomfortably so. The Shrine of the Last Heard had been one of her first after the disaster that befell Asur. Its memory of her was strong, her legacy permeating the bone and stone, down to the foundations of Ulthwé, this temple raised before any other dedicated to Khaine.

When the circuit was complete, she motioned for the warriors to take up their helms and stand. The hate was building, their anger growing. She watched each of them carefully, seeing the glassy look entering their eyes as their war masks started to form, cutting off empathy and compassion, sealing away memories of loved ones and kin.

'What of the words?' asked one, whom she knew from the shrine's memories to be called Tallithea. 'What of the mantra?'

'I am the Storm of Silence,' Jain Zar replied. She turned and took up the Zhai Morenn. On the edge of the blade was reflected the black fire from the sacrificial grail. She turned the weapon carefully, so that the gleam of the flame danced across the faces of the waiting Howling Banshees. As each looked upon the spark of darkness the transition completed, all sympathy and mercy and love falling from their thoughts at its passing. 'I need no words.'

When it was done they raised their helms and put them on, a physical analogue to the metaphorical donning of the war mask. Jain Zar could feel nothing of their former selves in the spirit of the shrine, all had metamorphosed correctly and completely.

No eldar remained in the chamber, only Howling Banshees, warrior-queens of the Bloody-Handed One.

Jain Zar put back her head and screamed and her daughters screamed with her, the ceiling of the shrine wreathed in coiling black flames as the candles of the night burst into fresh life around them.

While the final preparations were made, Jain Zar attended to the exarchs in the chamber adjoining the throne room of the Avatar, where the incarnation of murder had returned for the time being until Ulthwé was prepared to launch its attack.

Durothian of the Dark Reapers spoke first.

'It is not as wished, this war-plan of yours. Heed the Avatar.' There was nothing to be seen of the Dark Reaper exarch's face behind the skull mask of his armour and Jain Zar could not help but picture the face of the first eldar to have donned that attire.

'We do not need Khaine's fist,' Jain Zar replied. 'I shall lead the Aspects to battle.'

'You are only one, even a Phoenix Lord, not Lord Khaine himself,' Durothian argued. 'You are one Aspect, he is the many, the Bloody-Handed One.'

'This is not to be a massed attack,' she reminded the assembled exarchs. 'The slightest cut, a single thread to be severed, will change the course of the orks' fate. I have seen this – it can be done with just the smallest of forces.'

'The Avatar leads us, we follow, Daughter of Morai Heg,' said the Striking Scorpion, Tar-Duath. His powered claw opened and closed with agitation at having to deny the Phoenix Lord, but the words betrayed his decision. 'The banshee calls to us, I accept that, but it does not command.'

'Another battle, seen by Eldrad, will guide Ulthwé safe,' countered Napheriuth.

'Eldrad is wrong,' snapped Jain Zar. 'He will have the craftworld embroiled in a conquest that will see hundreds die and bring you to a disaster that will doom millions. Who is this seer whose words you value so highly? An upstart. He did not even live through the Fall and yet you are willing to follow him to such slaughter?'

'He is the guiding one, the seer of paths, who treads the oldest ways.' Another of the Dire Avengers, Louashafar, spoke this endorsement. 'Disaster he has averted, many times now, and in his words we trust.'

'He does not lead the seer council. Daensyrith is senior, and I have her full consent.'

'If seers are divided, that is their wrong. As one we have voted,' countered Louashafar.

Jain Zar looked at the exarchs and realised that they would not be swayed. Had she arrived earlier, before the rousing of the Avatar, she might have convinced them to take part in her small engagement. Now that Khaine's warsong sang in their hearts it was too late. They would follow their wargod to victory or ruin, and Khaine desired great bloodshed over all other considerations.

Louashafar made a valid point. Daensyrith was too

weak; she should not have allowed Eldrad to mount this counter-preparation. Even so, the Phoenix Lord knew better than to meddle without care in the affairs of seers, for they were subtle and prideful individuals.

She said nothing more to the exarchs, fatigued by their company and the sapping presence on her spirit from the Avatar behind the throne-room doors. She did not need them. She was the Storm of Silence and the Last Heard were hers to lead as she desired. Before the mighty war engine of Ulthwé brought its full power to bear and plunged them all into disastrous all-out war, she would slay this troublesome alien and change the course of the future to the betterment of all. In light of that development even Eldrad would have to concede that his plan had no merit.

It was not the strategy she had sought when she had arrived on the craftworld, but it was still the best hope for peace between Ulthwé and the other craftworld, Anuiven – and the opportunity to save the eldar from catastrophe.

16

From a balcony overlooking the terraces that led down to the Port of Last Starlight Eldrad could see the assembling warhost of Ulthwé. He sat on a low, padded stool, a moonlyre on his lap, idly drawing finger and thumb across the strings in improvisational composition.

The starfield visible through the force dome above the harbour area was filled with ships of the fleet sliding into and out of the three berths that had been designated for the war effort. Beyond the graceful outlines of the ships the stars sparkled with multicoloured flashes; the edge of the Eye of Terror's distortion. Eldrad knew that if he were to move to the other side of the craftworld, a journey of a day, he would look upon the seething depths of the Chaos Heart. Except for the seers and a few aesthetes, the majority of the population had moved away from those plates to the settlements that looked out to the untouched galaxy.

He had watched the procession of war materiel and crews for some time, detached from the skein to clear his thoughts. Below him, as small as mice, lines of black-armoured guardians formed around the yellow banners of their squads. There were only a few hundred, but their number grew with every pass as more inhabitants of the craftworld headed through the shrines of the Aspect Warriors.

Was it a remarkable achievement or a retrograde step? Eldrad respected the efforts of Asurmen to bring the order and discipline of the Path to the craftworlds, but did it have to focus on such a martial theme?

He shrugged to himself, flicking a thumb across his instrument to create a few rising discordant notes. The ability to fight was a necessary evil, and to control the natural urges that came with such bloodshed had proven an equal necessity. One only had to look at the troglodytic throwbacks of Commorragh to see the depths to which the unfettered eldar mind was capable of descending.

Wave Serpent grav-transports snaked along the boulevards to the loading quays, sliding effortlessly above the floor. Each stopped briefly for a squad of guardians to embark, so that the line seemed to be a single reticulating entity before it slipped through the immense gateways to the docks themselves.

'Looking on the works of your hubris, Eldrad?'

He turned at the sound of Daensyrith's voice. The seer was clad in her full regalia, runic armour over her robes, her rod of office held in one hand, a shield of wraithbone in the other.

'And he played on while the craftworld burned,' she continued. 'I should not be surprised that you enjoy stringwork so much, as you seem most adept at pulling those of your puppets.'

'You know well that I walked the Path of the Musician

while I broke from my seerdom. I find the similarities between divination and composition fascinating. It is not only the notes that we hear, but the space between them. It is not only the visions we see that are important, but the ones that we do not. Much can be inferred from the absence or negative.'

His fingers danced lightly, a jaunty air one would associate with the more raucous establishments where outworlders and outcasts, like those Jain Zar had brought with her, were likely to gather. Alien, unsympathetic countermelody rose and fell through his playing.

'Hubris?' said Eldrad, returning to her earlier accusation. 'To see the craftworld protected against all threats?'

'To set yourself against the will of Asuryan.'

'The gods are dead, Daensyrith.' He struck three descending melancholic chords. 'Those that survived the War in Heaven were consumed by the Great Enemy.'

'There is a burning idol that leads us to war that would speak otherwise of the death of gods.'

'Asuryan no more guides the hands of these Phoenix Lords than you are still an oracle of Morai Heg.' His playing became tempestuous, staccato. His gaze moved to look back across Ulthwé, to the roiling Chaos storm that could not be seen. 'A new power has risen, we must bend all effort to its resistance.'

'Without my knowledge of the ways of the hag we would have no seers,' Daensyrith retorted. 'I do not know what promises you have made to Charythas and Licentas but I hope it is worth the lives you are about to throw away.'

'Promises? You make it sound as though I am politicking in some fashion.'

'Do not play me for a fool, Eldrad. I know that you seek

governance of the council. You undermine my decisions and move against my will.'

'It is a council, not a tyranny. Your word is the beginning, not the end. If your arguments fail to convince, perhaps you should study a little more rhetoric.'

'Listen to me!' The whipcrack of her voice caused him to stop playing and look up. 'You are gifted beyond any other seer but your judgement is faulty. You think we can strike back at She Who Thirsts? You really think that dangling such false hopes in front of others will bring you the power you crave?'

'Deserve,' he said quietly. 'Power I deserve.'

He nodded towards the other's farseer's belt and at his thought her pouches opened, spilling out the numerous wraithbone runes from within. They spiralled up around Daensyrith, her face a mask of shock – a seer's runes were mind-bound to them, supposedly answering only to their thoughts.

'Power is relative, Daensyrith.' Eldrad stood up and laid down the moonlyre. 'How many of these runes did I first discover? You brought the wisdom of Morai-Heg? Superstition and blind flailing compared to the precision I have brought to our craft. One might as well mould raw clay into a lump and call oneself a sculptor to make comparison to your efforts in scrying. I have led us to new vistas of understanding. I have taken us on roads undreamt of by the mumbling oracles of Gal-Shathoth and Biel-Tanigh.

'I already have more power than any of you. I have seen further and down more pathways than the rest of the council combined. I have communed with councils on the far side of the galaxy. We are not alone but we act as if we are. A hint of a threat and we run to hide. Cowardly!

We shall not overcome the obstacles arrayed against us by avoiding them.'

He moved to the balustrade of the balcony and looked down at the Falcon grav-tanks and Vyper jetbikes swarming below.

'Take these orks. Jain Zar would have us nudge them down a different route, one that avoids Ulthwé for the moment. I say we exterminate them now and be done with it. Let us finish the task the humans did not. These brutes are growing in number again while our eye is drawn to brighter, more tantalising lights. They are distracting, so let us be rid of them entirely.'

'You would exterminate them?'

'If such a thing were possible, but I think not. Let us crush them for the time being and focus on worthier goals.'

'Survival is our only recourse now, Eldrad.' She sighed and her shoulders slumped. 'We must marshal carefully what little remains of our civilisation. Fortune and distance saved us from the worst of the Fall, and the Path brought to us by the Asurya has shown us the way forward. Do not think you can reclaim what we have lost. You look into the repositories and you walk back along the roads into the past, but you did not see what became of our people. We cannot, should not, return to that time. Let us diminish if we must, for to prosper again would be even greater folly.'

'How conveniently you throw away the future of those still with time to live it.'

'You did not feel the coming of She Who Thirsts, Eldrad. You are one of the generation born with the taint upon you, but free of the knowledge of what came before. You are blissful in your ignorance, you have no idea what we truly lost and what we gained.'

'An easy accusation to make, from one who saw our entire civilisation brought to ruination!' Eldrad snatched up his moonlyre and stepped to move past the other seer. He stopped and jabbed the instrument towards Daensyrith. 'You repent a little late for your trespasses against the eldar people. You wear your guilt like a mantle – do not try to hang it upon my shoulders. Your time is over, Daughter of Morai Heg, my time is coming.'

'You are too arrogant to lead, Eldrad. Such certainty only brings error. You are deaf to the wisdom of others, even the Asurya.'

Before he responded, Eldrad saw that one of Daensyrith's runes he had plucked from her belt was spinning – rotating vertically about its centre. The Banshee. He let down the barriers holding his mind in check and let his being flow into the infinity circuit, and through its conduits into the webway beyond.

A ship had left, the outcast vessel that had brought Jain Zar to Ulthwé. He felt the Storm of Silence slicing through the skeinsphere like an ice particle. She had the squad of the fallen Young King with her.

He spooled out into the skein proper, unravelling the threads of fate he had bound into his plan to attack the orks. Several of the pathways were fading, slipping from his grasp as Jain Zar's actions altered the course of the future.

One in particular, his own thread, started to split like an untwined cord, his certain fate becoming dozens of potentials.

He heard Daensyrith take in a breath and felt her

presence, urging him along one of the splaying pathways. Eldrad ventured after her web-ghost and came upon the sight of a great battle, Ulthwé in flames as green-skinned savages ran amok through the very docks below them.

Smoke choked the passages, staining the walls, while red rivers flowed along the quays, spilled from the piles of the dead. Strange two-limbed beasts bounded and whooped along the corridors while savages hollered their cries as they burst like a flood through the domes of the craftworld.

He shuddered, feeling the pain of the infinity circuit as alien psykers drove their copper staffs into its crystal veins, jabbering and shrieking while psychic bursts flew from their eyes. The spirits of his ancestors wailed at the desecration.

He pulled back and confronted the senior seer, heart racing.

'Call off the attack,' Daensyrith insisted. 'See what happens when you defy the will of Asuryan.'

'This is no punishment from a dead god, it is the goal of Jain Zar's mission.' The hubris of the Phoenix Lord riled him even more than the condescending tone of his superior. 'She wants to bring the orks to Ulthwé, not steer them adrift.'

'What a ridiculous notion. Why would a Phoenix Lord want to bring such savage war to the shores of our craftworld? It is your opposition that will bring the doom upon us.'

'Why indeed?' said Eldrad, retreating to his body. He felt the burning ripple of the Avatar's approach and cast an eye below. Many-coloured, led by their exarchs, the remaining squads of Aspect Warriors came to the gateways, the flaming incarnation of Khaela Mensha Khaine at their head. All others fled before the Avatar and its disciples, leaving the Port of Last Starlight deserted.

The ring of boots and the war-chants of the boarding squads filled the empty halls, distant and morbid, echoing as though from an ancient time. Certain phrases resounded, growing in volume from among the myriad verses.

Blood runs, anger rises, death wakes, war calls.

Matters were fast approaching the point of inevitability, beyond which the future could not be dramatically changed. He prided himself on seeing further than all others, but the finality of the ork attack had been like a veil drawn across his eyes.

Yet there had to be a different way that the others could not see, to steer the craftworld clear of the bloodshed Jain Zar seemed determined to bring down upon their heads. If the Storm of Silence could not be bowed, perhaps an even greater power of destruction could be turned to the cause.

Eldrad delved back into the skein, following the rune of Khaine's burning path into the heat of a thousand battles. He searched far and wide, tracking down distant futures beyond the sight of his fellows, but in all of them he saw the ork butchery falling upon Ulthwé. Such indiscriminate slaughter, unthinking, uncaring of the complex interleaving strands that made such a terrible thing possible.

In desperation, he hurled himself deeper into the web-void, chasing half-seen potentialities and almost-to-be fates. Here he found more promising earth on which to sow his plans – visions of the orks burning by their thousand as the Avatar led the army of Ulthwé against their repugnant cities and the ships of the fleet scoured their buildings from above.

Ignoring Daensyrith, he started to walk, heading back to the chambers of the seers in the distant craftworld heart. His body needed little guidance, and while he strode he used his thoughts to unwind the strands he had snatched up, working out how to manoeuvre the fate of Ulthwé and its inhabitants onto this profitable path.

He barely heard Daensyrith's demand. 'What will you do?'

'Whatever it takes to keep us safe,' he replied.

IX

Maugan Ra spoke over his shoulder as he led them across the grand lobby.

'I really did think that nobody would come. Nobody that had any purpose but ill intent. There has been a lot of that since the coming of She Who Thirsts.'

The first door through which they passed – the one by which he had arrived – took them into a small study, no more than a dozen paces across, with a winding stair of white stone at the back. The walls were lined with shelves full of data crystals, piled on each other, so many that some of them had spilled onto the thin-carpeted floor.

A chair and table were pushed into one corner, a low cot in another. Plates and other crockery were neatly stacked on the floor beside the stairwell. A crystal-reader sat on the desk, its projector the source of the light they had seen from the entrance hall.

'You live in here?' Asurmen regarded the chamber and its domestic contents. 'Just here?'

'No, of course not,' said Maugan Ra. 'I just eat, sleep and study here. My work takes me all over the library.'

'"She Who Thirsts". That's the second time you have used that title.'

'The new god.' Maugan Ra looked at them as if this were explanation enough. He greeted their incomprehension with a furrowed brow of uncertainty. 'It is real – our studies have proven it, even beyond the library.'

'Beyond the library?' Asurmen examined the data crystals more closely. 'You have not left since the Fall?'

'"The Fall?" How appropriate.' He sighed. 'No, I have not left the library. I could not, the masters might not survive without me.'

'You still tend them?' Jain Zar was even more confused than a moment earlier. 'Where are they?'

'This is going to get… complicated.' Maugan Ra moved to the spiral staircase and laid a hand on the banister. 'I suppose you should know. Follow me.'

They ascended several floors, passing through chambers devoid of contents but for empty crystal viewers and high-backed chairs. The archive pillars were all opened, their crystals apparently removed – probably those piled in Maugan Ra's chamber.

They finished in a long hall lined by high windows through which came the silver light of Biel-Tanigh's captured star. Rows of cushioned benches were set out around a central dais, as though for audience or conference. On the raised stage was a large plinth, and at its heart was a single globe, roughly the size of two fists together, swirling with white fog.

Jain Zar's eye was drawn to the sphere and its coiling, misty contents but Maugan Ra continued past, paying it no heed. He led them to the far end of the hall, to an alcove a little more than ten strides across. The floor within the space was tiled with white, as were the walls, with round gems set into the ceramic squares.

'I sometimes walk to pass the time,' Maugan Ra explained, 'but this way is quicker and I suppose you can have the grand tour another time.'

He touched a skeletal finger to one of the stones and the alcove melted away. Jain Zar's head buzzed for a few moments with echoes and pale brightness and then the white tiles reappeared, coalescing from a kaleidoscope of after-images.

She turned and found herself looking into another hall, smaller than the one they had left. Desks lined the walls to either side and more crystal repositories ran in a line away from the transporter. At one of the desks, about a third of the way down on the right, a figure sat hunched over the reader.

'Fatecaller Inniathanas,' announced Maugan Ra, stepping onto the lacquered wooden floorboards. 'One of the crow-touched. High Interrogator of the Third Sphere, Guardian of the Esoteric Arch.'

The robed figure did not move, his expression of intense concentration fixed in the glow of the crystal reader. Spindly fingers were splayed on the surface of the desk.

The Fatecaller still did not move as they approached, or give the slightest reaction to their presence. Coming closer, Jain Zar was unsettled by the stillness of the scholar, a feeling that deepened as they stood right next to the Fatecaller without a hint that he was aware of them.

His skin was covered with a fine tracery of lines, like gossamer threads so thin they could barely be seen individually. They flowed out of the sleeves of his robe as well, webbing him to the desk.

Asurmen held out a hand to brush away the filaments but Maugan Ra grabbed his arm with a shake of the head.

'I would not touch that,' said the Harvester of Souls. 'Daemon-web. Entropic residue from a warp intrusion.'

Jain Zar looked in disgust at the fine crystalline hairs and then at the Fatecaller. There was not the tiniest flicker of movement; no rise and fall of the chest, no twitch of a brow or eyelash.

'I assume he isn't dead?'

Maugan Ra gave her a pained look.

'Life. Death. Not obvious concepts in this place, in these times. Fatecaller Inniathanas continues.' He gestured to the desk beside the projector of the crystal viewer. A way-stone sat there, glowing fitfully. 'He is certainly still here rather than there, shall we say? His spirit is with us, not taken by She Who Thirsts.'

'You need to explain what you mean by that, and quickly,' said Jain Zar, raising her glaive a little.

'The guardians are not wrong,' Maugan Ra said with a sigh. 'You will not hurt me. They would not let you enter if they knew you would do me or the Fatecallers harm. Your threat matters not. I am happy to tell you what you need to know.'

Asurmen nodded, intent. 'Tell us everything.'

'We do not have time for that,' Maugan Ra replied. He waved a hand to encompass the room, and by extension the rest of the library. '"Everything" is quite a lot. But what is relevant, that we can discuss.

'The library of Biel-Tanigh was a place of learning, a study of arts and disciplines more philosophical than practical in nature. The Fatecallers were not immune to the spiralling decline of our people, far from it. Where others sought gratification from the flesh, the scholars were lured by the potential of the mind, of knowledge.

'Some became so engrossed in their studies that they forgot to eat and drink, others went mad, chasing answers to intangible questions that became ever more self-referencing and pointless. And competition... Not simply the pride of scholarly achievement but the desire to prove all others wrong separated the campuses, pitting college against college in pursuit of impossible intelligence.

'Reason, logic and humility were swept away by hubris and ritual. No longer did they seek to understand the universe for the good of all, but to control one another, to dominate the minds of lesser mortals. Biel-Tanigh became a place of death and perversion, where study was a religion and investigation was conducted through blade and flame upon the bodies of innocents.'

Maugan Ra turned his glum expression to Fatecaller Inniathanas. 'Like everywhere, the hopes and desires and quest for perfection fuelled the nascent beast that was growing within the warp. She Who Thirsts. A new god of Chaos, made from the spirit-stuff of our people. A hungering deity that thrives now on the energy of our dead.'

'How do you know this?' asked Asurmen. 'Time flows strangely in the webway but you cannot have been more than an infant when the Fall occurred.'

'I was a foundling, left by my parents as many were, in the hope that the colleges would raise me while they... Who knows what they desired, what immaculate pursuits distracted them from raising a child? Most of the scholars died, of course, as they have across society, but a few survived, the least-touched they claimed. Some fled the ghosts that came after, but twenty Fatecallers remained, and I with them for I was too young to know better, but old enough to carry food and work the garden systems.

'Broken from the grip of their obsessions, the Fatecallers were able to see what had happened, to use the Asurentesh to scry the fortunes beyond our realm and see the devastation wrought by the arrival of She Who Thirsts.'

'The "Heart of Asuryan",' Asurmen said sharply, noting the word Maugan Ra had used. 'What is this?'

'A seeing orb, very powerful and rare. The last of its kind, I think. You saw it downstairs.'

Asurmen started to move towards the transporter alcove. 'I must see it.'

'In time, you can. There is something else I have to show you first.' Maugan Ra picked up the waystone in front of Fatecaller Inniathanas. He nodded to the gem held in a socket upon Jain Zar's cuirass, and then to Asurmen's. 'The Tears of Isha, they are the key. I see you have yours. They are spirit-vaults, the immortal remains of all that perished. Psychic vessels keyed to our individual souls.'

'This much we have already divined,' said Asurmen, 'though their purpose is unclear.'

'I do not know if they have a purpose, they are a side effect, the inevitable consequence of She Who Thirsts devouring countless billions of our people. Waste product, you might say, though Fatecaller Viaillish was more poetic, and called them the Tears of Isha, wept from the life goddess of ancient myth.'

He placed the stone back before the Fatecaller, reverentially.

'We and She Who Thirsts are bound together, linked through that disastrous birthing pain that all but wiped out our people. When we die, our spirits will not be reborn into a new generation, as it was since the time of the gods. Now our souls belong to this new god. But the Tears of Isha capture our spirit, protect it from that fate. Save us from eternal damnation and torment.' He let out a lengthy sigh and looked away. 'For now, at least. I do not think there is a true salvation from this doom.'

'How do you know all of this?' asked Asurmen.

'That is another answer best shown rather than said.'

'Show us,' said Jain Zar.

They returned to the auditorium that held the device Maugan Ra had called the Asurentesh – the Heart of Asuryan. The sphere sat on its pedestal as when they had left, inert. Asurmen approached hurriedly, eyeing the globe with a mixture of suspicion and wonder.

'The name, why is it the Asurentesh?'

'It is part of a mechanism older even than the library,' explained Maugan Ra. He gestured for Asurmen and Jain Zar to stand back while he circled the pedestal, hands not quite touching the surface. 'The other parts existed in different places and times, linked through this central processor.'

'Processor? What does it do?' Jain Zar leaned closer, trying to peer into the milky depths of the crystal.

'One matter at a time, please,' said Maugan Ra. He placed his hands at strange angles on the rim of the pedestal, fingers irregularly splayed.

A sigh emanated from the dais and a brief flicker of a breeze touched Jain Zar's face. Lines of light emerged on the stand of the pedestal and crept across to its top, forming white fractures. Like a flower opening, the pedestal split, six sections parting to reveal a column of rainbow light beneath the Asurentesh.

The gleam of the light dimmed and then disappeared, leaving behind what appeared to be a slender tree trunk of gnarled white bark, no thicker than Jain Zar's arm. Branch-like fronds held aloft the central plate of the pedestal table.

Oval gems – waystones – had been set into the wood of the miniature tree, each aglow with its own energy. Jain Zar moved around the opened mechanism, counted eight Tears of Isha.

'The former Fatecallers?' she guessed. 'This is where you are keeping them?'

'I had not intended it,' said Maugan Ra. 'When the Fatecallers delved deeper into their studies they opened up our defences, to witness with their own minds the devastating majesty of the goddess we have created. They are enraptured now, as you saw. Alive, but gripped in the embrace of She Who Thirsts. These are the ones I could save, the others… They exist between damnation and freedom. Too long they have stared into the eye of destruction, not consumed but caught within its snare.'

'They are kept safe here? From… She Who Thirsts?' Asurmen crouched and looked closely at the spirit stones. He raised a hand to the gem at his breast. 'A permanent resting place?'

'More than that, and less.' Maugan Ra sat cross-legged next to the pillar and touched a finger to the closest gem. 'Not dead, not in our sense. Their spirits continue, they exist in a conscious state even if they do not perceive our world or the webweave any longer.'

'Imprisoned?' Jain Zar's throat tightened at the thought,

memories of her dormitory at the arena surfacing unexpectedly. 'Trapped inside those stones?'

'That is the truth of it,' Maugan Ra said sombrely, drawing away his hand. He stood up, languid, shoulders round.
'But that is not all. The stones, once occupied, generate…
They emit psychic frequencies that resonate with some
of the ancient matrix devices our ancestors built, such as
the Asurentesh.'

'The stones power the device,' concluded Asurmen. '"The
Harvester of Souls". You have turned them into a power
network?'

'Yes, that is one benefit.' Maugan Ra pushed lightly
against one of the raised sections of pedestal and the
device closed in on itself with another hiss. He touched
the completed pedestal with both hands and the
Asurentesh sprang into life, its inner mists swirling with
dabs of colour. 'We can also commune with the spirits
inside the matrix. In a fashion.'

He waved for them to approach.

'This room, the Asurentesh, was created to allow multiple viewers to access the same data networks, mine the
same psychic delving. The Fatecallers, the scholars that
built this library, did not just seek physical study. They
breached space and time, using the Asurentesh to draw
visions from across the fate continuum. Many could witness at once the same events, those past and those yet to
be, each from a unique perspective.'

He indicated for them to put their hands onto the dais.
Swirling lines like organic circuitry traced across the stone.

Jain Zar settled her weapon in the crook of her arm and
placed her hands on the pedestal. She allowed her gaze
to be drawn further into the mesmerising spiral of pale

colours within the Asurentesh. She relaxed and let her mind ride on the swirls and whorls, until shapes started to form. The hall, the library, the world faded from conscious thought, from memory, until she was all that she knew, all that had been.

She looked upon herself and saw the blood-soaked maiden within, unlocked from the prison she had created inside her mind. Jain Zar saw nothing specific, only glimpses of terrified faces and splashing crimson, of swift death upon glaive and triskele, countless lives washed away with a tide of blood. She heard the scream, piercing and long, the wail that heralds death. An eternity of slaughter.

Not an eternity.

There was an ending.

The visions became a blur of a passing age, but then stopped, a single vignette of war and devastation, of fires burning the sky and a plain of skulls torn asunder by the fury of battle. A goddess-god, ancient and young, beautiful and terrible, caught up in the flames, dragged into the abyss to share the doom unleashed upon its parent-children.

At the centre was stillness, the black eye of a skull that drew Jain Zar's gaze, dragged her as if into a vortex, to the shadows within, a place of frozen blackness and echoes. A pale ghost came to her, the ghastly maiden still, bound in chains, weeping tears of blood, mouth stitched shut with the sinew of fallen heroes.

Feeling choked, gasping for breath, Jain Zar broke free of the visions. Her head swam and she staggered away from the dais.

She felt strong arms holding her and came to her senses

sitting on the floor, Asurmen with an arm about her shoulders. His face was full of concern but in his eyes she saw something else, a hint of sadness.

'What did...' she began.

He shook his head, refusing to answer the question before it was asked.

'Better that we do not share these things,' he said. 'Are you well enough to stand?'

The dizziness had passed and she nodded, pushed herself to her feet and retrieved the glaive that had fallen from her grasp. She looked at Maugan Ra, who had a troubled expression – even more than it had been for the entire encounter. He glanced at the Asurentesh, at Asurmen and back to the sphere.

'Tell me of your journey,' he said to the Hand of Asuryan.

'It does not matter how we came here, but where we are heading,' replied Asurmen. He pointed to the Asurentesh. 'This, and the technology it wields, is our salvation.'

'There is no salvation,' said Maugan Ra. He looked close to tears, hands trembling as he fidgeted with the edge of the pedestal. 'You do not understand. All things shall end. Our people are dying, each generation hence shall diminish. Gone is our dominion, laid low by greed and self-worship. She Who Thirsts will prey upon us until the universe's ending. The stones are a temporary respite, not sanctuary. In time even they will fail.'

'We do not have to die alone,' said Jain Zar. The sharp looks from both of her companions showed that they too had seen something of what she had witnessed. 'Every time we fight we must face the prospect of losing, of death. It is that confrontation that makes the battle worth fighting.'

Jain Zar and the Hand of Asuryan looked at each other, sharing a moment of agreement.

'Come with us,' said Asurmen. 'Teach us more of the Tears of Isha and the Asurentesh. I will show you how to walk the Path, to shape despair into a weapon with which to strike back.'

'I am no warrior,' said Maugan Ra.

'Nor was I,' said Asurmen.

'I was,' said Jain Zar, 'and there is no secret to it. Kill before you are killed.'

She stepped up beside Asurmen and looked at Maugan Ra.

'But there is more to success than killing, more to life than victory.' She smiled at Asurmen. 'We walk a Path, its destination unknown. Walk it with us, Harvester of Souls.'

Maugan Ra swallowed hard and nodded, hesitantly at first and then with more vehemence.

'The Fatecallers are beyond my care,' he declared, voice cracking with emotion. 'There is nothing here but morbid ghosts.'

It felt fitting that the Asurentesh was installed in the shrine. The Heart of Asuryan did not seem out of place as Maugan Ra slid home the last of the Fatecallers' spirit stones into the central column, the unnatural light filling the space until the sections of the enclosing dais slid together. The shallow curve where the globe sat was empty, awaiting the Asurentesh itself, removed for their journey from Biel-Tanigh.

'It is fortunate that we found you when we did,' said Jain Zar.

'Do not trust to serendipity what can be attributed to

the hand of Morai Heg,' replied Maugan Ra. 'Complex are the threads of fate she winds.'

'I think that another steers our course,' countered Asurmen with a pointed look towards the statue of Asuryan. 'All is being set in motion by a decree as old as our people.'

'Is that what you saw?' asked Maugan Ra.

'We agreed not to speak of what we see in the Asurentesh. Conflicting futures and hidden pasts, the deaths of others, our coming doom... These things we must bear each to ourselves.'

Jain Zar had no desire to tell the others of the blood-swept vision that had assailed her, the memory of which still lingered close. She pushed aside such thoughts and tried to give herself something more cheering to think about.

'Whether by fortune or design, the Asurentesh shall help us find others more swiftly. Better than the navigational archives of an old yacht, at least.'

'That is very true.' Maugan Ra brought forth the crystal sphere from a black bag. It shimmered silver, still reflecting the rays of Biel-Tanigh's sun caught on its surface when they had departed. Slowly the silver turned to the pale yellow aura of the shrine, the distorted faces of the three Asurya bound to its perfect curve. 'We can use this to guide the search, and perhaps if we find more spirit stones – occupied ones – we can also save a few of our dead kin.'

'The dead guide the living,' said Asurmen. 'Our gods died aeons ago, yet still they reach down to us from the wreckage of the heavens to steer our destiny.'

Maugan Ra did not look entirely convinced by this as he set the Asurentesh into its receptacle. The moment the glassy surface joined with the pedestal it filled, the surface becoming a pinkish-red like ink spreading in water. The red deepened, flecked with black.

'What does that mean?' said Jain Zar, uncomfortable at the sinister change. She darted a look at Maugan Ra. 'What did you do?'

'Nothing.' He looked as confused as she felt. 'It has never done that before.'

Hair-thin traces of lightning crawled within the globe's surface, as if the whirl of darkness inside was a storm cloud trapped in miniature. Jain Zar felt all warmth being drawn from the chamber as ice crystals started to form on the plinth. The slender rune-circuit sparkled with psychic energy, fitful and disturbing.

In the cloudy depths something started to coalesce. A face that seemed both horrifying and immaculate, grotesque and divine.

It was then that Jain Zar felt something else, a certain knowledge of discovery, of being observed from afar. The sensation fluttered across her skin and crept along her spine, dancing its feathery touch into her chest to set her heart racing fiercely.

'We have been found,' whispered Maugan Ra, eyes wide with realisation.

A laugh echoed down the corridor outside the shrine, drawn out and callous.

17

Jain Zar was not a seer, but she could feel the competing strands of fate tugging at her soul. She had no desire to pit herself against Eldrad and the other seers of Ulthwé, but the Asurentesh had clearly shown her what had to come to pass to avert the cataclysmic confrontation between the eldar of Ulthwé and Anuiven.

It filled her with an unfocused urgency, a tension that forced her to prowl the decks of the *Swiftriver* as though possessed of mortal energy to burn off. She returned frequently to the bridge to demand updates of Answea. Already vexed at being asked to depart Ulthwé before her ship was fully repaired, the corsair captain eventually locked the access against her repeat visitor and cut off all internal communications.

The Phoenix Lord's unease came off her in waves, her agitation a deterrent to any contact with the outcast crew. Only one seemed capable of spending any time with her, her empathic senses dulled by a life of suppression.

She found Maensith in one of the maintenance bays

reviewing the state of one of the ship's Cloudcutters –
a short-range web-capable launch used for atmospheric
landings. Maensith was crouched below the tail wing,
the canopy of the hull split open to reveal glowing arrays
within.

'It hasn't seen action for a while,' the Commorraghan
commented as Jain Zar entered the brightly lit arched
hall. The Cloudcutter was a three-finned craft that sat on
a grav-cradle facing the outer doors, its shark-nosed fuselage blistered in several places with sensor nodules, the
distinctive jag of skeinweave antennae like whiskers along
its prow.

'They prefer void-prey,' Jain Zar replied, stepping up
behind Maensith. 'Choke them to death. Close on their
target, take down the shields with pulsar fire and then crip-
ple the life support systems before affecting an unopposed
boarding.'

'Well, the starcannons are still working, the crystals are
charged and the nav vanes are in order. It's just the control systems are… sullen? Neglected?' She stepped back
and shook her head. 'I'm not sure I'll get used to these
sentient infinity systems. The souls of the dead can be irritating and temperamental.'

'It sounds as though you might try,' said Jain Zar. 'To
integrate with the corsairs?'

Maensith shrugged. 'What choice do I have? Ships and
fighting are all I know. Can't return to the kabal, can't
live on a craftworld, don't have the natural rhythm to
be a Harlequin.' Her laugh was short and bitter. 'Answea
has said I can stay aboard for a while, learn how a corsair flies and fights.'

'What of the soul-hunger?'

Jain Zar knew the Commorraghan had to be feeling the vacuum in her spirit. It had been some time since she had siphoned the tortured spirits of her victims. It was likely that Vect had been spiritually starving her even before Jain Zar had taken her from Commorragh. 'You cannot live forever beneath the gaze of the Great Enemy.'

'As long as I don't spend too much time out of the webway, I'll be fine.' The words rang false and her voice sounded strained. 'I'll work out a plan.'

'The outcasts will turn on you if they think you're preying on them,' Jain Zar warned.

'Why do you care?' Maensith rounded on Jain Zar, eyes flashing with anger. 'What am I to you? A favour? A tool?'

'An eldar.'

The simple statement stopped Maensith mid-tirade, mouth still open. She frowned and eyed the Phoenix Lord warily.

'You don't mean that. You hate my kind.'

'I hate what you represent,' Jain Zar confessed, 'not what you have become. Do you think Vect threw me into his arena on a whim? He knows me, or something of me and where I came from. I was no different to you. None of us were, those that lived before the Fall. If any tell you different, except perhaps the Exodites, they are lying. Even those that fled on the craftworld took the taint with them.

'Amoral, indulgent, violent, sociopathic. Not one of us did anything for our fellow eldar. Some of us were forced to perform, in various ways, but we embraced our servitude. Before the coming of the Great Enemy it was no bondage that held us in thrall, it was our own desires. I was a blood-dancer because I courted death, as an end and as an ally. I never felt more alive than when I danced the white sands.

'So, I do not hate Commorraghans, though they refused to listen, spurned the teachings of Asurmen. The craftworlds heeded our warning though, and to them we handed not a hope of a future, but the hope of an ending. The Rhana Dandra, the Last War Against Chaos. Mutual self-destruction between our people and She Who Thirsts.'

'But it is a future-myth,' said Maensith. 'Not a strategy.'

'It will come to pass, it cannot be avoided.' Jain Zar looked around the bay and then settled her gaze back on the former kabalite. 'Yet it is not certain that we will be ready for it. One wrong step and the war will come too soon. The Great Enemy will triumph and our sacrifice, our lifetimes of struggle, will be rendered void. This quest we follow is to ensure that all proceeds as needed. Ulthwé cannot risk the future of all in some misguided sense of self-preservation.'

'What exactly is it that you have to do?'

Jain Zar did not answer immediately, wondering if she could explain to a mortal the overlapping sensations of destiny and unfolding potential that guided her instincts. And if she could, she was not sure Maensith was of the nature to be told such secrets.

Yet she had risked her life, her immortal soul, to settle her debt with the Phoenix Lord. She could have left on one of the outcast vessels departing Ulthwé during their short stay, but had remained aboard the *Swiftriver* until she had received Jain Zar's call for further aid.

'Thinking to save itself, Ulthwé will put another craftworld in the path of a great danger. Anuiven, the victim of this manipulation, will respond, attempting to redirect the threat to Ulthwé.' Jain Zar shook her head as the details of the visions, the terrible future as she understood it, unfolded in her thoughts as though she opened a package that had been placed there by the Asurentesh. 'The ripples echo back through time, as each seer council bids to pre-empt the machinations of their rivals. A cold war fought before hostility begins.

'They will fight through proxies, steering orks, humans, kabalites and others to interfere in the course of destiny, each trying to divine a strategy that ensured doom for the other and salvation for themselves. They will fail and, at a far distant time, will clash in open combat in the webway. That battle, the hate they have for each other that they bring to the war, will rupture the skein and allow the daemons of the Great Enemy to run rampant. Not only are both craftworlds lost, it will usher in an age of darkness we cannot survive. The Rhana Dandra will come early and we shall all be consumed by She Who Thirsts.'

Maensith swallowed hard and nodded her understanding. 'And the taint spreads to Commorragh and the Exodite worlds?'

'All is touched as the galaxy breaks apart and the birth that began with the Fall reaches its final apotheosis.'

'I can see why we might want to avoid that. So what is the issue? Surely the craftworlders wish to avoid that fate?'

'For all to live, one must die,' Jain Zar said quietly, giving voice to the impossible choice. 'Eldrad must have sensed as much. His power is immeasurable already. Raw, but growing and gaining focus with each pass. Even if he does not see the intricacies, he understands the underlying theme. Ulthwé or Anuiven, one or the other must perish to avoid catastrophe.'

Maensith brushed strands of white hair from her face, brow furrowed.

'So which are we doing? Dooming Anuiven or Ulthwé?'

'If the orks attack Ulthwé in the distant future, as I was shown, then they will be too weak to strike against Anuiven. Ulthwé will founder, and eventually the survivors will drift away, abandoning the craftworld to the grip of the Eye of Terror.'

'So we are not stopping the orks, we're just delaying them?'

'One ork will fall so that later another might rise. It is this other warlord, a generation from now, that will attack Ulthwé and forestall the conflict with Anuiven.'

Maensith felt dwarfed by these concepts, her ambitions petty when measured against such aeon-spanning events. It worried her, that she was meant to have some part to play in these galactic schemes.

'Why me? Of all the pilots you could have chosen…?'

'Fate.' Jain Zar was apologetic, knowing it was poor explanation for something so important. 'When I saw that I could not reach Ulthwé as I had desired, my first thought was of you. The memory of your ships, daring the webway storms above Tir-namagesh. I was guided to you just as, long ago, you were unwittingly brought to me.'

A thrum of power through the starship circuit cut off any reply Maensith might have given. Answea's spirit coursed through the crystal matrix, seeking Jain Zar. Finding her, it coalesced as a shimmering artifice on the deck beside the Cloudcutter.

'We are close to the ork world, Storm of Silence,' the projection informed her. 'Several Ulthwé warships are not far behind us.'

'We must act swiftly before forces move out of our control,' Jain Zar said. She looked at the apparition. 'Very well.

You must deliver me and the Shrine of the Last Heard to the world. I shall guide you to the place we intend to attack.'

'We are outcasts, we have no skeinseers,' replied Answea. 'I can breach the skeinway in orbit, but the webway does not run to the surface.'

Jain Zar looked at Maensith and then the Cloudcutter and back to the Commorraghan.

'Go back out into the physical realm, where my soul is shredded and drained from me with each passing moment?' Maensith shook her head, but there was no conviction in the gesture.

'Your thread runs alongside mine, child of Commorragh,' said the Phoenix Lord.

'The craftworlders are right,' said Maensith. 'To see a Phoenix Lord is ill omen.'

Engulfed by a flare of prismatic energy, the *Swiftriver* exited the webway above the planet just as a pale daybreak glimmered around the world's edge. A bay opened, spitting forth the Cloudcutter, a spark against the stars. This simple task complete, Answea not desiring to remain in real space longer than necessary, the starship turned and disappeared, sliding back through a shimmering veil to wait in the webway.

Guided by Jain Zar's instructions Maensith piloted the craft into the atmosphere, navigating buffeting winds and thick clouds to bring them soaring over a vast continent that dominated the southern hemisphere.

Even from this altitude it was not hard to find the orks. A pall of smoke blotted the sky above their city, casting a twilight gloom over the wild heath and woods around it. Vast swathes of the forest had been felled, chewed up by immense machines that continued to plough across the hillsides, beasts of roaring blades and splintering jaws that left tattered stumps and ash in their wake.

A constant stream of wheeled and half-tracked vehicles moved back and forth between the city and the harvesters, along highways of crude black tar and dirt tracks. They passed across swaying bridges and along canyons cut by chisel and explosive from the land, raw wounds in the flesh of the world.

Open-cast mines like huge craters marked the highlands, while dammed lakes and drained rivers gave up their resources to swarms of shanty-wagons and mud-barges that prowled the marshbeds trawling for whatever could be found.

The smokestacks of the factories belched forth smog and fire from furnaces that burned day and night, driving the engines of war industry. In dark workshops the humans that had once claimed this world toiled endlessly. Cut off for ten generations from the civilisation that had birthed them, living as little more than animals themselves, the humans had been dragged from their caves and mud hovels to labour beneath the alien lashes making wargear far beyond their primitive comprehension. A horde of small servant-caste greenskins seethed through the rough settlement, messengers and functionaries, couriers and tinkerers.

'Not here.' Maensith glanced over her shoulder from the controls. Jain Zar looked out through the canopy from behind her, scouring the horizon. Beyond her the squad of Howling Banshees stood ready in the Cloudcutter's main compartment. Jain Zar pointed to the right, towards the forested highlands. 'Over there.'

Nothing more than a shadow against the dark masses of cloud, the Cloudcutter rolled at Maensith's command, banking them in the direction indicated by the Phoenix Lord. At first Maensith could see nothing of worth, just the expanse of wooded mountainsides occasionally torn by the erratic incursions of ork machinery.

But through the trees and along the winding tracks she saw something far below. Movement on the ground, boiling out of the city like ants swarming from a nest.

The orks were on the move, columns of buggies and bikes racing into the wilds through a sea of greenskins. Like a spreading stain the ork horde pushed up into the foothills, clanking, fume-belching battle-fortresses leading the advance, gawky armoured walkers trampling and stomping alongside the mobs of alien warriors on foot.

From the battlewagons and armoured giants flew flags and pennants of dark yellow decorated with black checks and flame designs. Snarling, frowning moon devices were painted onto the slab sides of the vehicles and stitched upon the crude banners. Everywhere Maensith looked she saw the splash of yellow paint on armour, sewn patches of brightness amongst the metal and coarse cloth of the orks' raiment.

Using the visual magnification system Maensith looked ahead, scanning the distant peak for some sign of the orks' target. It took only moments to locate the enemy stronghold. What she had taken to be an odd but natural formation rising from the swathe of woodlands was nothing of the sort – the entire top of the mountain had been carved into the likeness of two immense orks squatting back to back, hands on knees.

They crouched over two huge cavern entrances, their

eyes and bawling mouths hollowed-out gun platforms, ramparts cut along arms and legs. More orks poured forth from this subterranean citadel. Judging by the grey and brown clothing they wore, they belonged to a different allegiance, a preponderance of blue skull devices adorning their gear.

They came not on mechanical monsters but natural ones – ponderous, gigantic creatures decked with skull-marked thick plates over their scaled hides, battle towers and armoured gondolas upon their backs. Cannon muzzles jutted from the ports of immense battle chariots pulled by more of the gargantuan quadrupeds. With them rode ork cavalry on the backs of blunt-nosed reptiles, dragging at reins made of thick chain, digging serrated spurs and hooked goads into their mounts.

For all that their initial appearance was of some throw-back species – if such a thing were possible amongst the already degenerate ork-kind – these savages were not without technology. Outlandish forcefields crackled and spat from generators atop the backs of more war-beasts. Leader-caste warriors in plates of powered armour watched over the attack from chariots held aloft by sputtering anti-grav engines pulled by snarling, part-canine, part-porcine animals.

The mountain itself vomited forth this tide of cruel menace, choking the paths and roads down from the peak with a solid flow of brutal aliens in numbers as great as the host that had been spewed from the city of the lowlands. It was impossible to know what sudden spur had pitched these two ork tribes against each other but from what she knew of the green-skinned primitives there would be no peaceful accord to end the hostilities.

'One warlord will rise, the other will fall,' said Jain Zar, as if reading her thoughts. 'The strands of fate separate in this place and at this time. One triumphs, will conquer all and from this world will lead its horde into the stars and, eventually, to the shores of Ulthwé. The other is victorious? Another destiny, and Ulthwé is free to escalate its conflict with Anuiven several generations hence.'

'Which one do we want to win?'

Jain Zar stepped beside the Commorraghan fugitive and scanned the magnifier across the teeming multitude pouring down the mountain. The artificial eye settled on a particularly immense beast of burden that was standing on a spur of rock aside from the main advance. A huge ork commander stood close at hand on the promontory surveying its force, surrounded by a group of subordinates in overlapping plates of armour.

'The battle hangs in the balance, it is too late and we are too few to swing the tide of the whole clash one way or the other. I am not a seer, I cannot see the subtle turn that will speed destiny on our preferred course. To ensure that one succeeds, we must kill the rival. Swiftly now, while it stands apart from its horde.'

Maensith sent the impulse to dive into the Cloudcutter's guidance spirit, but at the moment it dipped from the cloud cover crimson warnings flashed across the displays. The sensors detected multiple incoming signals, and autonomous systems located the threat and highlighted them through a collection of secondary displays that rose up from the console like a cluster of bubbles, at the heart of each a blunt-nosed ork aircraft. Eight in all, screaming through the mountain thermals, each uniquely constructed, painted in yellow, their wings and fuselages laden with improbable-looking bombs and missiles.

'We can outpace them,' Maensith assured her companion, directing more power to the engines to increase the rapidity of their descent. Barely half a dozen heartbeats passed before a second wave of warnings flared through the systems and another batch of view-orbs glittered into being. Six monstrous winged beasts ascended from tunnels dug in the roof of the mountain, each three or four times larger than the ork fighter-bombers soaring up towards their citadel. Green, leathery wings studded with armoured rivets ponderously brought the monsters higher, gun-filled gondolas swinging beneath their yellow-scaled guts. Slabs of metal clad their bucket-jawed heads, a pilot's cabin built low between each set of broad shoulders.

Their course took them directly between the plummeting Cloudcutter and the giant beast of the ork warlord.

'The fates are conspiring against us, Phoenix Lord,' Maensith growled. 'Shall we avoid them, or fight?'

The question was answered before Jain Zar spoke, as two of the ork flyers broke away from the others, turning towards the incoming eldar craft. Flares of tracer bullets screamed up towards them, far wide of the mark but a signal of intent. Larger cannons barked from low turrets between the beasts' wings, filling the air with explosive detonations and shrapnel. Shrieks of alarm cried out from the spirit of the Cloudcutter.

Maensith pushed all other considerations from her thoughts and concentrated on weaving and rolling through the incoming barrage of wild fire. The beating of immense pinions meant the ork creatures rose and fell in erratic timing with their salvos, each burst of fire making up for lack of accuracy with sheer weight of shells and bullets. Casings trailed like smoke from the climbing beasts.

Perhaps detecting their intent to speed straight past, the ork pilots directed their mounts to slow and then hold station, staying in place with churning flaps of their wings while their gondolas continued to spew torrents of fire crazily at the jinking eldar craft.

'Between them,' said Jain Zar.

Maensith stalled the protest at the thought of plunging purposefully into a crossfire. There wasn't time to think, simply respond, so she banked the Cloudcutter hard and rolled it into an even steeper dive, heading directly towards the two flying behemoths.

They were moving too fast for the alien gunners to track, the flash of fire trailing after the speeding ship. As the orks continued to lay down a mindless barrage in the hope of catching the speeding eldar craft, Jain Zar's plan became obvious.

The Cloudcutter flashed between the two ork flyers. So caught up were the gun crews with hitting the descending ship they paid no heed to each other, so that a wall of bullets and shells slammed into each flying beast from its counterpart. Leathery flesh exploded into bloody fountains and armoured turrets sparked and rang with the unintended fusillades.

Snarling and bellowing, the beasts turned on each other, enraged by the mutual attack. They fell on one another with fangs and claws while the crews, distracted from their original intent, merrily continued to blast away at each other. Bound with tangles of twisted metal and hide-piercing talons the monsters spun and spiralled groundwards behind Maensith as she activated the gravitic impellers to slow their dangerously precipitous descent.

'There is not enough room to land,' Maensith warned Jain Zar. The ork leader's titan-mount had crashed through the trees with its bulk rather than following a road, leaving a splintered trail but no even ground. She spied a burned clearing not far away. 'How about there?'

'Close enough,' said Jain Zar. 'But do not wait for our return.'

There were other shapes moving through the trees – orks on foot issuing from secondary tunnels and caves. The landing spot would soon be overrun.

18

Grit and ash swirled from the pulse of the Cloudcutter's gravitic engines as the Commorraghan renegade lifted off again, leaving the warriors of the Last Heard standing amongst the debris of the orks' forest clearance. Wind-borne cinders already darkened the armour of Tallithea's shrine-sisters, smearing a grey coating on the ivory of their plate, leaving dirty streaks in the red plumes of their helms.

The gleam of seven power swords drawn in unison lit the gloom of swirling ash, seven glimmers of pale blue beside the white shine of Jain Zar's glaive.

Certainty radiated from the Storm of Silence, quelling the trepidation that had risen in Tallithea when she had set foot upon the alien world. The desire to fight was swiftly growing, fuelled by the knowledge that the enemy was close at hand, tempered by the presence of her aspect's founder.

'Follow me, as swift as death, as silent as the tomb,' said the Phoenix Lord, heading into the swirling ash cloud.

Tallithea followed on her heel, the rest of the shrine-squad in close attendance as they reached the treeline. In the distance the boom of large-bore guns and crackle of side arms echoed up from the mountain valleys with swells of orkish chanting and the bellows of gigantic warbeasts.

The sound deadened as they moved beneath the pale canopy, stepping softly and quickly over a layer of dropped needles and mulch. Raucous shouts permeated the close trunks, coming from half-seen hunched figures moving through the woods ahead and to the left, heading downhill.

Jain Zar turned them away from the line of the orks' advance, their speed allowing them to outpace the front-runners of the green-skinned mobs hurtling down the slopes. Having moved out of sight, the eldar cut uphill again, heading directly for the ork warlord Jain Zar had asserted was the target. Whatever happened, the Phoenix Lord had made clear during the final leg of their descent, the alien commander was to be slain.

Tallithea didn't know why this ork was important, nor why they interfered in what was obviously an alien civil war. She realised with some reluctance that she did not care. It mattered nothing to her why they were here, only that they were. This was battle, and she was a warrior. It was her place to fight, following the lead set by the Storm of Silence.

She was a Howling Banshee, a blade of the Last Heard, the omen of doom. Let seers and autarchs concern themselves with grand strategy, she served the singular purpose of Khaine. To slay.

The gestalt desire of her sisterhood was a welcome

aura around her, comforting and invigorating in equal measure. From Anothesia and Nadomesh, Kathllain and Idomen, Laiesh and Tulvareth she felt a tangible bond connecting them together.

Anxiety gave way to excitement as they sprinted through the shadows of the trees, every stride taking her closer to confrontation. Her pulse beat steadily, her thoughts clear of distraction, centred upon the task to come.

Guttural snarls alerted them to a group of orks emerging from lair-holes not far ahead. The squad looked to Jain Zar, to see if she would avoid these foes as well.

'No time,' she told the sisters. 'We go through them.'

The Phoenix Lord increased her pace and they accelerated with her, speeding lightly over roots and stone, as surefooted as if they had spent their lives in these woods. Slaloming through the close-growing trunks they were almost upon the aliens before the orks realised they were not alone.

The banshee scream burst out of Tallithea without conscious effort. From her and the others a nerve-shredding wail pulsed like a storm front of splintering bark and swirling leaves. The psychosonic waves hit the orks as they turned, engulfing them with nerve-ripping intensity, glazing eyes and numbing reflexes.

The Silent Death – that legendary weapon that had claimed so many foes – scythed from Jain Zar's hand to decapitate a pair of orks staggering with ropes of drool falling from their gaping mouths. The Last Heard opened fire with their pistols, unleashing a hail of shurikens that slashed into crude armour and tore open green skin to reveal dark flesh beneath. A few orks fell, but several times their number remained, some with mono-edged discs sticking from hardy alien flesh and padded jerkins.

Jain Zar burst into the dazed foe with flashing sweeps of the Zhai Morenn. Tallithea had but a moment to admire the curve of the blade's arcs and the spray of alien blood before she lashed her field-sheathed blade across the throat of the nearest enemy. It stumbled back, clawed hand raised to the wound.

Tallithea turned, leaping to thrust the tip of her blade down into the face of another ork, riding the collapsing body to the ground. Straightening, she heard the grunt of a foe behind. Too slow she turned, shock convulsing her sword-arm as the ork whose throat she had slit slammed a spiked mace into Tallithea's midriff. Her armour took the brunt of the impact but the blow robbed her of her breath and hurled her sideways to trip over the corpse of the ork she had dispatched.

She spun to a crouch and took a breath to scream again, but before she could release it Jain Zar appeared, the Blade of Destruction parting the greenskin from groin to shoulder in one cleaving strike.

'An ork does not fall easily,' Jain Zar admonished her. 'Strike twice, thrice, to ensure it is dead.'

Nodding, Tallithea turned away. She saw a bone-armoured body on the ground among the dismembered carcasses of the aliens. It looked out of place, like a brushstroke that had gone awry or a chisel mark that had marred a perfectly sculpted feature.

She was no longer aware of the presence of Idomen. She felt a momentary disappointment that her sister had fallen to such crude foes, and knew dispassionately that when her war mask fell she would grieve for the fallen shrine-maiden. For now she regarded the loss without emotion as she crouched to pluck Idomen's shining spirit stone from the breastplate of her armour.

'More are coming but we do not have time to fight them all,' Jain Zar said, gesturing towards the increasing din coming from up the mountain.

Her blood fired by the brief clash, Tallithea sped after the Phoenix Lord with light steps and a joyful heart.

The trees soon gave way to the trampled wake of the war-lord's beast, a broad swath of snapped and splintered trunks. Coming out into the meagre daylight, it was immediately apparent why the alien commander had chosen this location, as the vista stretched almost the entire length of the mountain valley below. The lead forces of both tribes clashed across a river, riders and bikers sparring and swerving through the spume of a ford while gun-trikes sped over a rickety bridge further down the mountain.

The larger hordes were closing with the inevitability of tectonic plates, the potential impact as earth-shattering. Warbeasts and battle engines pounded towards each other exchanging hails of rockets and shells, advancing amidst a sea of smaller walkers and creatures, a tide of green-skinned brutes baying and howling in their lust for battle.

Close to the forefront of the city-tribe's attack rose a war machine larger than any other, a many-decked mechanical idol of a raging god, its turrets and ports ablaze with mounted weaponry and fusillades from the orks crowded within. Arcs of green energy leapt from the eyes of the god-titan, building in power.

Jain Zar knew she looked upon the throne-machine of the creature that would humble Ulthwé and save millions of her people. It felt strange to be indebted to an alien warlord, whose part in the fates to come was no more conscious than that of a natural disaster that sweeps all before it.

Ahead the king-ork of the mountain fortress was heading back to its huge mount, perhaps hoping to meet its rival head-on. He was followed by his entourage of slab-armoured thugs; if they were able to clamber aboard the mighty beast it would be all the harder to slay the commander.

Urging on the Last Heard with her thoughts, as though dragging them after her like the train of an elaborate gown, the Phoenix Lord sped across the broken wood and uneven ground. The Scream That Steals started to build inside, ready to be unleashed the moment she was within range of the orks. With it she felt the bloodthirst of the shrine-squad building, taking her power from her and feeding energy back at the same time, the Storm of Silence and her Howling Banshees becoming a solitary weapon aimed at the ork's heart, guided by a single will and desire.

They had covered perhaps half the distance when the mist-shrouded and smoke-filled air above the clashing hordes bent and warped, blistered suddenly with dozens of golden portals. Falcons and Wave Serpents, Nightwing fighters and Vampire bombers sped from the webway.

Red flares of brightlances and the azure spark of starcannons coursed through the press of greenskins pouring up the mountain. Scatter lasers and shuriken cannons reaped hundreds of lives from the throng of aliens. The bright flash of pulsars lit the gloom, a dozen weapons converging on the engine-god of the city. Ammunition stores burst into flame at their touch, armour ran in molten rivulets under the intense barrage of lasers that sliced apart armoured turrets and punched through engine blocks. Smoke billowed from a score of rents in the machine's armour.

The coloured splashes of Aspect Warriors pouring from Wave Serpent transports dissected the advancing ork attack in many places, perfectly coordinated to isolate and destroy the most threatening alien warriors. Black Guardians followed in their wake and jetbikes circled the flanks, cutting down the greenskins in their path with ruthless volleys of shurikens and laser fire.

Jain Zar slowed to a halt, ill feeling rising as she watched a fresh salvo of fire flash down from the speeding craft in the skies above. Stabbed with brightlance and pulsar, the god-engine gave up all resistance, its boilers and furnaces breaking open to engulf the teetering structure foot to head in purple and orange flames. Secondary detonations wracked the machine, hurling flaming debris onto the warbikes and battlewagons clustered around the war engine.

The Last Heard gathered around their Phoenix Lord, snarling in spite, echoing her dismay.

Jain Zar looked at the collapsing ruin of the warlord's battle tower and knew that she had failed.

19

A hundred runes danced across the skein. It was a thing of beauty, the combined efforts of Ulthwé's seers conducting the strands of fate in concert with each other. Daensyrith led the psychic symphony, directing the great swell of the battle, arranging the foundations of the warhost's movements. Around her, the council teased out individual destinies, manoeuvring squads and even individuals to make best use of the surprise of the orks. Exarch and Aspect Warrior, Falcon pilot and Avatar, the unfolding fates of all swayed and flickered in transit from the future to the past.

Eldrad was content to play his part, monitoring the attack up the left flank of the city-tribe of orks. He sent Striking Scorpions and war walkers on a course that would intercept alien reinforcements bundling out of their crude transports alongside the river that cut through the battlefield. A Wave Serpent disgorged its squad of Black Guardians so that their starcannon could cover the advance, its plasma bolts ready to ward off a burgeoning ork bike attack.

The farseer saw this playing out not on the mountainside but across the interlocking fragments of fate that made up the skein. In his mind's eye the present and the future overlapped. The Striking Scorpions cut down the ork nobles with their whirring chainblades while the war walkers sent flurries of brightlance fire into more transports, turning them into half-tracked pyres. To his thoughts the starcannon had already turned the ork warbikers into slag and charred flesh.

The edifice of the skein quickly shifted like sands beneath their feet; once-futures disappeared, replaced by whole new mazes of potential. Fundamental changes spread out along the paths of possible outcomes, splintering fractals that broke the plan into a thousand strands.

Eldrad did his best to rein in the rapidly multiplying fates, his runes spinning and careening from one strand to the next as he sought out the best outcomes. He saw eldar dying, hacked down by thuggish aliens, blasted by their primitive weapons, crushed beneath vehicle rollers and tracks. The Striking Scorpions were surrounded, the war walkers left as burning wrecks on the riverside. The bodies of Black Guardians littered the mountain in pools of blood and mounds of severed limbs.

Around him flew the runes of the others as they tried to bring the rampaging fates back under control.

An urgent impulse spread through the threads, originating from Daensyrith. The head of the council demanded communion.

'We must work as one,' Daensyrith demanded. 'We begin again, starting with the Rune of Khaine. All must spring from the Avatar's fate.'

The seers closed their minds together, pulling with them

dozens of strands, bending the skein with the pressure of their thoughts so that the splintering future started to coalesce around the burning rune of Khaine. Eldrad moved to join them, snatching up such fates as he saw best served the effort, seeking to trace the source of their creation so that he might add his thoughts to the new strategy.

Yet even as he sought out these beneficial futures, he demanded answers.

'What has changed?' he asked the others. 'What did we miss?'

'The orks are united against us,' replied Astrothia. 'We hoped to divide them, but we face two foes, not one.'

'Impossible,' replied Charythas. 'We saw clearly that the orks continue to wage battle against each other even as we fall upon them. What could change so dramatically in a few moments?'

What indeed? Eldrad merged his threads of fate with those of the others, conjuring together a makeshift plan to keep the tides of battle in their favour. As he did so he searched the skein for an answer, seeking to know how they could not have foreseen the unity of the two ork tribes against a common foe.

He found one particular thread that stood out of place. It cut across everything else, a singular line through fate that briefly touched others but was not bent from its course nor knotted to any other.

The Rune of the Banshee sped along its length, spinning rapidly, flickering with life.

Jain Zar.

Before he had a chance to delve deeper along this strand, an impulse from Charythas brought him out of his contemplation, dragging his thoughts back to the here and now of the mortal world.

Eldrad stood beside the Wave Serpent that had carried him and Charythas to oversee the left flank of the eldar attack. From their vantage point they could see about half of the battle, the interplay of precise eldar attacks against the rushing brutality of the green-skinned savages. Though it lacked the clarity of the skein, the combined elements of clean eldar vehicles cutting lines through the rampant ork horde possessed its own raw beauty.

But there was nothing beautiful about the thousands of orks streaming down the mountain, roaring, trumpeting beasts of war at their heart. They were led by an enormous scale-skinned creature as tall at the shoulder as a wraithknight. Four immense tusks jutted from the riveted plates that clad its head, its body decked in howdahs and gun turrets. Cannons belched forth fire and smoke, their barrage ripping a swath through city-orks and eldar alike. Three other warbeasts flanked the monster, adding their own fusillades to the weight of shells falling upon the swift eldar formations. Crackling shields from generators mounted on smaller beasts around them fizzed and sparked with incoming laser and plasma, deflecting the fire of the eldar.

'Jain Zar did not kill the mountain warlord...'

Eldrad watched with trepidation as the orks from the peak fortress attacked alongside their commander, steering towards the heart of the eldar rather than smashing into the city-tribe as the council had foreseen. Faced with annihilation, the orks of both settlements were willing to fight together beneath the banner of the still-living warlord.

A flare of fear and pain rippled across the skein, followed

by a cold wind of loss. Below, Eldrad could see a thicket of Black Guardians trying to hold back the incoming beasts, several dozen of them, gathered about the smoking wreck of a downed Wave Serpent.

Even before he dived into the skein, Eldrad knew what had happened. The absence of Daensyrith was immediately apparent, a vortex at the heart of the seers' threads.

'We must leave.' The thought came from Hathesis, one of Daensyrith's closest allies. 'The battle here will be too costly. If we withdraw now, we can minimise the damage.'

'What of the fallen?' replied Eldrad. 'We have lost dozens of kin, their spirit stones lie unclaimed among the savages. Would you abandon the souls of our people to an uncertain future?'

Eldrad's runes flew from his pouches at his command and circled in long orbits as he slid his thoughts back into the deep skein.

'What choice do we have?' said Astrothia. Her spirit flashed this way and that, highlighting the rampage of the ork warlord. The rune of Khaine guttered and died in the vision as the shell of the Avatar was crushed beneath the metal claws of the titan-beast. 'Five times that number again will fall in saving them.'

Out in the far distance, nearly a lifetime away, Eldrad saw worlds burning, the rampage of the orks changed but unchecked. His own rune floated alone in the darkness, far from the sight of the others, beyond their understanding. He could not even reach back to show them that the doom had not been averted, that the dying was for nothing.

It was almost too much to contemplate, staring out into

the infinite emptiness of the future, where paths of fate became so divided they ceased to exist. He felt the bitter cold to the depths of his soul and knew that he alone had been set upon this road. There was not an eldar alive that could walk it instead.

Waiting in the abyss was She Who Thirsts, a bottom-less maelstrom consuming all that was left of his people. He looked down into the storm, watched the expansion and contraction of the god they had created, pulsing and writhing, waiting to feed on the last eldar soul.

And despair fled before the sight, for Eldrad knew beyond any doubt that he would not allow it. From death's grip itself he would find a way to rob the Great Enemy of victory, to starve She Who Thirsts.

And in making this decision he saw that the void was not empty but filled with glittering strands, each as slender as a single fate, uncountable millions of billions, eldar and alien alike, all woven together to create the skein itself.

Upon this canvas were woven brighter threads. The lives of great leaders and thinkers, warmasters and emperors. In gold filament they stood out, but they were as much part of the mass as anything else, not entirely unique in the cosmos.

He found his own strand, saw the many knots and kinks and winding curves that still stretched far into the future, five lifetimes of the eldar and more. Alongside were the hundred others, those where his life ended short. As his mind flashed past he watched himself brutally cut down, turned to cinders, imploding beneath psychic assault and a hundred other deaths equally unpleasant. He saw him-self turned to crystal in a dome of Ulthwé, his unfettered mind disappearing into the fractured infinity circuit of the craftworld. He saw his spirit stone consumed by a greater daemon of Chaos, his soul the plaything of immortal beings. He felt the crushing weight of his own demise a dozen times, falling into darkness with his quest unfulfilled.

But he saw also that one strand, the path that took him on into the future unbound, to the end itself when all things would be decided. It could be done, if he had the skill and the will.

More pressing concerns crowded these fleeting thoughts, for though such musing took only an instant of reality, matters were swiftly progressing in the mortal world.

Eldrad seized upon the closest threads of the future and examined them in detail, finding the strongest that did not contain the ork attack on Ulthwé. There were a few, but they differed only in detail. Each contained a single moment of decision, a knot in time where fates converged and then diverged.

He plunged his thoughts into that knot, unpicking the threads of the individuals involved, finding his at the heart, inextricably linked to the rune of the Beast, the signifier of the ork warlord.

He and the other farseers stood before the onrushing might of the titan-beasts, the cracked remains of the Avatar beside them, the smoking shells of tanks and Titans scattered over the battlefield. Summoning all of his power, Eldrad threw himself into the raw power of the webway, feeling the leach of She Who Thirsts tug at his soul as he dared the immaterial realm to bring himself face to face with the ork warlord on its fortress-mount.

Even as his Witchblade scythed down on the monstrous ork the mauls and axes of its nobles smashed apart his rune armour in sparks of psychic feedback, their blows raining down on his crippled body, dashing out his brains across the cold metal floor of the beast's howdah.

And Ulthwé would be saved, the might of the ork army never quite reaching the critical mass it required to break out into the stars. Robbed of their leaders, the aliens would fall to fighting among themselves once more, no threat to any but their own.

Letting the visions fall away, he signalled for the others to join him, assuming his place at the head of the council without consultation. It mattered little if he was to die shortly, but there was some satisfaction in taking up the mantle of leader for the time being. With Charythas beside him, an escort of guardians behind, he mounted the Wave Serpent and sent a thought of command to the pilot, directing her to the thickest fighting ahead of the main ork counter-attack. There he would lay down his life for Ulthwé.

The sleek transport lifted up with a whine of anti-gravitic engines and turned its nose towards the battle, undulating shimmers of energy from its protective field enveloping its hull. Eldrad sat down opposite Charythas, who grasped with both hands the haft of his singing spear.

'I saw… I saw what will happen. The price you will pay.'

'What else did you see?'

'What else? I saw Ulthwé saved. Is there anything else that matters?'

Eldrad thought of this, remembering that he alone had been able to reach his thoughts into the coldness of the distant fates. The other seers knew nothing of the grander spiral upon which they walked.

'No, I suppose not.'

Eldrad considered the recent twists that had brought him here. But for small things, his fate would be different. It was hubris to think that they could control the anarchy that ruled time, make sense of the impossibly complex network of interlocking futures. Yet they tried their best and he was better than any other. It vexed him that he had been unable to solve this puzzle, that Jain Zar had backed him into this impossible position. Had she known what would happen if she left the warlord alive? Did she think he would shirk his sacrifice, to allow her horrifying intent to become realised?

His thoughts fluttered on the skein seeking the strong thread of the Phoenix Lord. It was simple to locate, at the heart of all that happened yet barely touched by the fates of so many others, fates that abruptly ended.

His mind reached into the vastness that was the spirit of Jain Zar and felt a cold howl move through him. She was in her Cloudcutter, rising up over the ongoing battle.

'You will not win,' Eldrad told her. 'Though it costs me my life, I will not see the orks defile the craftworld of my people. Ulthwé will be saved, even if you demand my life forfeit.'

The returning thoughts from the Storm of Silence were a frosty whisper that left an icy taint on his soul.

'I demand nothing, Eldrad of Ulthwé. You are the far-seer, the one that cheats fate. Sometimes fate will not be denied. Morai Heg has cut the thread, the banshee has called forth your spirit.'

'It's so pointless!' Eldrad's frustration burst out like a nova on the skein, illuminating the threads with his incandescence, showing what would come to pass. 'You have achieved nothing, Jain Zar, except the deaths of hundreds of eldar and the demise of one of your greatest allies. I would have saved our people, Storm of Silence. Did you never consider that perhaps we might work together? You need not have struck blindly, a missile forged by Khaine and cast by dead Asuryan's hand. What good we could do if you were not the victim of fate but its mistress.'

'What is done cannot be undone.'

'Kill the warlord,' said Eldrad. 'You can still do that. Whether by your hand or mine, it dies and Ulthwé will be saved from its assaults. All that remains is whether you demand I die to preserve nothing!'

Cold black flames lapped at his spirit. There was no reply and he thought he had further angered the Phoenix Lord. Yet when he pulled back from the distressing contact, he saw that the skein was frozen, held in a moment of balance and stasis.

Such power! Whole worlds turned on an instant's thought when one moved as the immortals moved. To have been in such company would have seen Eldrad elevated to the highest echelon, wielder of the fate of all eldarkind.

The future rolled on again, gaining momentum and motion as the decision was made.

Blazing white through the winding threads of fate, the rune of the banshee shone like a rising star.

Casting his mind to the present, Eldrad saw with his projected vision the Cloudcutter of the Phoenix Lord stop in the air. Silhouetted against the pale sky, it performed a sharp stall-turn and then accelerated groundwards, diving hard towards the ork army.

X

Jain Zar's first reaction was to head for the shrine of Khaine and the armoury beside it. A call from Maugan Ra stopped her. He pointed to the crystal dome of the shrine, directly above the Asurentesh's pedestal. It seemed as though rivulets of liquid sapphire poured down the outer surface until it was covered with a haze of cerulean shimmer.

The three of them ran to the shrine entrance and saw the same curtain of energy sliding across the skylights of the passageway outside. The flux of power continued to descend, falling like a curtain across the many archways that broke the corridor between the shrines of Asuryan and Khaine.

As the azure flickering touched the ground it paled and disappeared, leaving nothing but a faint gleam on the edges of the stones and windows. Jain Zar put her hand towards the closest archway. She felt resistance in the air and a tingle of static through her fingertips, where tiny blue sparks crackled.

'Thankfully the Asurentesh knows how to defend itself, it seems,' said Maugan Ra. He took a step back towards the shrine of Asuryan but faltered as he saw something outside.

Jain Zar saw it too, through the arch, beyond the towers and domes of the shrine campus. The sky had turned black. Not just the dark of night but impenetrable; the structure of the webway that encased them had become solidified shadow.

Storm clouds started to boil free from the enclosing umbra, thunderheads that flickered with purple and scarlet lightning. Voices swept over the shrine, as though distant screaming carried on a wind. The clouds bubbled and thrashed with inner turmoil, descending and expanding, swallowing the central tower, creeping down each storey like the edge of an eclipse.

Soon all was shrouded in darkness, only the sapphire gleam of the Asurentesh's shield lighting the exterior. Shapes appeared in the darker fog, half seen, pressed up against the openings for an instant, disappearing when the three eldar turned at the sound of a sigh or scratch.

Eyes appeared from the twilight, pairs of red unblinking gems. Tittering laughs and the scampering of clawed feet echoed down the corridor and skittered across the roof.

Asurmen looked at Maugan Ra, who was staring in fascination at the apparitions skimming through the dark cloud – fleeting, half-bestial things that wore the features of eldar.

'What has found us?' demanded the Hand of Asuryan.

Maugan Ra managed to break his gaze from the

nightmare unfolding around them and turned a dead stare towards his companions.

'She Who Thirsts.'

'I told you,' Maugan Ra pleaded while Jain Zar pulled her cuirass from its stand, 'I am not a warrior.'

'Stay here,' Asurmen told the newest of the Asurya.

Jain Zar held the breastplate to her chest and allowed it to fold its embrace around her, forming hard plates from the mesh-like underweave. Placing her hand into the accompanying gloves, vambraces grew up her arms, the one on the left sweeping up into a high shoulder guard. Thigh plates grew down her legs and encased her feet with a protective sheath.

Asurmen armoured himself beside her, eyes fixed on the arch that led back to the shrine of Khaine. Through the door they could see the access tunnel, where ill-formed shapes cast shadows in the light.

'We hold the shrine of Asuryan,' he told Jain Zar. 'Whatever happens, we cannot allow them to take the Asurentesh. It is not coincidence that these foes have come at the moment we have brought it out of the library.'

Jain Zar nodded, fitted her mask – fashioned in the screaming face of the banshees of legend – and took up her glaive and triskele.

'Whatever comes, we shall destroy them.'

The two Asurya left the armoury together, leaving Maugan Ra standing at the door. They crossed the open space of Khaine's shrine, weapons at the ready. Together they stepped out into the corridor that led to the shrine of Asuryan.

The archways and crescent skylights filled with shifting,

leering faces. Jewel-eyed creatures licked serpent tongues across the transparent barriers and scratched with grotesque lobster claws. They tapped and rasped and snarled and hissed, their agitation increasing to a frenzy as the two eldar stepped into view. Slashing and biting, the daemonettes thrashed at the ward that kept them at bay, every strike eliciting tiny golden sparks from the mystical barrier.

'I do not think it will hold forever,' said Jain Zar. She steeled herself as they passed along the passage, her skin crawling with revulsion at the horde of un-eldar scrabbling to gain entrance to the inner sanctum. Like the ghost-crowd at the arena, it seemed as though every face that stared at her belonged to one of her victims, born again into immaterial form to torment her with her murderous past.

'Even if the barrier holds, we cannot remain here forever,' Asurmen replied. 'Our food, our future, is beyond these walls.'

Jain Zar stopped and met the stare of one of the daemonettes clawing at an open archway. Tendrils of psychic energy crawled from the creature's long claws with each pounding blow against thin air. It stopped and regarded her with multi-faceted eyes of ruby red, head cocked to one side.

It raised a claw and drew its tongue along the serrated edge, dripping silver daemon blood from the laceration. Droplets slid over its lips and chin and pattered against its exposed breast.

Disgusted, she drew back and the daemonette threw back its head and laughed, its screeching cackle drilling deep into her senses, sending a shockwave along her nerves. The daemonettes cavorted, teasing and taunting and beckoning to her. The sneers goaded her. Trembling, rage rising, she reacted, stepped forward to lash out in anger.

Asurmen's grip on her shoulder was tight, holding her back just a pace from breaking the line of the psychic ward.

'Not yet,' he said quietly. 'They will steal your power, turn your desire to kill against you.'

She nodded and turned away from the writhing daemon mass, closing the doors in her mind that trapped the banshee-spirit crying to be unleashed. Eyes downcast, set upon the floor, ears deaf to the wordless wails and chittering around her, she followed Asurmen to the shrine of Asuryan.

Stepping across the threshold was like surfacing from water, a sudden easing of pressure, light and cool after the heat and oppression that had filled the walkway.

Asurmen crossed to the Asurentesh. The globe was almost black, just a few flecks of red left to mark its surface. Pulses of energy boiled the inner cloud, each beat darkening the sphere further.

'I do not think we have much time left,' said the Hand of Asuryan. He turned to the doorway and drew his sword. The spirit stone in its hilt gleamed blue, brighter than Jain Zar had seen before. The gem on his chestplate was similarly invigorated, as was her waystone.

The sensation was not pleasant, like hot nails slowly pushing into her body. The stone reacted to the presence of the daemons, and the psychic bond described by Maugan Ra became a physical pain. It felt not only as if the energy pushed deeper into her, but the sinews and threads entwined through her pulled taut, the barbs in her spirit hooking and dragging as the daemons tried to prise free her soul for themselves.

Jain Zar pushed aside the distraction, focused on the fight that was to come – one of the few techniques of the arena that still had a use.

She glanced at the Asurentesh. The last flicker of red disappeared, leaving a lifeless black orb.

The relief from the psychic pressure vanished; the weight of the daemonic presence crashed into the shrine like water into a breached submersible, flooding everything with overwhelming, suffocating power.

The wash of immaterial energy staggered Jain Zar, physically bowing her beneath its onslaught as the tide continued to press in. Behind the wave of force came the daemonettes, shrieking in triumph, baying like loosed hunting hounds.

Asurmen's vambraces spat a hail of shredding discs, each shuriken edged with a golden flicker of energy as it slashed through the first daemons. Limbs and heads fell, turning to silvery dust before they touched the ground, bodies crumbled to metallic mist amid the storm of fire.

Recovering from the daemonic surge, Jain Zar threw her triskele. In Asur it was no ordinary weapon; its curving course followed the movement of her hand, spinning through half a dozen foes before sweeping back to her grip. She caught it, spun on her heel and hurled the triskele again, parting the bodies of another handful of daemons. As it flew, the triskele drank in the glittering remnants of the daemonettes, absorbing their power. Twice more she hurled the weapon, black flames burning in its wake as a further score of foes fell before the daemons were upon her.

She met their attack with her own charge, the blade of her glaive sweeping out to sever lashing claws, to score deadly wounds across throat and chest. Jain Zar moved constantly, the blade tip weaving figures of eight, feather-light in her hand. She ducked a whirling claw and struck its owner, lashing the glaive up through its gut and chest to turn the daemonette into a fountain of falling silver particles.

She erupted from the closing pack, her passage carving whorls in the silver vapour of their demise. The triskele was in her hand again, spinning towards the shrine entrance where more daemonettes forced their way into the sacred chamber.

Where Jain Zar was death in motion, Asurmen was a pillar of defiance. He swayed and adjusted his feet, always a moment ahead of his foes but never forced to take more than a step. The Hand of Asuryan ducked and dodged without haste, never where the raking claws of his foes cut the air. Vambraces spitting deadly hails, he fought at the centre of a silver whirlwind, his sword an azure blur that annihilated the bodies of the daemonettes with its slightest touch.

Jain Zar snatched the triskele out of the air as it returned to her. She spun to confront the foes behind her, but they paid her no heed – they advanced towards the Asurentesh, claws snapping with anticipation.

Jain Zar was already throwing the triskele and breaking into a charge as Asurmen called on her to stop the daemons. Her missile decapitated three, and the blade in her hand despatched the same number again in the following moments.

She looked back and saw that as hard as Asurmen tried

to hold the archway, more daemonettes poured around him, using the dissipating bodies of their companions to shield themselves. So intent were they on the Asurentesh that they came straight at Jain Zar, barely registering her presence, faces twisted in desperate craving for the Heart of Asuryan.

There were simply too many for Jain Zar to destroy. For each that fell to her weapons another and another sprang forward. Asurmen retreated, firing the last volleys from his vambraces, and stood by her side to defend the Asurentesh.

A claw caught the side of Jain Zar's mask. Another left a welt across her arm guard. Her defence was failing, the need to strike down so many foes leaving her open to attack. Asurmen was similarly beset, blade now held double-handed as he lashed swinging blows through the horde, all skill and finesse abandoned.

Jain Zar's whole existence extended only as far as the mass of screaming, snarling faces in front of her. Hers was a universe of claw and glittering blade and nothing more. Time itself seemed to bend to her will, slowing so that she could rain more blows upon her enemies.

Yet it was not enough.

Another claw strike nearly knocked her grip from the haft of her weapon, leaving blood trickling from the wound.

The pain was sharp, far harsher than anything she had experienced, an injury to her spirit as well as body. Her chest burned with the force of her waystone even as her limbs grew numb with fatigue.

Just as she thought she could not swing her blade again, the daemons crowding upon her swaying vision exploded into silver tatters. Within the space of two heartbeats a score of foes evaporated into dispersing dust.

Through the expanding cloud she saw a figure at the arched entrance, clad in the black of midnight.

Maugan Ra.

He held a shuriken cannon, its tip gleaming with energy as he fired again, unleashing a fresh storm of projectiles into the backs of the daemonettes. Like embers caught in a hurricane the daemonettes were swept away by the fusillade until the last disappeared in a swirl of silver rags.

Peace descended, the clamour of melee silenced.

Maugan Ra lifted the shuriken cannon, his gaunt face a mask of shock.

'I thought you weren't a warrior,' said Jain Zar.

'There is no secret to it, apparently,' the Harvester of Souls replied hoarsely. 'Kill before you ar–'

A darkness enveloped Maugan Ra. It lifted him, hurling his flailing form across the shrine to crash into the far wall. He fell limp and unmoving.

Something monstrous pushed itself across the threshold of the shrine, a pulsing cloud of purple and bone and black that glittered with the light of a thousand stars. As it passed beneath the archway it coiled upon itself, as though it were smoke forced into a glass vessel to form a shape – a body that extruded two bestial legs, four arms growing from the torso, an elongated bovine head sprouting from a slender neck. Eyes like polished sapphires coalesced out of the collapsing firmament, beneath a brow from which six horns appeared, twisted and curling through a mane of white hair.

Hoofed feet stepped onto the tiles of the shrine, which smouldered beneath the touch of the daemonic presence. Serrated claws like those of the lesser daemons though far larger tipped its lower arms. The upper limbs ended in elegant hands that gripped the hilts of two long swords, their curved blades exactly like those Jain Zar had seen wielded as pairs in the blood arena. From pale pink flesh seeped patches of darkness, hardening into slick black plates studded with fist-sized golden rivets in the shape of eldar skulls.

It extended a claw, not in threat but greeting, and bent a leg in supplication. When it spoke, the daemon's voice was a chorus of whispers, disturbingly paternal and flirtatious at the same time.

'My children...'

20

A lifetime spent in Commorragh had exposed Maensith to the most perilous situations, with even her closest allies a moment away from becoming deadly enemies, surrounded by ruthless, ambitious murderers and thieves. Her earliest memories were of killing her two siblings, poisoning her sister and slicing the throat of her brother as he slept.

Such a life bred highly attuned instincts for danger, and every one of them was jangling insanely as Maensith turned the Cloudcutter towards the ork warlord and opened the engines to full speed.

'Get us as close as you can,' Jain Zar told her, holding the frame of the arched door to the piloting compartment.

'And then we are even?'

'Even? You think you are still in my debt?'

'I owe you a lot, even if that is an uncommon, distasteful feeling. You freed me.'

'For my own ends. I needed a pilot.'

Maensith turned and looked at Jain Zar, surprised that the Phoenix Lord had misunderstood her.

'That wasn't what I meant. I thought you would... You must know what it is like, being trapped by yourself, unable to escape the prison you built with your own hands?'

The Storm of Silence tilted her head, regarding Maensith for the space of several heartbeats.

'I see. That sort of freedom.'

'Yes. The only kind that counts, I think.'

Something rattled against the hull, sporadic fire from the ground. Maensith returned her attention to the controls. 'I thought I had power over my destiny, and you showed me how little control I really had. No more. I choose to do this, not for my sake, not because of fear or favour, but to honour what you have given me.'

Muzzle flash and tracers flared from the seething green horde below. She centred her thoughts on the tower-laden behemoth of the ork warlord, easing the Cloudcutter from side to side, up and down, to present a harder target to the ork gunners.

'And perhaps all I get to choose is how I die,' she added, and found that the thought was oddly satisfying. 'That's more than I ever had before.'

She sped them over the heads of the orks, dodging rockets and airbursts, pushing the Cloudcutter to its limits.

'We are approaching too fast,' Jain Zar warned as the titan-beast loomed large in the canopy like a cliff face.

'Trust me,' Maensith said with a smile, knowing that for the first time ever she actually meant the words.

Past the Storm of Silence, through the slightly grey-blue blast filter of the canopy, Tallithea could see the immense bulk of the orks' warbeast. It looked more like a fortress with thick legs and a blade-sheathed tail than a creature born of the natural world. Over the heads of raging green-skins and rampaging alien walkers it grew larger and larger, making a mockery of perspective.

'Hold on to something,' the Commorraghan told them.

Tallithea's fingers found purchase on the edge of a bench, digging into the memetic fibres that held her in place.

The sudden deceleration was like a blow to the gut, punching the air from her lungs despite the compensating flex of her Aspect armour. Fingers tight, she held on as Maensith activated the orbital brakes, energy grapples designed to slow descent from space, now deployed to halt their horizontal progress.

The pilot wrenched the craft into a tight roll, inverting them as inertia carried them along their axis so that they passed backwards over the spinal towers of the fortress-monster, bleeding energy as an amber glow of heat along the wings and fuselage.

The portal gate sighed open at the rear of the craft, directly above the main keep-howdah just as their momentum came to a halt.

Jain Zar bounded past and leapt from the Cloudcutter without hesitation. A heartbeat later Kathllain followed and Tallithea found herself on her feet, leaping into the open sky a stride behind Tulvareth.

She fell only a short distance, landing lightly on a thin metal awning above a three-strong battery of breech-loading cannons. Dropping down onto the stunted slave-caste crew, the Howling Banshees cut them down in moments, so swift that not even a warning shriek escaped the short greenskins.

Jain Zar had not even struck, but moved intently towards

the main body of the howdah, the Silent Death burning ebon in her grip. A larger ork moved into the doorway. A heartbeat later its head hit the rusted metal of the decking and its body fell backwards into the chamber beyond.

Vaulting the corpse, the Phoenix Lord led them into the dim ruddy light of the interior. A few servant creatures scuttled from their path, yelping and hissing. Metalwork steps ahead led them to a viewing platform where the warlord and its cronies watched the unfolding battle, standing beside the turntable of a crackling energy cannon.

'Save your wrath for the great ork,' Jain Zar told them, speeding on tiptoe up the steps.

The Howling Banshees were like a slender sword wielded by a single hand, punching into the crowd of orks clustered at the rail to observe the unfolding battle. The closest noble fell to the Blade of Destruction, armour rent by two swift blows, leaving room for Jain Zar to bound towards the warlord itself.

The Last Heard felt the thoughts of their founder reaching into them, dragging their own hate and anger to the surface. As one the squad directed their war shouts at the warlord, ignoring the slowly turning orks to focus their ire on the object of their wrath.

The rage came from inside Tallithea, intoxicating and strong, a surge of pure hate that brought joy in the wake of its leaving.

The shout of doom erupted around Jain Zar and she added her own voice to the shockwave that emanated from her shrine-daughters. Intent upon the warlord, she was one with the hurricane of rage that swept over the massive greenskin, lifted up by the power, her blade-arm guided by its strength.

The effect was staggering, bursting across the warlord in a spume of distorted air, cracking the plates of its armour, forcing it backwards.

The gleaming head of the Zhai Morenn crashed against the warlord's chest in a fountain of sparks, ricocheting from crackles of green power emitted by a hidden field generator. Jain Zar drew the blade back and struck again, as quick as a serpent, twice more, thrusting towards the fanged maw of the warlord.

She gave no thought to the other orks, concentrated solely upon the slaying of the alien commander. Eldrad had opened her eyes to the consequences of her actions, the true cost of averting the war with Anuiven.

Jain Zar would not buy the future with the blood of so many. Blind, the seer had called her. Bound, she felt, forced to follow the fate set out for her. Eldrad had shown her that another path was possible.

The ork swept a lightning-wreathed claw, forcing the Phoenix Lord to duck, giving it time to regain its balance. Around them the sisters of the Last Heard slashed and spun and fired their pistols, creating a near-solid shield around their aspect's figurehead.

The ork swung its claw again, bringing it down towards Jain Zar's head. She slipped aside, throwing the Silent Death point-blank into the monster's face. Its helm cracked under the spinning blades of black fire, exposing a face composed more of scar tissue than unblemished flesh. Red eyes full of alien rage regarded her from the depths of the helm's remains as she snatched the Jainas Mor out of the air.

Jain Zar heard a cry and felt the sudden silence of the daughter called Anothesia. An instant later and the soul of Laiesh gave its last wail before fleeing to the sanctuary of the Howling Banshee's waystone.

Two more lives given in exchange for the seer's. It was no bargain, and yet Jain Zar knew it was also the only promise of a future. She understood now why the others had looked to Eldrad. She was willing to surrender herself to his fate for a moment, to be his blade and not her own.

Her scream came again, hitting the ork warlord with its full force. The creature stumbled, blinking and frothing as synapses misfired, fingers twitching within the powered claw-gauntlet.

Double-handed, she drove the point of the Zhai Morenn into the ork's exposed throat, pushing until she felt bone part and the head came away.

The Phoenix Lord rebounded from its falling corpse, vaulting and twisting in the air to land with a roll beside her surviving daughters. Her blade lashed out to slash the leg from a charging ork noble, leaving it to fall into the blades of Tallithea and Nadomesh.

It seemed that they were surrounded by a wall of green bulk and armour, ringed within the confines of the viewing platform. Inaccurate pistol fire started to spit down from the cannon position above them, sending sparks up from the rail and deck.

A sleek black shape scythed into the orks, the wing of the launch cutting into armour and flesh like a blade. Almost out of control, it thudded into the deck, crushing another noble beneath its bulk.

Jain Zar saw Maensith staring wide-eyed from the pilot's position. Many of the orks had been knocked in all directions but were still alive, groaning and snarling on the deck. There were scant moments in which to leave.

'We take the fallen,' Jain Zar told her daughters, seizing up the corpse of Laiesh. It felt light in her arm as she ran towards the open bay of the Cloudcutter, the rest of the Howling Banshees tight around her carrying Anothesia's body.

Two orks followed them across the threshold of the launch – a bold move rewarded by half a dozen gleaming blades parting armour and flesh in a flurry of blue light and bone armour. Scattering ork parts fell out of the open portal as Maensith accelerated away, rising steeply from the back of the behemoth with rounds of fire zipping against the hull and hissing past.

Jain Zar looked down at the battle falling away below her and saw that the confrontation was far from over. The death of the warlord secured the safety of Ulthwé's future generation, at the cost of another dying below. And in the back of her soul she felt the ache and the joy of the Great Enemy as those that spawned its vile existence spent their lives to protect nothing more than survival until Rhana Dandra.

Such was to be the fate of all eldar, to live in sacrifice knowing that there was no paradise to come, only the bliss of oblivion freed from the grasp of She Who Thirsts.

XI

'I am your saviour,' the daemon continued, rising to its full height, horns not quite touching the domed ceiling of the shrine. 'You have fought well. Your reward is nigh.'

'We need nothing from you, spawn of the else-sphere.' Asurmen raised his sword in defiance, though he seemed pitifully small in comparison to his adversary.

'You may call me the Mistress of Dreams, the Master of Delights. Your hearts' desires are mine to grant. We are one and the same, birthed together, entwined in spirit.' Gem eyes regarded them both, the flicker of daemonic energy edging every facet. 'Bountiful Slaanesh would have you as lords amongst the eternal court.'

Jain Zar could sense its hunger, a deep longing that echoed inside her heart. A craving awoke in her, to hear again the savage glee of the mob, to weave the blood-dance before an immortal, appreciative god.

What glories she would achieve, to fight eternally, to indulge her bloodthirst without remorse or hindrance. Not even her mortal frame would be a limit to the wonders of murder she would unleash. Form would mould to her will, to be manipulated at a whim. Extra arms? A stinging tail? A tongue of blades? Serpentine hair? No fancy was too extreme, no method of bloodletting forbidden.

She saw herself reflected a dozen times over in the eyes of the Keeper of Secrets, adored as a warrior, worshipped as a demigod by a legion of followers who would sing her praises to the highest heavens. She saw an audience turning on itself, rending and slaying for her approval, for the slightest glance in their direction. Their roars, their anticipation and satisfaction lifted her up to the highest pinnacles of ecstatic revelation on a surge of adulation.

The reflection changed, becoming a truer image, showing the mask she wore.

Harbinger of doom, bringer of fate, daughter of Morai Heg.

Daughter of Khaine the Bloody-Handed.

The Howling Banshee.

This was who she was. The gift of slaughter belonged to Khaine and no other. It was his spirit that fuelled the fire of her rage. To embrace the offer of the daemon was a denial of this truth, to shun that which had kept her alive for so long. Rage, unquenchable and deep. A curse for some, a gift for her.

Asurmen had brought her to this brink, but she had to plunge into the dark abyss herself. Not simply to let the banshee burst free but to embrace the nature of the thing within her spirit, the smouldering shard of Khaine buried in the breast of all eldar.

It was not extinguishing that ember that would bring her peace and freedom; such an end was impossible. To accept it, to nurture it into full flame, that would give her power, that would give her control.

She saw the daemon's true purpose. Another that sought to enslave her, to cage her will to its own ends.

Jain Zar broke free of its hypnotising glare and knew the daemon for what it truly was – a pawn of a greater power with no more will than the blade in her hand.

It saw her refusal, sensed her rejection. A sneer rippled across its face.

'You have chosen eternal torment,' it hissed. 'I sought to have you as my companion, bride for eternity, but you shun my offer. Know that I am the Pleasurable Death, the Enticing Doom, Keeper of Secrets. Mortals do not refuse the gifts of N'Kari and live. Everlasting Slaanesh shall feast on your vanity for all time.'

The daemon lunged, claws and blades directed at Jain Zar. She leapt out of its reach, hurling the triskele back-handed as she rolled. It struck the creature in the middle of the chest. A welter of black sparks fountained from the blow. Yet the weapon stuck there, wedged into the mystical plate of the daemon's armour.

Asurmen was at the daemon's side in the next moment, the edge of his blade crashing against an upraised arm. Two more blows he rained down with lightning speed until the Keeper of Secrets turned and swept him aside with a contemptuous swing of a longsword. Asurmen recovered, parried the next attack and speared the top of his sword towards the throat of the daemon. A claw snapped about the blade, dragging Asurmen closer.

He let go of his sword and threw himself back as a second claw sought to rake out his entrails. Jain Zar met with her glaive the sword descending towards Asurmen's head, deflecting the blow. Her weapon shivered from the impact but she held tight, turning its downward swing into a rising strike across the thigh of the daemon.

Golden droplets sprayed from the wound, eliciting not a shriek of pain but a cry of bliss from the Keeper of Secrets. A claw punched out, catching Jain Zar's shoulder guard. She moved with the blow, cartwheeling out of reach as fragments of armour scattered from the broken pauldron.

Swords raised, claws open, the daemon of Slaanesh towered over her.

Everything that had come before rose from the depths of Jain Zar. Every hurt heaped upon her, every bloody victory she had won for others' pride, every drop of blood spilt in the cause of self-gratification; all of her fear and pain and rage became an inferno that could not be contained.

But she did not let it go, not at first. Just for the briefest of instants she honed the pain and fear, controlling it rather than letting it control her.

A singular moment.

Jain Zar screamed.

She released her rage as a focused lance of power rather than a hammerblow. The sound broke over the Keeper of Secrets in a drawn-out wail. Its near-white skin blistered and bubbled as it staggered back from the psychic onslaught. The armour upon its pale flesh and the blades in its hands shattered into black shards. As the breastplate fell away the triskele stayed in its flesh amid trickles of gold from the wound it had inflicted.

Asurmen struck, the tip of his blade punching into the weakened breast of the daemon. It recoiled as more golden sparks erupted from its body. Reeling, N'Kari swept out its claws, shrieking and slashing blindly.

Jain Zar crossed the distance with three easy strides. She leapt upon the Keeper of Secrets, using one of its outstretched arms as a step to jump again. The edge of her glaive whipped across the throat of the daemon as she somersaulted over its shoulder.

She landed in a deluge of golden rain, the litter of the daemon's destruction falling around her like sparks from a forge.

Jain Zar remained still for several heartbeats, crouched upon the tiles of the shrine as daemon energy cascaded down upon her.

She searched for the banshee, but found nothing. Of the wild spirit nothing remained. She and her bloodthirsty companion had become one.

There was no fear left. Stillness reigned. Peace.

The Storm of Silence.

21

Jain Zar sought out Eldrad after the battle and found the seer with his companions from the council. As she approached she saw two spirit stones floating above his outstretched palm, one a deep blue, the other glowing amber. She could feel the souls within, but their voices were muted, as though shut behind thick glass.

'It would be a waste to mix their spirits with the great wash of the infinity circuit,' Eldrad told the others as she came into earshot. 'We can continue to commune with them, to use their potency. The mind of a seer is intended for a better resting place than the grid that sustains the craftworld.'

'I do not think Daensyrith and Holtharin would have wished this,' said Astrothia. She looked to her peers but none raised their voice in support. 'Very well, it is clear that the wisdom of Daensyrith resides only in a few.'

Eldrad saw the Phoenix Lord and broke away, intercepting her before she reached the others.

'You have my thanks, Storm of Silence.'

'And you are in my debt, Eldrad of Ulthwé.'

'I did not know that was the extent of the bargain. Am I to be a base commodity?'

'You can settle the debt by making a simple promise. Remember this day. Remember when the banshee called your name. Your doom has been set, I have simply delayed it.'

'And what would you require to continue to delay that fateful moment?' There was disdain in his voice, but also caution. 'Are you threatening me?'

'Serve our people, Eldrad,' she told him. '*All* of our people. Today you have been spared, and your destiny will be great. Do not waste that opportunity on selfish loyalties. Know that my coming here is a warning and should you stray, others of the Asurya will cross your path to set it straight again. Or end it.'

'Threats? Between the likes of us? Is that how immortals deal with one another?'

'You are not an immortal. Not yet.'

But she knew from the surge of satisfaction that emanated from the seer that he missed her point. She could imagine his thoughts at the utterance of those last two words. She was no seer, but she was the banshee, daughter of the hand of fate, Morai Heg, and she knew when she was in the company of one whose thread would travel all the way to the Rhana Dandra. But Eldrad did not need to know that.

'Farewell, Storm of Silence, do not take it harshly if I say that I hope you never travel to Ulthwé again.'

'I will, many times,' she replied. 'And though it will presage blood and death, you will also be glad of my presence for in me is your salvation. There will be many hard decisions ahead, but hold true to our people, heed the wisdom of Asuryan as brought by his heralds, and you will repay this day.'

The sudden presence of Jain Zar was almost overwhelming, causing Tallithea to shake with emotion. The circuitry of the craftworld was alive with the Phoenix Lord's approach and a confusion of fear and excitement coursed through Tallithea as she waited at the dock where the Phoenix Lord's ship was berthed.

She almost fled, but at the moment before her nerve broke the Storm of Silence stalked through the high arch of the quay. Jain Zar turned towards her immediately, as if she had been expected. She stopped a few paces away, the chill of her presence prickling across the exposed skin of Tallithea's arms.

Out of her armour, dressed in a smock of silvery-green scales, she felt even smaller next to the Asurya, who seemed more than ever a figure of legend, a statue from the gardens brought to life. The shrieking mask was terrifying, the glint of the Blade of Destruction beguiling.

'I'm sorry,' sobbed Tallithea, bursting into tears. It was all too much, a rush of contending feelings that could not be stopped. 'I can't do it again!'

'Rest, child, and speak easily. Cannot do what, Tallithea?'

'Wear the war mask. I took off my armour and let the mask fall away and I felt sickened by the thought of what I had done.'

'You remembered the battle?'

'No, nothing that terrible. But just the knowledge of it, the idea that I fought and killed and... I don't know what else I did, but it makes me weak to think of it. And I could

GAV THORPE

die! The fear, all of that terror hidden away behind the mask, it's crept into every part of me. It took everything just to leave my chambers to come here.'

'And why have you come? For what are you apologising?'

'I've failed you, Jain Zar. I've failed my shrine-sisters, and the memory of Danaesh. I wasn't strong enough.'

Tears streaming, she turned away, but was stopped by a gentle touch at her elbow. She could not resist as Jain Zar eased her closer, into the mane that fell from her helm, its icy touch oddly comforting, bringing clarity through the haze of conflicting thoughts. The Phoenix Lord laid an arm about her shoulders, so tender it was impossible to think that the act was performed by one who had spilled the blood of so many foes.

'My child, be glad, not sorry. This is not a failure, it is success. Had Danaesh been with you, he would say he was proud. The failure is his, to be trapped on the Path of Khaine. You are free of the grip of the Bloody-Handed One, freed of the hate and anger that can consume us.' Jain Zar straightened and wiped away the tears on Tallithea's cheeks with the tip of a black-gloved finger. 'It is still within you, the war mask, and you will be called upon to wear it again before your spirit travels to the infinity circuit. Many times Ulthwé may need you, for this is a dangerous universe. But you are strong enough to walk away from the temptations of battle and the thrill of combat. That is a beautiful thing.'

Shuddering, taking a ragged breath, Tallithea nodded her understanding and thanks. A thought occurred to her, bringing with it a profound sadness.

'What of you, Jain Zar? Can you escape this Path?'

'One distant day, I will be free,' replied the Phoenix Lord.

'My Path shall be upon the bodies of my foes. Yet it takes me to the Rhana Dandra, the ending of all, beyond which I shall, as will all our people, eventually know peace.'

ABOUT THE AUTHOR

Gav Thorpe is the author of the Horus Heresy novels *Deliverance Lost*, *Angels of Caliban* and *Corax*, as well as the novella *The Lion*, which formed part of the *New York Times* bestselling collection *The Primarchs*, as well as several audio dramas including the bestselling *Raven's Flight* and *The Thirteenth Wolf*. He has written many novels for Warhammer 40,000, including *Rise of the Ynnari: Ghost Warrior*, *Jain Zar: The Storm of Silence* and *Asurmen: Hand of Asuryan*. He also wrote the *Path of the Eldar* and *Legacy of Caliban* trilogies, and two volumes in The Beast Arises series. For Warhammer, Gav has penned the End Times novel *The Curse of Khaine*, the Time of Legends trilogy, *The Sundering*, and much more besides. He lives and works in Nottingham.